PRAISE

Close Call

"With its bracing twists and turns, this thriller is an immensely entertaining dive into the high-octane world of competitive tennis."

—Tess Gerritsen, *New York Times* bestselling author

"Whip smart and instantly entertaining! Only Elise Hart Kipness—with her depth of experience, insider access, and storytelling savvy—could so rivetingly reveal the tense and taut behind-the-scenes world of sports: the relentlessness of competition, the desperation of ambition, and the power of desire. Kipness knows her stuff and will have you turning pages as fast as you can."

—Hank Phillippi Ryan, *USA Today* bestselling author

"Elise Hart Kipness serves up an ace with the latest installment of her addictive series that mixes pulse-pounding crimes with the high-stakes world of elite sports. This time, intrepid sports reporter Kate Green faces a race against time to save a top tennis pro who has been kidnapped smack bang in the middle of the US Open. *Close Call* is another winner in a series that just keeps getting better."

—Lisa Gray, *Washington Post* and *Wall Street Journal* bestselling author

Dangerous Play

"Kipness knows her territory the way Messi knows the pitch. *Dangerous Play* is a surefire winner."

—Reed Farrel Coleman, *New York Times* bestselling author of *Blind to Midnight*

"Crime comes to the Olympics in the captivating new Kate Green thriller. With a flair for conveying the complexity of friendships, and a meticulous eye for anything sports, Elise Hart Kipness delivers another big win."

—Tessa Wegert, author of *Devils at the Door*

"Kipness writes with impressive authority and specificity about the worlds of sports and sports reporting, and her skillful treatment of the human relationships at the heart of the mystery makes this a must-read thriller!"

—Sarah Stewart Taylor, author of the Maggie D'arcy series

"Kipness' depiction of the world of women's sports, featuring crisp character portraits, is both relevant and well executed. A brisk whodunit set in the world of women's soccer that arrives at an appropriate moment."

—*Kirkus Reviews*

"With keen insight into the world of sports reporting, Elise Hart Kipness takes readers on a riveting journey through the world of competitive soccer and the reporters who cover their triumphs and defeats. *Dangerous Play* is a masterfully plotted murder mystery, and the perfect sequel to *Lights Out*. I can't wait for the next Kate Green adventure!"

—Wendy Walker, bestselling author of *Mad Love*

"Elise Hart Kipness's expertise in the world of sports reporting shines through in this pulse-pounding thriller that's perfect for fans of Harlan Coben's Myron Bolitar books. The twisty plot will keep you turning the pages, while intrepid reporter Kate Green is a character you can't help rooting for."

—Lisa Gray, *Washington Post* and *Wall Street Journal* bestselling author

Lights Out

"*Lights Out* is a thriller that starts at breakneck pace and never lets up. Kate Green is a great character—you'll want her to be your best friend, but she already has one, and she has to answer the question: Is she a murderer? In this striking debut, Elise Hart Kipness writes with heart, empathy, and psychological insight into evil that exists where you least expect it. She has created a main character who is real and warm and tough and faced with the biggest mystery of all: Who in her world can she trust? You don't have to love sports to love this book, but either way, Kipness's inside knowledge will pull you right in."

—Luanne Rice, *New York Times* bestselling author of *The Shadow Box*

"With a TV sports reporter protagonist, *Lights Out* blasts onto the thriller scene with something completely new and exciting for seasoned readers of the genre. The book is teeming with plausible suspects, each with a compelling motive and secrets they'd kill to keep, but always returns to the question of whether or not we truly know what those closest to us are capable of. This is fast-paced suspense you'll want to read in just a couple of sittings, and with an ending that hints at more intriguing layers of our protagonist's story to come, I can't wait to see what Elise Hart Kipness delivers next!"

—Megan Collins, author of *Thicker Than Water* and *The Family Plot*

"When a basketball superstar is murdered in his gated home, all eyes look to his wife and circle of insiders for possible suspects. Drawing on her experience as a national sports reporter and longtime resident of suburban Connecticut, Elise Hart Kipness takes us inside both worlds in this scandalous, page-turning thriller!"

—Wendy Walker, international bestselling author

"What a fantastic debut! A unique protagonist, an interesting setting, and a story that grabs you from the beginning and keeps on building. I couldn't put this book down and read it in one sitting!"

—Chad Zunker, Amazon Charts bestselling author of *Family Money*

"Elise Hart Kipness's debut novel, *Lights Out*, is the kind of gripping, tightly paced domestic suspense mystery sure to delight fans of the genre as well as general readers. Set in the high-stakes world of professional sports, the book pits an appealing female protagonist against an increasingly slippery killer who will stop at nothing to evade capture. Elise Hart Kipness is a writer we are sure to hear more from in the future!"

—Carole Lawrence, acclaimed author of *Cleopatra's Dagger*

"*Lights Out* is a seminal triumph in mystery writing, as original as it is polished. Elise Hart Kipness's sterling debut takes us inside the world of professional sports on the one hand and a female reporter cracking that particular glass ceiling on the other. A crime thriller of rare depth and societal implications, *Lights Out* shoots straight and hits the bull's-eye dead center."

—Jon Land, *USA Today* bestselling author

CLOSE CALL

ALSO BY ELISE HART KIPNESS

Lights Out

Dangerous Play

CLOSE CALL

ELISE HART
KIPNESS

THOMAS & MERCER

Published by Thomas & Mercer, Seattle

www.apub.com

EU product safety contact:
Amazon Media EU S. à r.l.
38, avenue John F. Kennedy, L-1855 Luxembourg
amazonpublishing-gpsr@amazon.com

ISBN-13: 9781662527876 (paperback)
ISBN-13: 9781662527869 (digital)

Cover design by Caroline Johnson
Cover image: © Jose A. Bernat Bacete, © Juergen Hasenkopf / Getty; © Maarten / Getty Wouters

Printed in the United States of America

Dedicated to my aunt Sylvia Moss and my father-in-law, Irwin Kipness. While you never saw my work in print, I will always be grateful for your support during my journey.

PROLOGUE

The floor feels cold beneath her body. Damp, wet. She tries to push herself up but can't move her legs. Or hands. Something thick and rough binds her limbs. Her cheek aches, and a sticky, wet liquid fills her throat. She swallows and realizes it's blood, pooling in her mouth.

Help, she screams, but her lips don't move. A tight adhesive covers her mouth. Metallic and thick. Electrical tape?

A heavy fog holds her brain, pressing against her thoughts like she's been drugged. Has she?

A memory pokes through of him. Yelling. *You don't deserve this,* he said. *You destroy everyone who cares about you.* She tried to push by as he blocked her path. She didn't take him as a threat. An asshole, sure. But not a threat.

He grabbed her arm. She remembers a fist against her face. Then nothing.

Where is she? She blinks, and blurry images slowly come into focus in the dark. Concrete block walls. Mud color. Grimy. An old stationary bike. The kind where the handles move back and forth. One of the pedals missing. She shifts her eyes to the right of the bike, spotting an old television, a large cobweb in the corner of the screen.

Her eyes search for light. If she can make out these images, there must be some source. She tilts her head up and realizes how low the ceiling sits. If she stood, she could reach her hand up and touch it. Sweat breaks out across her skin as the ceiling seems to descend, pressing from the top, a terrifying inverse of the stretching room at Disney World's Haunted Mansion. She squeezes her eyes shut to banish the image, her breath shallow. Heart pounding against her chest. Did he take pleasure putting her somewhere that would trigger panic?

Stay strong, she chides herself, forcing her eyes open again in search of the light. Just a glimmer will help calm her. Sun perhaps? Or a lamp? Her eyes scan the rest of the space, stopping at a tiny window in the upper corner about the size of a milk crate. Bars stretch across the small opening. Like a prison. It's a cellar or a basement. But her prison.

Terror overtakes her body; arms flail against a pipe; her legs bang the ground. In her mind she's shaking the whole room with her power. She needs to get out. The room grows smaller. Sweat covers her skin. It feels like a hand squeezes her lungs.

She's aware of a creak. And more light. But she can't focus.

"Calm down," his voice orders. He turns on the television by the stationary bike and switches the channel to the US Open.

"I thought you'd want to see your match." He laughs, turning up the volume as the commentator announces a shocking development in the world of tennis. The anchor reports that she's withdrawn from the US Open due to *personal issues* and would like the media and public to respect her desire for privacy.

Fury floods her body. This was supposed to be her moment. She peers up at him. A tear drips down her cheek, salty.

"I set the rules of the game," he sneers, bending down, his face inches from hers. "And you can't win."

Terror mixed with indignation ricochets through her, like a circuit. Will this be how her life ends?

CHAPTER 1

TWO DAYS BEFORE THE KIDNAPPING
US Open—Day One

The US Open is much more than a sporting event; it's a scene. A happening. But this time I don't have to report on the *atmosphere*. I'm here for my in-depth segment on the women of the US Open. Specifically, the two women dominating headlines. Lucy Bosco, the most vilified woman in tennis. Or, according to her public relations team, the most misunderstood. And Brynn Cole, the young rebel under pressure to prove she's a serious competitor and not just a spoiled child from tennis royalty.

As someone who's had her share of knocks from the media, I want to do a deeper dive into these women. Do they deserve the shade thrown their way? Is sexism a factor? Do they need to recalibrate? Not just that—what drives them? As a former Olympic soccer gold medalist, I could never imagine playing a sport like tennis. I'd miss the teamwork. I'd hate to be out there alone. But I imagine these women thrive on it. Otherwise, why play?

"Kate—you ready?" my stalwart cameraman grumbles at me, popping another piece of nicotine gum into his mouth.

"Absolutely," I say, careful not to poke the Bill bear—who has taken grumpy to a new level, after kicking his cigarette habit following a heart attack three months ago. *If you don't stop smoking and start taking care of yourself, you'll be dead in a year,* the doctor told him.

"Don't look at me like that." He steps aside to make way for a group of middle-aged women rushing toward Arthur Ashe Stadium, visors pulled down against the late-afternoon sun.

"Like what?" I ask, watching the women in their tennis whites. Dressed as if they were actually going to play, instead of watch the matches.

"With pity in your eyes." He scowls.

"It's not pity—it's concern," I reply, studying Bill's leathery skin and sallow complexion, which haven't improved since he stopped smoking.

"Even worse," he grumbles, then spits into the grass. "Let's go." He turns his back on me, and I follow as he winds his way to the media entrance on the side of the brick facade below the main stadium. We flash our press passes and walk into air-conditioned halls with bright-white walls on one side, glass and chrome on the other, making our way to one of the small interview rooms we reserved for the hour.

"Real subtle." Bill snorts as we study the room, covered in USTA wallpaper.

"Just so no one forgets who runs the tournament," I add, laughing. Bill sits down next to his camera and stretches his long arms over his head; his wrinkled button-down rises over his jeans.

He points to my face, eyes assessing me. Without saying anything, I take out my makeup bag and remove my compact. My foundation has melted down my cheeks in ugly stripes. I get a tissue, wipe my face clean, and cover my pale skin with another layer of foundation. Next, I pull out my black eyeliner and apply it around my blue eyes, trying to ignore the small wrinkles that recently sprouted in the corners. Not bad for forty-four, but not great. Last, I take out the powder and dab the puff over my skin.

"Better?" I ask Bill.

"Better," he replies, flicking on the television above our heads and turning to our station, TRP Sports. One of the new young anchors sits next to a tennis commentator, discussing the first day of the tournament.

They show highlights of Lucy Bosco's quick match against her first opponent.

"Bosco's a fierce player. When she's at the top of her game, she's unbeatable," the anchor says. "Does it surprise you that she's talking about retirement?"

"Not really. She's old for a tennis player, thirty-seven. And, from what I hear, she's been putting off a double knee replacement. It's hard to come back from that kind of surgery at her age," the commentator says.

"True," the anchor responds. "I was surprised by something today." She giggles, making me cringe. "What Lucy did after the match." The video now shows Lucy engaging with the fans. "She signed autographs."

"Part of the new Lucy 2.0 campaign," the commentator replies before the anchors switch to the results of the men's morning matches.

"2.0." Bill snorts. "As if signing a couple of autographs can change someone."

"Don't knock it," I say. "You're working on the 2.0 version of yourself. A smoke-free Bill."

He grimaces, but I see a little smile creep across his lips.

Half an hour later, Lucy Bosco strides into the room wearing street clothes: jeans and a crisp white T-shirt. She looks harder in person, with sharp features, an angular jaw, and a regal, hawklike nose. "Nice match," I say, referring to her morning win against the unseeded player.

"It's easy when your opponent can't play," she says in typical Lucy fashion. Her younger brother, who has taken over all her public relations, glares at her.

"I mean, my opponent showed some nice skills and will probably become an excellent player as she develops," Lucy says, and I'm glad to see she has a sense of humor.

"That was off the record," her brother adds, pointing to his assistant, who stands close to him making notes on a tablet. Lucy's brother, Conrad, is famous in his own right among the political elite. He's what's known as a fixer. Think Kerry Washington's character Olivia Pope, from *Scandal.*

"Sure," I say, knowing Lucy will show her true personality at some point. After all, we plan to spend the next two weeks shadowing her during her off time at the Open, including a trip to her hometown and old haunts tomorrow. Something she hasn't shared with the press.

"Why don't we start with some general questions," I suggest as Bill clips the microphone to Lucy's T-shirt.

She folds her long muscular arms across her chest and leans back in her seat, legs extended. Basically, putting as much distance between herself and me as possible.

"What originally drew you to tennis?" I ask.

"I started playing in Poland, where my parents and family come from," she begins, her voice monotone. I already know the basics of her story. But I'm looking for emotion. Nuance. Her brother said Lucy's ready to share more aspects of her past. "By seven years old I showed real promise, so my parents shipped me to my uncle, who happened to know a prominent tennis pro."

"Your uncle played on the circuit himself."

"Yes," Lucy says, tucking a piece of auburn hair behind her ear. "He just never could break into the top two hundred." I hear pride in Lucy's voice. *I'm better than my uncle.* I wonder how that made her uncle feel. Did he enjoy seeing his niece thrive or resent it?

"Does your uncle come to your matches?" I ask.

"No," Lucy says, glancing toward her brother, who asks if we can move on.

"Sure." I make a mental note to pursue that topic at a later date. What were the dynamics between Lucy and her uncle? Where is he these days?

"It must have been hard to be separated from your parents and siblings," I continue.

"It was," Lucy says, her voice void of emotion. "But I couldn't talk about it to anyone. My opponents would hold it over me. You have no idea how brutal things can be in locker rooms," she says, oblivious to the fact that I spent plenty of time in locker rooms. Did she not see the news last year about all the bullying my teammates and I experienced as teenagers playing soccer for the United States? Heck, the story won me an Emmy. Clearly, Lucy lives in a narcissistic bubble. Then again, being a top-seeded tennis player does take focus.

"Why share this information now?" I ask.

"I'm less concerned about what my opponents think—"

"And more concerned with what the public thinks?" I finish her thought for her when she doesn't.

"If people are going to hate me, at least I want it to be for the right reasons," she says, holding her head high, in a way that reminds me of a member of England's royal family. Lucy definitely gives off *keep your distance* vibes.

"And what about sponsorships? A better reputation could help win over endorsements," I say, bringing up the fact that despite her achievements, a surprisingly small number of sponsors support her.

"That's true. But that's not why I'm doing it. I'm fine—I am a ten-time Grand Slam champion," she snaps, the competitiveness coming through.

"Let's return to the question about your family, shall we?" I say, and she nods.

"My parents and siblings all made it to the US four years later and moved in with my uncle and me. Conrad was about seven when he arrived in the States." She motions to her brother, who is the second oldest in the Bosco clan.

Lucy's childhood contains multiple stories of tragedy and trials. Sibling jealousies. Poverty. Her mother's tragic accident. But I decide to hold off on asking those questions just yet.

I can't avoid all the sticky topics and move on to her marriages. "Word is you're separated from your husband?" I say, referring to Nico

Pappas, a top-two-hundred player, known more for his underwear commercials and man buns than tennis strokes.

"Not separated," she says. "Our 'issues' have been blown way out of proportion. We're still together. He's meeting me here soon, in fact."

"That's great," I add, surprised.

"Just because I don't have the best track record with men . . ." *Two divorces by thirty-seven.* "Doesn't mean anytime my husband and I fight we're heading for divorce court."

"My mistake," I say, hoping she won't storm off and end the interview, something she's been known to do.

As if on cue, the door opens and Nico steps into the room.

He gives his magazine smile, apologizes for barging in, then winks at Lucy. She blushes and smiles back, like a little girl. Nico turns to me and Bill. "I promise to be quiet." He puts his fingers to his lips like he's locking them and throws away the imaginary key.

"Let's continue." Conrad moves his hand like he's stirring soup.

"That was a sweet moment between you and Nico," I say to Lucy. "Hope it's all right to include it."

"Of course," Nico booms. "An honor to support my beautiful wife. And happy to answer any questions you might have for me," he adds.

Conrad turns to Nico with a warning glare. There's certainly no love lost between these two. Nico puts up his hands in surrender.

"Since Nico is here," I say, "tell us a little about how the two of you met."

"It was four years ago at Indian Wells. Nico got knocked out early," Lucy says matter-of-factly. Out of the corner of my eye, I see Nico wince. And Conrad smile. "My coach at the time suggested we hit together. My hitting partner had twisted his ankle the day before. And Nico became my hitting partner," she says. "And then my husband."

I wonder what Nico thinks. Does it bother him that she reached the level of tennis he never managed to break into? I glance again at

Nico, who went from all smiles to texting furiously on his phone. Lucy seems oblivious.

We wrap up the interview and confirm our meeting tomorrow in her hometown of Glenport, Long Island. As they walk out, Lucy reaches for Nico's hand, and he bats it away. So much for the happy couple.

CHAPTER 2

Evening sets over the USTA Billie Jean King National Tennis Center; a slight wind blows across the concrete grounds as the sun dips lower in the horizon. Night tennis fans replace day fans, like changing tides. Many of the evening crowd still wear their work clothing, coming straight from their Manhattan offices. About a twenty-minute limousine drive from downtown, if that's your mode of transportation. Or a fifty-minute subway ride, depending on how many transfers. The moneyed rush to their fancy boxes and private dining spaces, while the regular fans find stadium seats in the upper decks of the main stadium or muscle their way onto the aluminum stands on the outer courts.

The changeover gives Bill and me an opportunity to grab a bite before the next match.

"Should we eat in the media cafeteria or head to the food vendors?" Bill asks, knowing my opinion. For a media cafeteria, the one here isn't bad. But the Open's food court features a variety of popular vendors, all offering mouthwatering options.

"You already can guess my answer." I laugh at him, scanning the choices in front of us.

"What are you thinking?" Bill looks at me. "A burger or Mexican?"

Normally, I'd jump at getting the burger, but I'm thinking there will be healthier choices for Bill at the Mexican stand.

"I'm not dying," Bill grumbles at me when I don't answer. "I just quit smoking. Stop acting like it's my last meal."

You might be dying, if you don't change your habits, I think but hold my tongue. Bill needs to avoid red meat. In fact, we should get salads, but I'm sure if I suggest that, he'll implode.

"Mexican," I say, hoping Bill will pick the vegetarian option. Or at least chicken.

"Not a burger?" He sounds irritated.

"Nope."

We take our food to one of the square metal tables bolted to the ground and pull over the matching white metal chairs from an empty spot. I glare at Bill's food, a beef burrito that he chose after I'd placed my order for the vegetable option. He's toying with me. At this rate, we could have had burgers.

"I'm also getting ice cream," Bill says, shooing a pigeon from his feet.

"Damn," someone grumbles over my shoulder as liquid sloshes onto my foot. I look up at a man dressed in a suit jacket, loosened tie around his neck, juggling three beers. "Sorry," he mumbles as I jump from my seat to avoid another dousing of beer.

"Are you kidding me?" I shout at his back, reaching for a napkin. He ignores me, disappearing in the growing sea of people. "What are you laughing at?" I snap at Bill.

He just smiles and hands me another napkin.

"Now I smell like a frat party," I mutter as I wipe my shoes and push my food away, no longer hungry.

"Ice cream will cheer you up," Bill says, picking up both our plates to dump in the garbage. I follow him out of the Food Village and across the East Plaza, passing a multitude of drink vendors—from Grey Goose to organic nitro cold-brew coffees—and head to a quiet spot in the back by one of the outer courts. Underneath the stands sits an outdoor setup, completely incongruent with the Open: wicker-style furniture made of plastic, with cushions. The couch and love seat resemble something you'd expect in a suburban backyard, not under the outer court at one of tennis's Grand Slams. But, at least now, we seem to be among the few who have discovered it.

I get two scoops of coffee ice cream and don't even wait around to police Bill's choice. He comes back with a single scoop of sorbet, making me wonder if he'll behave better if I stop nagging him. Great! A third child.

"What time is our next event?" Bill asks, his lips turning pink from the raspberry flavor.

"Seven," I say, looking at my phone. "That gives us a half hour. We can cover the match and then listen to the press conference."

"Why is there so much hype around this girl?" Bill asks, scraping the bottom of his cup with the plastic spoon.

"For one, Brynn Cole is from tennis royalty." I swallow a big spoonful of ice cream. I'm anxious to get a look at Brynn and her family. A lot of stories focus on their status. Generations of elite tennis.

"And the kid—Brynn, she's adopted, right?"

"Yup." Brynn's adoption fascinates me because it brings up the question of nature versus nurture. Obviously, Brynn must possess athletic genes. But would she have become a tennis phenom if she'd been adopted by a different family?

Bill crumples his cup and loops it at the garbage can.

I laugh when the cup hits the rim and bounces onto the ground. "You better clean that up, my friend."

"Didn't Brynn also beat Lucy recently?" Bill asks, walking to pick up his cup.

I stand, too, finishing my last spoonful. "Yes," I reply. "Brynn beat Lucy in five sets a few months ago. It really put Brynn on the map as a contender and not just the child of famous players. But one win doesn't beget a star."

"It does *beget* media attention, though." Bill laughs as we walk to Court 7, where the bleachers remind me of the metal stands from my daughter's Little League games. Except these are packed with people.

"You'd think Serena Williams was playing back here," Bill says, muscling his body between me and a woman trying to save a spot on the bench with her program. While the outer courts don't, in fact, draw the big names, they tend to feature the most heated matches in the early days of the tournament. The players fighting to make it through the first rounds. In fact, Brynn's relegation to an outer court drew some criticism in the media. At seventeen years old, she's ranked in the top one hundred in the world and has won some important tournaments leading up to the Open.

She certainly maintains star power, evident by the fans crushing around the court, including standing along the edges of the stairs to get a view.

Brynn Cole walks onto the court in an edgy tie-dyed tennis skirt and matching tank. Her long brown hair, pulled back in a ponytail, tinted to match the pastel colors of her clothes; a row of diamond studs lines her ear. Her TikTok-famous go-to fake eyelashes framing confident amber eyes.

"That's a secure seventeen-year-old," Bill whispers to me as the crowd roars for Brynn.

"We'll see," I reply, suspicious that sometimes overconfidence in teens is used to hide insecurities.

I scan the player boxes and spot Brynn's parents on the sideline. Their demeanor and dress are opposite from their daughter's. Both wear tennis whites—the mother, no visible makeup, her blonde ponytail peeking out from a white visor, designer sunglasses covering half her face. The dad, Brynn's coach, looks buttoned up in his Lacoste classic polo.

Brynn waves to the crowd, basking in the cheers, while pointing her cell phone outward to record the fans.

"My God," Bill grumbles. "This is a bit much, don't you think?" Brynn shares incessantly over social media. Every argument with her parents finds its way onto her feed. Tons of videos talking about her feelings, her frustrations, her food choices, a hangnail—*everything* ends up on her posts.

Not a curated account to build sponsorship or brand. Brynn shares her adolescent angst with the whole world playing armchair psychiatrist.

It's a generational thing, I guess. To an extreme. Even my twins, now freshmen in college, think Brynn overshares.

A new thought pops into my head. Does the phone help Brynn hide? If she's peering out at the world, can she keep the world from peering in? Maybe she'd rather be at the forefront of the narrative so the outside world can't see something deeper and more troubling?

Brynn serves first, and the ball flies off her racquet at Williams-sisters speed. But goes wide. She double faults, then loses the game.

She glances at her father, who stares at her with a deep scowl. Instead of shrinking, Brynn appears defiant. Shoulders back, head high, she waits for her opponent's serve, making quick work of that game. And winning the next.

"You ever think of playing tennis?" Bill whispers to me as the women switch sides.

"Not a chance," I answer. "It strikes me as the loneliest sport in the world."

Brynn wins the first set and then quickly wins the second, showing the crowd why she's the player everyone's talking about. She possesses a killer serve and devastating forehand. She's also quick on her feet, running down every shot.

After she shakes her opponent's hand, she glances at the player box. Her father gives a small nod, his eyes now hidden behind small rectangular sunglasses, even though it's night and the only thing to hide from is the crescent moon. Next to him, Brynn's mom stands clapping for her daughter. A tennis superstar in her own right, Brynn's mom won multiple Grand Slam doubles championships.

At the press conference, Brynn sits at the front table, hands clamped together on the surface.

"Brynn," the first reporter calls. "How do you feel?"

Brynn stares straight ahead and smiles. "I feel great. I did my job out there, and I'm looking forward to my next match."

"What's it like to be at the US Open as a top-one-hundred player?" another reporter asks.

"It's a dream come true," she shoots back.

"Your style of play is often compared to Lucy Bosco's. What do you think of that?"

She pauses as if waiting for all eyes to focus on her. "I think I play like Lucy did when Lucy was *young*."

A hum of whispers overtakes the room, commenting on her audacity or confidence, depending on their spin. Either way—that line will be the lead in everyone's story. I glance at Brynn's father, who gives his daughter a thumbs-up. Let the psychological warfare begin.

CHAPTER 3

I sit in my driveway, staring at my home in the dark. Usually when I arrive late, the lights shine, and I rush inside, eager to catch up with my twins. But they both left a week ago for college. My heart sinks a little as I step out of my car and head up my brick walkway into my small Victorian home, an outlier of a house in the affluent suburb of Greenwich, Connecticut.

I flick on the lights and make my way through the narrow hallway into the kitchen. Even the bright-yellow paint doesn't lift my spirits. I grab the wine from the fridge and pour myself a large glass.

The only benefit to having the house to myself is that I no longer need to conceal my side project—an investigation into my biological father's past. I stare at the papers that cover my cramped dining room table—bits of evidence I've collected over the past two years. Progress but not definitive proof that Liam Murphy continues to hide the real reason he was shot and abandoned my brother and me when we were kids.

One more day, I remind myself, thinking about my meeting tomorrow, which should provide me with the conclusive proof I've been seeking.

The grandfather clock in the hallway chimes a low, hollow gong-like sound. I stifle a yawn listening to the twelve beats and head upstairs to my cozy bedroom, with its white wicker furniture, slanted roof, and soft comforter. I fall asleep, but I'm aware of a disturbance in my dreams and a feeling of foreboding that takes hold of my thoughts.

CHAPTER 4

ONE DAY BEFORE THE KIDNAPPING

I wake with a start to the sound of my phone ringing. "Hello?" I push myself against the headboard, noticing that the sky remains dark outside my window.

"Kate," the voice of my boss, Charlie, from TRP Sports cuts through the haze. "Are you awake," he says, not asks. Knowing perfectly well that I'm not.

"Does it matter?" I snap, not responsible for pre-coffee behavior.

"I waited until six to call. There's been some unexpected changes with your show," Charlie starts as I slide out of bed and shuffle downstairs.

"I'm listening—"

"We need to move your tennis story up to this Sunday."

"This Sunday?" I say, adrenaline ramping up. "That's a whole week earlier. Jeez, Charlie. Why? That's going to be a tough turnaround. I'll barely be done with the interviews."

"A combination of things—one concerning your cohost," he says, letting that sit in the air. My cohost, also known as my ex-boyfriend David Lopez, has been growing more and more hostile. Not just to me but to Charlie and the TRP staff in general. "He's not going to be ready with his story."

A spite delay, I can't help thinking. "You said a combination of reasons," I say, turning the coffee maker on.

"The new bean counters. They're micromanaging the hell out of me and think it would be better to have the tennis piece during the first week of the US Open."

The bean counters descended on TRP Sports and the rest of NetWorld Media last year, right after the chair of the corporation and his son landed in federal prison. Largely a result of my investigation. The unintended consequence of the arrests is that our station is up for sale, and the new board of directors wants to cut budgets to make TRP Sports more appealing to buyers.

"If I try to argue with them?" I ask, watching the coffee drip into the carafe.

"Wouldn't matter," Charlie replies. "See how much you get done, and we'll circle back in a few days. Okay?" he asks but hangs up before I can even respond.

That's an empty offer. I down my coffee and get dressed. No choice but to power through with some long days and, hopefully, productive interviews.

CHAPTER 5

Glenport is technically part of Long Island's Gold Coast, but the glaring exception. The idle rich settled to the east and west of this town, leaving Glenport's rocky beaches and swampy wetlands to the working class.

I drive past abandoned storefronts and modest homes, slowing down to turn into an industrial park with a stone and granite yard to the right and a storage facility to the left. The tennis center sits straight ahead, a bare-bones concrete building, with a giant domed roof.

An arch of blue and green balloons swings softly in the breeze over a platform facing fifty folding chairs. I get out of my car, then walk the parking lot in search of Bill and his van. I don't spot him but see Lucy sitting in the driver's seat of a black SUV idling in the front row.

I knock on the passenger window and hop out of the way as the door opens and Nico steps out. His hair wet and pulled back in a ponytail. "Good morning, Kate Green," he says with a little bow. "How exciting for Lucy that she gets to return home for this reunion. What a lovely little facility."

I glance at Lucy to see if she notices Nico's tone, but she either doesn't or doesn't care. He excuses himself and heads toward the activity, saying he wants to make sure everything is in place for his wife.

"I thought most players don't like driving during tournaments," I say, making myself at home in her passenger seat, the smell of leather and lemon strong inside the car.

"I'm not like most," she snaps, then straightens her back and sighs. "Driving helps me clear my mind."

"I get that," I say, also a fan of driving my little BMW convertible around. I take out my phone and text Bill to see how far away he is. Even though the ceremony will only be a small part of our story, I'd still like to get the video. Bill responds he's almost here. "Traffic!"

"How does it feel returning home?" I ask Lucy, noting her hands clenched around the steering wheel, knuckles white.

"My brother would be mad if he knew you were talking to me without him." She turns to me, eyebrow raised.

"But the whole point of this story is to give you the chance to open up. Something Conrad said you wanted to do," I reply, knowing I won't have an extra week to *charm* her into sharing.

Outside, a group of people unravel a vinyl sign welcoming Lucy home. She presses her lips together but doesn't explain why she's agitated. Something I will push her about later when the camera is rolling. What about home makes her uncomfortable? And it's not like I'm trying to be salacious. Conrad came to me saying Lucy wanted to do this no-holds-barred interview to, in his words, *bare her soul.*

In the meantime, there's no reason to delve without the camera going, so I sit in silence as more cars pull into the lot, including a bus with children dressed in bright-yellow LUCY BOSCO TENNIS ACADEMY T-shirts, some down to their knees.

"Cute kids," I remark.

She turns to me, voice low, "Do you know why Conrad thought you'd be trustworthy over other reporters?"

"You didn't help him decide?" I ask.

"I was busy," she says in her matter-of-fact *bordering on insulting* tone.

"Maybe because I'm a fellow athlete," I suggest. "Or because I know how harmful inaccurate coverage can be. You probably are aware of the fact that I've had my own run-ins with the press."

"You have?" She releases the steering wheel, turning to me.

I don't know whether to feel offended by Lucy's ignorance or envious of her blinders. I tell her about the gotcha video from two years ago that showed me cursing out an NBA player. "He deserved it," I explain. "But only part of the video got caught on tape."

"How did you redeem yourself?" she asks with genuine interest.

"I nearly died trying to catch a killer. In the end, that became the bigger story." In front of us, the children pour into the seats in front of the stage, their giggles reaching the car. "I didn't force you into this story. You came to me," I remind her.

"Technically my brother did," Lucy says, more to herself than me.

"I promise to be fair. I'm just here to tell your story."

"Mine and Brynn Cole's." She looks at me with a smirk.

I want to ask Lucy about Brynn, specifically Brynn's comment last night where Brynn compared herself to a *young* Lucy. But I want that on camera and on the record.

Lucy returns to surveying the area as a limo pulls up and a woman emerges from the back seat. Lucy's body stiffens as she watches the thin, small woman, who looks like she's playing dress-up in a baggy suit jacket and pointed heels.

"Is there a problem?" I ask Lucy.

"Would you excuse me for a second," she says. I can take a hint and step outside into the hot, humid air. As soon as my door shuts, Lucy picks up her phone and turns her back to me. A phone rings about ten feet in front, and I see Conrad answer. He's too far away for me to hear what he's saying, but his brows are knit in frustration.

CHAPTER 6

"Ready for work, boss." Bill approaches, tripod swung over his shoulder, camera in hand, lollipop in mouth.

"Nice to see you chipper," I reply. "Guess you didn't hear from Charlie today."

"Bad news?" he asks as we walk to the back of the audience, where a small platform sits for cameras.

"He wants our story for *this* Sunday," I reply.

"That's crazy." Bill opens his tripod and sets it on the platform. "You know Charlie, though. That deadline can still shift three times."

"Still, now we have to assume Sunday," I reply. "The worst of it was that Charlie woke me at six this morning to tell me all this."

"Pre-coffee? That couldn't have gone well," he says, and I laugh. Bill and I are the same person when it comes to coffee. And anyone in their right mind knows not to talk to us until we've had at least one cup.

Bill attaches the camera to the tripod as Lucy emerges from the car, escorted by Nico. I step behind Bill so he can get the video of the two of them striding toward the stage.

Lucy steps onto the dais, shaking the mayor's hand and flashing a smile as the mayor whispers something in her ear. The interaction feels forced in light of the anxiety that crossed Lucy's face when she first spotted the mayor from her vehicle.

"Here we go." Conrad approaches, coffee in hand. Conrad wears a crisp white oxford, hair gelled to statue-like firmness. "It's going to be a great day." He smiles, then takes a sip of his drink, which leaves a little foam on his lip. My coffee envy disappears as I realize he's drinking one of those silly frilly options.

"What's the deal with Lucy and the mayor?" I whisper to Conrad as the mayor welcomes everyone to the event.

"Absolutely nothing," he snaps, no longer smiling. I know he's lying, which I hate. But it's more my curiosity than a story element—I need to focus on my piece since it airs five days from now.

Lucy approaches the podium, unfolding a piece of paper, and reads from the document, thanking the residents of Glenport and a few local sponsors, then pauses. She starts to read a word with an *m*, my guess—*mayor*, but skips over it. Conrad's color rises. My eyes move to the mayor, who clenches her jaw but shows no other outward sign of irritation.

Lucy turns to address the kids in the front row. "I hope you will enjoy playing tennis here. And to help ease any financial burdens"—she moves her eyes up to the rest of the audience—"my foundation will create multiple scholarships for promising athletes."

A smattering of applause breaks out from the audience.

"That's a nice moment," Conrad whispers. I ignore him and his attempt to influence my story.

The mayor picks up a pair of large scissors and motions for Lucy to walk to the blue ribbon tied to poles in front of the entrance to the dome. The kids line up behind the two women.

Lucy reaches for the scissors, but the mayor holds on tight, forcing Lucy to share the moment. As soon as the photographers walk away, Lucy drops the scissors and turns to leave. Nico reaches for the mayor's hand, holding it in both of his. She blushes as he says something to her. I look for Lucy, who watches from the edge of the stage. And I wonder again, What is going on between Lucy and her husband, Lucy and the mayor, and possibly, the mayor and Nico? This feels more like a soap opera than a tennis story.

CHAPTER 7

Lucy stalks toward Conrad and, by extension, me.

"I can't believe you invited your high school flame." She shoves Conrad in the arm.

"She's not here because we dated—she's the mayor," Conrad says and then looks at me and mouths, "Off the record." The bus carrying the kids in yellow T-shirts pulls past us; diesel fumes mix with the rising heat. A few of the kids press their noses against their windows, waving to Lucy. She ignores them, but I wave, watching them giggle.

"The *mayor* had nothing to do with the construction of this facility, Conrad." Lucy glares at him, still focused on their discussion. "She fought us on the permits. Now she gets to waltz in here and act as if she was part of providing our town something new and shiny. She's a leech."

Conrad takes Lucy's arm and pulls her away from me to a grassy area on the edge of the lot. I watch the two of them, voices now hushed but their movements animated and angry.

"Welcome to the Lucy-and-Conrad show." Nico sidles up to me eating a granola bar.

"What do you mean?" I ask, noting to myself that sibling tension would very much be part of a tell-all exposé.

"They fight all the time." Nico kicks at a rock on the ground. "It's exhausting." He lets out a heavy sigh to punctuate the point. I wonder about Nico; does he mind playing second fiddle to his wife? Because he strikes me as a person who very much enjoys being at the center of things. Before marrying Lucy, he was known as a player—off the court.

"Do you and Lucy fight?" I ask, keeping my voice soft in the hope he will feel comfortable confiding in me.

"We used to," he says, his dark-green eyes fill with sadness. "Fighting is Lucy's love language. When she starts ignoring you, that's when you need to worry."

Conrad and Lucy return, and Nico pulls out his phone as if he's in the middle of reading something extremely important.

We caravan into town, where Lucy and I leave our cars in the local lot. I hop into the TRP van with Bill, while Lucy and Nico pile into Conrad's Mercedes. I'm anxious to get moving with the rest of the day—the meat of the story. Lucy at her high school should provide good fodder for my piece. We have permission to videotape Lucy at the school as long as we don't shoot video with any students who haven't given explicit permission to be part of the story.

I'm most interested in sitting down with Lucy in her high school library and looking through her yearbooks. I love the idea of seeing what memories pop up. Maybe some unguarded Lucy 2.0 material.

The other spot I'm looking forward to interviewing Lucy at is her old neighborhood tennis courts down the block from where she grew up. The fact that they are now dilapidated will be an interesting backdrop for our main one-on-one interview, which is at the end of the day. Conrad insisted it be then, but I'm a little concerned Lucy might be tired, irritated, or both. I would rather have gotten to the main interview earlier in the day.

Bill turns at a purple-and-yellow sign reading **Glenport High School**, with a digital message flashing below. **Welcome Home, Lucy Bosco.** He pulls the car over and jumps out, then grabs his camera to get the setup shot of the sign.

"Got it," he says, climbing back in the van. He drives up the hill, where a parking guard motions for him to pull into a spot along the curb.

"Welcome," a gray-haired woman smooshed into a tracksuit gushes. "Welcome, welcome, welcome to Glenport High School," she repeats. "I'm Sophia James, but everyone around here calls me S.J. I'm the head of the physical education department." She shrugs. "Gym, but they don't like that word anymore."

"Nice to meet you, S.J.," I reply as she shakes my hand up and down like a seesaw.

"We have quite the time planned. I'm just plumb over the moon about this," she says and introduces us to the welcoming committee, made up of the tennis team, the captains holding a bouquet of sunflowers in a vase filled with tennis balls.

"Isn't that the most adorable thing you ever saw?" S.J. emotes. "These girls came up with it themselves."

Conrad jogs over, all business. Then S.J. reaches up and hugs him. "Conny." She releases him but holds on to his arms. "Look at you, look at you."

Conrad breaks into a genuine grin, telling S.J. how happy he is to see her. She pats him on the arm and focuses on the car as she waits for Lucy.

Conrad looks over at me, blushing. "What?"

"Nothing, Conny," I reply with a grin.

Bill hoists the camera onto his shoulder and points it toward the car, waiting for Lucy and Nico to emerge.

S.J. rushes to Lucy and wraps her in an even bigger hug than she gave Conrad. Lucy bends down to return the hug, a wide smile on her face. Bill pushes closer to capture the rare show of joy from Lucy.

"Here's our very own star." S.J. glows as she talks to Lucy. The captains of the tennis team approach and present the flowers for Lucy, who remarks on how clever the vase is before handing it off to Conrad. Bill takes a few more shots of Lucy with the tennis team, and then S.J. tells the girls to return to class.

"Where to first?" I ask, anxious to move away from all the staged video.

“Let’s go look at Lucy’s trophies,” Conrad says.

“Well, of course, but then we need to go to the library. I’m busting to show you both the yearbooks we pulled out. You’ll hardly recognize yourselves. So many memories,” S.J. says, and I’m suddenly Team S.J. and her suggestion to get to the library.

Bill puts wireless microphones on S.J., Lucy, and me before we enter the school. A security guard lets us inside, and I immediately smell frozen pizza—the kind shaped in rectangles. Every high school smells like this.

We wind our way past metal lockers to a glass trophy case. S.J. stops and points out all Lucy’s trophies. “And she won those her freshman year.” S.J. beams with pride as Bill videotapes her. “By sophomore year, Lucy moved to the Junior ATP tour. In fact, the school arranged Lucy’s academic schedule so she could finish her classes by noon and then leave for tennis.”

“Not every place is so accommodating,” I say, thinking about some of the issues I had at my high school when I needed to travel for national and international tournaments.

“Not everyone has S.J. in their corner,” Lucy says, putting her arm around her proud teacher.

“Do you have a favorite trophy?” I sidle up next to Lucy, staring at the shiny gold trophies.

“I think the state singles championship. My mom traveled with me to Buffalo for that tournament,” Lucy says, and I notice a cloud cross S.J.’s face.

“Your mom was quite a woman,” S.J. says, expression solemn. A bell sounds the end of a period, and the halls flood with teenagers, like termites swarming. High-pitched laughter and yelling.

“Which was your locker?” I ask Lucy as we press against the walls to avoid the rushing bodies.

“I’m not sure,” Lucy says. “No one used their lockers here. We’d carry all our stuff in our backpacks. The school’s so big that there was never enough time to return to your locker and make it to class.”

An argument breaks out at the end of the hall, and I see a thick boy in a football jacket shove a smaller kid. S.J. sprints over to break up the fight.

"It wasn't the easiest place to go to school," Lucy says, apparently to no one. S.J. returns as a second bell rings, signaling the start of the next period. The few remaining students quickly disperse, including the boys who were fighting.

S.J. leads us upstairs, through a hall to double doors with a plaque on the side that says **Library**. We wind past round wooden tables with low seats pushed in, making our way to the back, where a large window faces the school's parking lot. Bill grumbles at the glare from the sun.

"We need to move you to this table." Bill motions to a table farther from the window.

"I thought the sun would be a benefit." S.J. seems embarrassed, like she put out the wrong silverware for a fancy dinner.

"A lot of people make that mistake," I say as we move the yearbooks to the new table.

Finally, we sit down in front of the books, Lucy between S.J. and me.

"This is going to be so much fun," S.J. says again, pulling out a purple-and-yellow hardcover album with the words **Class of 2003** written on the front. "Your freshman year." S.J. beams.

She flips through the pages to the sports section, turning to the tennis spread. "Two pages," S.J. says to me, explaining most teams only get one. I stare at the photos, starting with a color picture of the team in their purple-and-yellow tennis skirts, holding a large trophy. Lucy stands in the front, looking un-Lucy with a huge smile across her face. Her hair pulled into a high ponytail; her features soft.

"Tell me about this photo." I point to a picture of Lucy and another girl, arms around each other's shoulders. The other girl has purple-and-yellow streaks in her long black hair. The caption reads **Besties**. I'd love to interview one of Lucy's high school friends, especially because she doesn't seem to have any friends on the tour.

Lucy doesn't say anything, but S.J. laughs. "You just met her at the ribbon-cutting ceremony—she's the town mayor—Heather Liu." S.J. reaches over and turns the page. "Look, there they are again." She points to a photo of the girls at lunch, mouths open and tongues out, seemingly locked in an inside joke. "They were inseparable."

If S.J. knows about the tension between Lucy and the mayor, she doesn't show it.

"Tell me your memories when you look at these photos," I ask Lucy, hoping for some emotion.

"I was really young," she says, studying the picture. "When you're a kid, you don't really know what motivates people."

"What do you mean?" I say, feeling like I'm pulling teeth.

"Nothing. It was a fun time back then. When I left for the tour, everything became more intense."

Talk more, I want to scream. *Expand your answers.*

"Tell me about this team." I turn back to the page with the whole group. We'll discuss her time on the tour later. This video is about high school.

"It was high school." She shrugs, and I fight the frustration bubbling up inside.

S.J. must sense the tension too. "I bet Lucy will have more to say about the photos in this book," she says, reaching for another yearbook, this one from her senior year. "You can see her prom photo with her dashing boyfriend."

I stare down at the photo of Lucy in a butterscotch dress with a puffy skirt and large corsage on her wrist. Her hair sits piled on top of her head in a pineapple bun. The boy wears a navy tuxedo with a matching butterscotch vest and bow tie.

"He was a nice guy." Lucy smiles at the photo of the boy with light-brown hair, freckles, and a giant smile. "Ian Reese."

"Clearly not an athlete," Nico scoffs, studying the thin freckled kid with braces. Lucy ignores Nico as she stares at the photo. "I remember when he asked me to the prom. He came to one of my matches, and when it was over, we walked to a back court where he had written *Prom?* in tennis balls." Lucy smiles at the memory. Finally.

"He always was a sweet boy." S.J. pats Lucy's hand.

"Was?" I ask, picking up on something.

They ignore my question, and S.J. turns the page. "Look, there you are with Ian at graduation."

"I had a tournament right after the ceremony, and he went with me from the ceremony to the match, skipping his family's graduation party." She smiles at the memory.

"I hope you won at least," I reply.

Lucy actually laughs. "I did. Always."

"You still in touch?" I ask, trying again to suss out why there's weirdness around Ian. He'd be a fantastic person to speak with.

Lucy exchanges a look with S.J. but doesn't speak.

Conrad fills the silence. "He's not going to want to be interviewed, if that's what you're wondering."

"The poor dear," S.J. jumps in. "He had an accident about a year after graduating from high school. Tragic really. He's around but not the same." She shuts the yearbook. "Is it time for my interview?" she asks, looking eager for her fifteen minutes of fame. Either that, or she wants to steer the conversation in a different direction.

I'm thankful to see Lucy and Nico excuse themselves, saying they'll meet us at the car when we're done. I only wish Conrad would leave too. But there's no way.

Sitting across from S.J., I start by asking her about Lucy as a high schooler.

"She was just wonderful," S.J. gushes. "She devoted herself fully to everything she touched, whether tennis or her classes."

"How would you describe her childhood?" I ask.

"She had a hard life," S.J. says, and I ask her to elaborate. The school bell rings, and Bill holds up his hand for us to pause until the noise dissipates. From the window, I watch students pour out of the building. S.J. explains that seniors are allowed to leave school during their lunch period. *Lucky them,* I think.

The noise dies down, and Bill signals for us to resume.

"Can you explain why Lucy's childhood was so hard?" I prompt S.J.

She clasps her hands on her lap and nods to me. "Nothing came easy for Lucy. Poor dear. She came to this country not speaking a stitch of English. Before anyone bothered to teach her the language, they plopped her onto a tennis court and hit balls at her day and night. By the time the rest of her family arrived, she had acclimated, and they were new and dependent on her."

S.J. goes on to describe Lucy as a leader at Glenport High School. Someone admired and appreciated. But also, someone who kept her guard up and didn't have many friends.

"Except for Heather and Ian?" I ask.

"Yes," S.J. says, but the talkative gym teacher doesn't elaborate on that, instead telling stories about all the teachers who loved and admired Lucy. "We always knew she'd be a superstar," S.J. says.

I finish the interview, and Bill starts breaking down the setup while I thank S.J. for speaking with us. Conrad leaves first, but S.J. waits to walk us out.

"Ms. Green," S.J. whispers.

"Yes?" I look down into her worried eyes.

"Stay away from the Ian thing. I shouldn't have brought it up. It was insensitive of me. And it has nothing to do with Lucy and tennis."

"Kate!" Conrad calls from the lobby, walking toward us, clearly not happy to see S.J. and me whispering together.

"Please." She grasps my hand in hers, eyes pleading. I pull my hand away and keep walking. I don't say anything to her, because I don't lie. And her plea has only made me more determined to figure out what happened to Ian and Lucy.

CHAPTER 8

It's 1:00 p.m., and as much as I want to get on with the day, I know we need to stop for lunch. At least we will eat at the restaurant where Lucy waitressed as a teen—a two birds with one stone kind of stop. Eat and get a sense of Lucy's teen stomping grounds. Not to mention the Mac-n-Cheesy is known for its mac and cheese, and anything with carbs and cheese is a good break in my book.

Not to take a pun too far, but I'm happy to see the restaurant doesn't present as *cheesy* but more of a quaint log cabin–type feel. There's a corner bar on one end and wooden chairs and tables on the other. Large rustic chandeliers cast a yellow glow over the wooden interior. Lucy explains that this place is all about comfort food and that she ate enough macaroni and cheese here to last a lifetime.

"That's still what you're going to get. Right?" Conrad smiles, seeming to relax in these surroundings.

"Well, I do have to carb load before tomorrow's match." Lucy gives him a sly smile in return. Conrad explains how Lucy got him a job in the kitchen while she worked here. "It wasn't as glamorous as waitressing," he says. "I was stuck in the back washing dishes. But it was fun."

We sit at a round bleached-wood table in the middle of the room with five matching chairs. Conrad steps past Nico to sit on one side of Lucy while I slip into the seat on her right. Bill next to me, leaving Nico standing in front of the last empty seat. Nico looks like the kid who just lost at musical chairs.

"Is everything all right?" A young waitress steps over, addressing Nico, who remains standing.

"Absolutely." He flashes her a pinup smile and asks where the restrooms are. She blushes and points to the corridor behind the bar.

Lucy's shoulders tense as she watches the waitress gaze after Nico.

Conrad coughs, and the waitress turns toward us and hands out the heavy red menus.

"I've never seen so many variations of macaroni and cheese," I say, scanning mac and cheese with mushrooms, cauliflower, bacon. On and on.

Lucy ignores me while staring at her menu, leaving Bill to grunt his agreement. Bill must feel sorry for me because he offers to share a mac and cheese. And *salad.*

"Deal," I reply. "If we can get the mac and cheese with truffle oil."

With the lunch negotiation settled, I close my menu and take another look around the restaurant. About half the tables are full, many with young mothers with toddlers. There's also a handful of people at the bar, watching a TV screen in the corner and drinking beer. Nico returns and takes his seat, making a big show of winking at the waitress, who giggles.

"This is actually where Lucy met Ian," Conrad says, and I notice Nico's head snap back.

"He worked here?" I ask.

"No—his younger brother washed dishes with Conrad, but Ian would come by to do his homework," Lucy says.

"He came to flirt with Lucy. Homework was the excuse," Conrad adds as the waitress returns with bread for the table, placing it in front of Nico.

"Whatever happened to his brother?" Lucy asks, head high, ignoring her husband.

"Runs the pharmacy across the street," Conrad replies, reaching for the bread.

The door to the restaurant opens, and a large group of women pours inside dressed in business attire. One points in our direction, and they start whispering.

I notice Lucy's shoulders tense again, but she continues talking. "I thought the brother, Greggory, planned to go to med school."

"Plans change," Conrad says to Lucy, a deeper message communicated between them.

"That's a shame. All Greggory talked about was getting out of this town," she says, staring at the women as they settle at the table behind ours. And I feel like Lucy is talking about herself as much as Ian's brother.

The mac and cheese arrives and proves even better than promised. As I enjoy the decadent cheese and pasta, I try to imagine Lucy and Conrad as teens working at this place. Lucy joking around with her boyfriend, Ian. He looked so cheerful in the yearbook. So sweet. I wonder what happened to him.

Stay away from the Ian thing, S.J. warned. But why?

Two of the women in business suits approach our table. "Lucy!" The taller one with thick foundation and too-bright lipstick speaks. "How nice of you to return home."

"We're so happy to see you." The other woman raises her plump arm in an exaggerated gesture.

"You remember us. Right?" the first one asks, eyes boring into Lucy.

"How could I forget the two of you?" Lucy responds.

The two women smirk as if they discovered a new power.

"Well, ladies." Conrad stands. "Nice of you to come by." He puts his arms out like he's herding geese and shoos them away, telling them we are in the middle of a business meeting.

"Jerks," Lucy mumbles under her breath. I will ask Lucy more about the girls in her high school during our interview. S.J. did reference that Lucy's early life was difficult. Were these women part of what made it hard?

Conrad calls for the check and hands it to Lucy. Something about the act makes me cringe. Not that I don't think women can pay just like men. I'm not into that whole chivalry thing. But it seems expected. Like she's the gravy train.

"I've got the bill." I take the check from Lucy. "It's on TRP Sports."

Outside the restaurant, I spot Reese Pharmacy diagonally across the street and ask if that's the family pharmacy that she and Conrad were talking about.

"It is," Lucy confirms, staring at the faded blue-and-gold awning.

"Lucy, remember they used to have the best fudge there?" Conrad says, raising his eyebrows, and I see glimpses of a younger brother trying to cheer up his sister. "Let's go get some candy."

Her lips turn up, and she gazes across the street. "Maybe we should swing by for old times' sake?" Lucy says. We all stare across the street as a police car sounds in the distance, the siren getting louder. The car speeds past, lights flashing.

"That's not as uncommon as you'd think," Conrad says and then leads our group across the street.

"Do you really think it's a good idea to have fudge before your match tomorrow?" Nico says as we approach the pharmacy.

The one thing I already learned about Lucy is that you don't tell her what to do. She glares at Nico and opens the door to the pharmacy, a bell jingling as she enters. Nico shakes his head and follows.

The scent of talc powder mixed with peppermint hits my nose. I feel like I've stepped into an old-world general store reminiscent of the one from *Little House on the Prairie*, a show I loved to watch the reruns of with my mom and stepdad.

There's a penny (quarter) candy section on the left and a glassed-in counter full of fudge and chocolate. Bill, Lucy, and I walk to the counter, inspecting the options—fudge with caramel, fudge with marshmallows, vanilla fudge, maple . . .

My phone rings with a call I've been anxiously expecting. I excuse myself, walking toward a private corner of the store.

"Nancy!" I greet the woman on the other end, who has information about the night my father was shot and nearly killed. The night my mom gave my dad the ultimatum—his family or his job. The night—I'm more convinced than ever—my father has been lying about for most of my life.

"Hello, Kate—" Nancy says. I hear hesitation in her tone. Immediately I sense I'm not getting my hands on the material.

"Is something wrong?" I ask, thinking about the box Nancy told me she found in her mother's attic labeled with my father's name, Liam Murphy.

"I can't meet you tonight . . ." Her voice catches.

"I can swing by your house if it's easier," I offer. We've been negotiating about the box for a year. First, Nancy's sister didn't want to share it. *We're just asking for trouble.*

Her sister moved away and told Nancy to do what she wants.

"No," she says. "I'll swing by your house in the morning, early—6:30 a.m. I need to head out of town, but I'll explain in person."

"Are you sure I can't just swing by your house in a few hours—" I suggest again, feeling like she's about to vaporize.

"Sorry, Kate," she says, cutting me off. "I need to get off the phone. See you tomorrow." She hangs up before I can get in another word.

My heart falls as I stare at my phone. Despite her promise to come to my house tomorrow morning, I feel like something is slipping away. She sounded distant. Distracted.

Focus, Kate, I tell myself. You have a story to do. I walk down the aisle in search of everyone and stop at the end by the prescription counter. Conrad stands in front of the pharmacist, leaning close in conversation. From my vantage point, it's hard to tell the mood: collaboration or collision.

I walk closer and see Conrad's face flush. Collision. My eyes move to the pharmacist, a broad man with a full beard that tapers to a point, making him look like a Disney villain.

"How dare you bring your sister here," the pharmacist hisses at Conrad.

"I don't understand . . ." Conrad sounds confused. "Greggory, what are you upset about?"

"Of course you have no idea. Your family just does what it wants, no matter the consequences to anyone else."

Conrad looks up and sees me. He pulls his lips into a tight line. Lucy walks over, despite Conrad's hand motions to stop her.

"You have some nerve, lady." Greggory glowers at her.

"What do you mean?" Lucy sounds shocked.

"Get out," Greggory says, voice raised. Conrad takes Lucy's candy and throws it down on the floor, then grabs his sister's arm and pulls her down the aisle. No one speaks.

"What was that about?" I ask as we step onto the sidewalk, the sun beating down on us.

Conrad doesn't say anything, just shakes his head. The women from the Mac-n-Cheesy cross the street in our direction.

"Let's get going." Conrad starts toward the cars. "Time for the big sit-down interview." Conrad tries to sound cheery, but his tone rings hysterical. He pushes Lucy into the Mercedes, refusing to give me an opportunity to ask again about the incident with Greggory.

I hop in the van with Bill, who holds out a paper bag with chocolate raisins. "I got them from the cashier in front," he says by way of explanation.

"Did you see the standoff between the pharmacist and Lucy?" I ask Bill.

"I did," Bill says, pouring a bunch of candy into his mouth and then passing the bag to me. "Something's certainly got that pharmacist riled up. Are you going to ask about it?"

"Not yet," I say, taking a handful of chocolates.

Bill nods as he pulls the car into the road. "No reason getting Lucy and Conrad angry until you know if the information is relevant to our story."

"Agreed," I reply, deciding to first research Ian and Greggory Reese before raising the issue with Lucy.

CHAPTER 9

Two tennis courts lie before us in varying stages of disrepair. Conrad shakes the latch of the gate. It creaks, and he pushes the door of the broken fence open. Grass sprouts through cracked concrete. The lines of the courts are faded, and one net sags between posts; the other net is missing.

"Can we talk"—Conrad looks at me—"privately?" He leans in, and I smell cinnamon gum on his breath. Bill walks to the first court and starts setting up for the interview, while I follow Conrad to the edge by an old bench covered in acorns.

"As you can tell, the incident at the drugstore took Lucy and me by surprise." He takes a deep breath. "Upon reflection"—he clears his throat—"I didn't calculate the amount of jealousy and resentment we'd encounter in Glenport. That's on me." He puts his hand over his heart to emphasize he's taking full blame for something I find more interesting than disturbing. His self-importance comes across comical, but I keep a straight face.

"You see," he continues, like he's sharing a secret, "Lucy and I are the ones that 'got out.'" He uses air quotes to make his point. "And people here are more jealous of our success than I expected."

A horn sounds in the distance, as if to punctuate his point. Or possibly cut off my response? But really, we just need to get on with the day.

"Okay," I say to Conrad. "Let's start the sit-down. That's most important anyway."

He blinks hard, seeming surprised I'm not giving him more pushback, but follows me to the spot where Bill is opening one of two folding chairs. For the main interview, Bill also sets up standing lights and a reflector. I take one of the clip-on mics as Lucy snakes hers through her designer shirt and attaches it to her collar.

"Ready?" I ask Lucy.

"Ready." She nods.

"When was the last time you played here?" I ask.

"Oh gosh—decades," she says, looking around. "I haven't been back to Glenport since my mom passed away." She looks wistfully past the courts and out at the full trees, seeing something I don't. Maybe a memory of her mother? Since she brought up her mom, I decide to start there, even though that wasn't my original plan.

"Tell us about your mother—" I leave my question open ended, hoping she will feel more comfortable sharing.

"My mom was the best." She smiles. "Always encouraging me without pressuring me."

"What do you mean?" I ask.

A plane flies overhead, and Bill signals for us to stop, as the sound drowns out our voices. The noise dies down, and Lucy resumes. "My mom always told me that if I'm not happy playing tennis, I should quit. Of course, it would have been impossible to really stop. We both knew that, but it was nice that she acted like I had a choice."

"Can you explain why you felt you didn't have a choice?"

"It's not that I *felt* I didn't have a choice. I *didn't* have a choice." She folds her arms over her chest. "I'm from a poor family in Poland. All my parents' money went to send me here. They did that with the expectation that I would provide for everyone else. And I don't say that with resentment but as a fact. I had a gift that could raise our family up. I understood that even as a young child."

A rabbit darts onto the edge of the courts, catching my eye. It stops, looks at us, and scurries under a hole in the fence, disappearing within the overgrown shrubs.

"My parents sacrificed for me so I could support my family once I turned professional. I was the oldest of my generation. My money went to pay for Conrad's, our other brother's, and my cousins' college tuition. I paid off the family's mortgages, bills. And I'm happy to have done that," she says, not sounding happy about it at all.

"That must have been hard. I can't imagine the pressure you were under. What if you lost?"

"Losing was not an option," Lucy says.

"And what about now?" I ask. "Are you still taking care of everyone?"

I see Conrad shift, but he doesn't say anything. My mind returning to lunch and how Conrad just handed over the bill to Lucy.

"I still help out," she says, looking down at the ground. I decide to let this line of conversation go in hopes of getting Lucy to expand on her mother, a topic Conrad indicated Lucy wanted to speak about.

"Your mom died in a car accident?"

"Yes, it was devastating," Lucy replies, her lips quivering. "It was a hit-and-run. They never found the driver of the other car." I remember reading about that. A witness saw the accident and identified a female driver. She also got the license plate. Turned out to be a stolen car. By the time the police found the vehicle, it had been torched.

"Cops believe bank robbers hit our mom," Lucy says, her eyes watering. She takes a breath, fighting back the tears. "There had been a spree of bank robberies at the time. The assailants always stole a car and then torched it after. It fit."

"It was just after you made it into the finals of Wimbledon?" I say, leaning forward.

"Yes, I had just spoken to my mom a few hours earlier. She was so excited. *This is your moment,* she had said. Wimbledon was the first Grand Slam I won. I know she would have wanted me to stay and play—" she continues, alluding to the public decision Lucy made to play in the finals after she learned her mother had died. Some journalists skewered her for that—accusing Lucy of being heartless.

"Let's move on," Conrad interrupts. I nod but make a note to ask Lucy more about this topic.

"Tell me about playing on these courts as a kid," I say, motioning to our surroundings.

"The courts were in much better shape." She smiles, breaking the tension. "My coach at the time made me meet him at five forty-five every morning, starting at age seven."

"What was he like?"

"Awful," she blurts out and then glances at Conrad, who nods at her. "He always yelled. I didn't even speak English, but his anger came across loud and clear. *Terrible. Lazy. Again.* Those were the first English words I learned."

"That must have been hard."

She nods but doesn't speak, just looks down at the ground, kicking at some weeds.

"Did your uncle intervene?" I ask.

Lucy's head snaps up. "The opposite. He laughed when the coach called me names. Then at home, if I complained, he told me to toughen up. *Life's hard. You're lucky you have a gift.* He said that a lot."

"How long did that coach train you?"

"Until I was old enough to choose for myself," she says.

"Is that when you switched to Zane Cole?" I say, knowing the answer is yes.

She presses her lips together and nods.

"What was he like?" I ask, planning to get Lucy's reaction to Brynn's comment yesterday.

"Zane Cole is a bully," she says. "But he's also an expert coach. He has the rare ability to find his players' weaknesses and teach them how to fix them. I stayed with him until I mastered everything I needed and then left to work with my present coach—Franklin, who is good and, while not kind, not a complete jerk."

"What a compliment." I laugh.

"It is in tennis." She smirks.

"Did you hear about Brynn Cole's comment yesterday?" I ask. "Where a reporter compared her style to yours—"

"And Brynn said she was like a young version of me?" Lucy finishes my sentence. I nod, anxious to hear her reaction, which I expect will be filled with anger.

"Good for her," Lucy says and laughs. "You need confidence in tennis."

"Assuming you both win your next few rounds, you will face Brynn. How do you feel about that matchup?"

"I look forward to it," Lucy says.

Another plane flies overhead, and we pause. Lucy explains that the richer towns that border Glenport lobbied the county to make sure air traffic avoided their affluent havens. As the noise dies down, I move to a different topic. "Did you make friends on the tour?" I ask.

"No," Lucy replies. "How can you be friends with competitors? Frankly it seems stupid to me. Your survival depends on beating them."

We talk more about the tour, her locker room philosophy, and childhood. The sun breaks through the shade of the large trees, and Bill stops us. "Maybe we could get the two of you walking and talking," Bill suggests. "Over there in the shade." During the break Conrad reminds Lucy to explain why they built the new Lucy Bosco facility.

We start walking the length of the courts, behind the baseline, Bill walking backward, camera trained on us.

Lucy follows Conrad's directions, speaking robotically as she explains that lower-income kids need an opportunity to play.

"Not many courts in town?" I ask, stopping, worried Bill will trip on the crumbling cement.

"Country clubs," Lucy says, emotion entering her voice. "That's where the girls from lunch played. This town is divided between the haves and have-nots."

"I imagine that was hard," I say, wondering where the haves live because so far, we've only seen modest-to-rundown homes.

"It made me tough." She lifts her chin and glances at Conrad, who's motioning with his arms for her to expand. Show vulnerability. Make herself more relatable.

Lucy takes a few steps toward the center of the baseline and looks across the court. "I was different than them. I didn't speak the language well; I didn't have money—but I was also better at tennis than everyone. If I had stayed down, I probably would have been fine. But I shined. And those girls didn't like that."

"What did they do?"

Lucy shakes her head. "Just mean-girl stuff. It's really not a big deal. Can we move on?" I agree, and we start talking about her plans for retirement.

When we finish, I ask Conrad if we can still swing by his and Lucy's childhood home.

"Sure," Conrad says as Lucy shoots him a surprised look.

"No one mentioned stopping there to me," she says.

"Dad's not home," Conrad says to Lucy, and I wonder why Lucy would want to avoid seeing her father. This woman has layers of complexity I've yet to discover.

CHAPTER 10

Conrad suggests we walk to their house. "That way you can see the path Lucy took every day to the courts," he explains. "It's only a few blocks."

I move next to Bill, who holds his camera in one hand, equipment bag slung over his shoulder. The chairs and lights already returned to the van.

Bill slows his pace, his breathing heavy, and puts his equipment down for a minute. I reach for his bag, but he blocks me. "I don't need you carrying stuff for me."

"Let's finish the interview at the house and then call it," I say, checking my phone, which shows 4:30 p.m. "It's been a long day."

He lifts the camera back up, and I sneak around him and grab the bag.

"I need the exercise," I say.

"You're a piece of work," he replies, but doesn't fight me. We pass ranch-style homes on small plots of land with large scratchy shingles reminiscent of the 1970s. Most homes appear well cared for, with fresh coats of paint, potted flowers, and a few gnomes scattered on lawns.

Up ahead, Conrad, Nico, and Lucy stop in front of a similar style home in need of love, with the paint peeling off the siding, weeds sprouting from the gutters, and the front railing ajar.

"This was our house," Conrad says as we approach. "Our father still lives here. But he promised to be out," Conrad says again to Lucy, then fishes keys from his pocket and unlocks the door. Must and cigar smells greet us. Conrad flips a switch, and a yellow fixture shines a dim light on the living room. I wait for Lucy to step inside—she hesitates like a cat ready to flee at the slightest suggestion of trouble but eventually moves into the hallway.

Bill proceeds past Lucy into the living room, camera on shoulder to videotape the old photos on a bookshelf. I step in behind him, studying the tarnished frames of Lucy holding trophies won as a child. Nowhere can I spot a picture of her days winning Grand Slams. Tucked in the corner sits a faded wedding picture. "Are these your parents?" I pick up the photo and turn to Lucy, who hasn't moved from the hallway.

Conrad walks over to me and takes the photo from my hands. "Yes," he says, placing the frame back where I found it.

"Lucy looks just like her mom," I reply, studying the image of the poised, striking woman next to a soft young man with thinning hair.

Conrad runs a hand through his own hair, as if worried seeing his father in the photo would make Conrad turn prematurely bald. Satisfied his hair remains firmly on his head, Conrad suggests we follow him into the kitchen.

"Our father's getting feeble," Conrad says as we enter the kitchen with a pile of dishes in the sink and frozen-meal cartons scattered on the counter.

"Give it a break," Lucy scoffs. "He never took care of himself. As if he cleaned a dirty dish in his life."

"Check out the backyard," Conrad calls, ignoring his sister. He opens the back door and leads us onto a patio that abuts a square grass yard fenced in with wooden slats.

Lucy sprints outside, seemingly gleeful to leave the house. "This is where I would continue practicing after we left the courts," she says, explaining how she'd hit tennis balls against the side of the house.

Bill picks up his camera and takes a little video of the yard before Conrad suggests we go back inside. "I'm sure you want to see Lucy's room," he says and leads us down the hallway to a room with a pink blanket and floor-to-ceiling trophies.

There are a few photos on a small white desk, including one of a young Lucy with Zane Cole. "You look really happy here," I say, picking up the photo of her and the coach, who has his arm around Lucy.

"Yeah," she says, taking the photo and placing it face down on the desk. "It was before I realized what an asshole he is," she replies.

"That's my mom." Lucy points to another photo of the woman from the wedding picture. "And that's my uncle." I study the photo of the man who also looks like Lucy and her mom but has hard eyes and a downturned expression.

"Did they get along?" I ask.

"Mostly out of necessity," Lucy replies.

"Hello," a male voice calls in conjunction with the sound of stomping feet moving quickly through the hallway. "Conrad! Lucy!" The voice gets louder.

"You said he wouldn't be here." Lucy gapes, staring at her brother.

"Dad promised he would stay away," Conrad replies, biting his lip.

Lucy glares at her brother, then squares her shoulders and steps into the hallway. For a moment, I think she might make a run for it. But that's not her style.

"Lucy!" Her father approaches as Bill and I squirm out of her room, then stand behind her in the hallway. The father walks over and tries to wrap Lucy in an embrace. She holds her hand out like a traffic cop. "We aren't going to do that."

"Fine. Fine," he mumbles. "But I'm glad you're still here." He glances at me and Bill and then back at his children. "Two minutes, Lucy. Please."

"To talk about what?" She folds her arms across her chest, staring at the balding man in front of her.

Nico steps next to Lucy and puts an arm around her. "You shouldn't have come here," Nico says. "Conrad asked you not to."

"Give it a break, underwear boy," the dad growls at Nico, and I see a fire behind the sunken eyes of the old man.

Lucy squirms away from Nico's arm. "Two minutes," she says and follows her father into the dining room. We hear voices raised but can't understand their words. They speak in what I assume is Polish. Only Conrad follows the conversation, and from his expression, it's not good. The father's tone goes from angry to whiny to furious.

"Nie! Nie!" Lucy cuts her father off and storms back to the hall and out the front door.

The rest of us follow Lucy onto the front porch. "The nerve of that man," Lucy fumes. "He wants more money."

"I can't believe he just showed up like that," Conrad says, standing next to Lucy. She turns her head to gaze down the street as her father peers out from the front door. I see Conrad mouth "Sorry" to his father. Lucy catches it too.

"You knew?" she screams at him.

"Shhhh." He takes her arm and pulls her across the street and out of earshot from me.

"This family is full of drama." Bill grunts, putting his camera down on the sidewalk.

The screen door from the home on the right snaps shut, and an elderly woman steps toward me, shaking her head. "You'd think they'd have grown out of it by now." She wrinkles her already wrinkled brow.

"What do you mean?" I ask, moving toward her.

"Since they were kids, those two, always fighting. Sometimes so late at night, they'd wake my husband and me. May he rest in peace."

She wipes age-spotted hands on her apron. "Making cookies." She smiles at me, introducing herself as Estelle Springer. "And I know who you are. My grandson watches TRP Sports all the time." She smiles again and asks if I'd sign an autograph for him.

"I'd be happy to," I reply.

She pulls a pad and pen from her apron pocket and gives me her grandson's name.

"What did Conrad and Lucy fight about?" I ask, handing back the pad.

"They fought about everything. Such a shame. Made their mom crazy, may she rest in peace." I remember Nico said fighting is Lucy's love language. But Estelle certainly isn't portraying their interactions that way.

"Were you close with the family?" I ask as she bends down to pick up a soda can left on the sidewalk and steps toward her trash can.

"We were neighborly." She tosses the soda can in the garbage bin. "Oh my, the cookies. I hope I didn't burn them. Thanks for the autograph." She taps her pocket and rushes back to her house. I return my gaze to Conrad and Lucy, who are still arguing. Nico stands to our left, buried in his phone, and I almost feel sorry for him, clearly the third wheel.

"Looks like Conrad and Lucy reached a truce." Bill juts his chin in their direction as the two walk toward us, Conrad's hand on Lucy's back. Behind them I notice a silver sedan, idling in a parking spot.

"Sorry about that," Conrad says. "Family can be complicated."

"Family stuff can get tense," Lucy adds, trying and failing to put a light spin on the events.

Conrad suggests we call it a day.

"That's fine," I agree.

"One thing," Bill adds. "I'd like to get B-roll of Lucy and Kate in town."

"Video of us walking and talking," I explain, adding that we won't use the sound, just the video.

Lucy looks toward Conrad for his approval.

He puts his finger up, reading something on his phone.

"Conrad," Lucy calls. He apologizes and hastily gives his approval, while reminding us only video. And everything Lucy says must be off the record. "I'll need to head out as soon as we get to town," Conrad says to Lucy. "Something important came up at the office."

We caravan back to Main Street; Conrad drops off Lucy and Nico before he drives away.

I take out a mirror and hand it to Lucy so she can pat down some stray pieces of her hair.

"I don't know how you deal with all this primping." She hands me back the compact, and I powder my cheeks and apply lip gloss.

"It's my least favorite part of the job," I reply, putting my makeup away.

Bill instructs us to stroll down Main Street, past the restaurant where we had lunch, and over toward a bench.

"I'm going to get a coffee for the road," Nico yells as Bill signals for us to begin.

I try some small talk with Lucy, so it looks like we're engaged in conversation, but she's only supplying one-word answers. As we talk about the weather, I notice how tired Lucy looks; dark circles have emerged under her eyes.

"How would you normally spend a day before a match?" I ask her.

"I try to move a lot to avoid getting stiff. Spending the day walking around was good for me physically. But emotionally—well, this was probably a bad idea the day before a match. But it is what it is." She looks off to the right, where a boy runs through tricks on a skateboard. "Still, it's just the early rounds," she adds.

"All set," Bill tells us, putting the camera down by his side. "I'm supposed to pick up food for a family barbecue. Mind if I run?" Bill asks me.

"Not at all," I reply. "Get a tofu burger!" I call after him, but he ignores me.

"Tofu?" Lucy asks.

"He's trying to eat healthy," I explain, and she nods. Lucy and I walk across the street to the lot where we left our cars.

"Thanks again for doing the interview," I say to her. "I look forward to seeing your—" I stop midsentence, realizing I left a bag in Bill's van. "I need to run too," I say to Lucy, explaining that I need to catch Bill before he leaves. I jog in Bill's direction and spot him standing by the van holding my bag.

"Thanks. And sorry. I hope I didn't make you late." I take the bag from him.

"It's okay. Want me to drop you at your car?" he asks, opening the front door, but I can see he's agitated.

"I'm fine. It's just a few blocks from here."

He nods and closes the door, then starts the engine. I throw the bag over my shoulder and stroll back down Main Street. This part of the street is less built up, with only a few open shops. I pass a nail salon and barber, then an empty storefront with a **For Lease** sign taped to the window.

An old convertible drives toward me, Ariana Grande blasting from the speakers as the teenagers in the back seat raise their hands in the air as if they are on a roller coaster. The sight brings my brain to my kids, now off in college. My daughter, Nikki, is thriving in her new environment. But Jackson seems on edge. *Freshman nerves,* I tell myself again, knowing that I'm supposed to give him space.

Returning to the lot, I'm surprised to see Lucy's SUV still parked in the same spot. I'm about to call out to her, when I notice she's speaking with the pharmacist, Greggory. Her fists squeezed in tight balls by her side.

In contrast, Greggory's body is all movement. Arms flying in front of him. Face darting in different directions like a bobblehead. His words carry through the air. I stop walking, watching from the sidewalk.

"Do you have any idea how you ruined my family?" Greggory's voice carries through the air.

"I ruined your family?" Lucy says each word slowly as she takes a step closer to him.

"Ian's accident was your fault." Greggory rubs his forehead. "He gave up everything for you—"

"I gave up everything because of him—" Lucy screams, her voice cracking.

"What are you talking about?" Greggory puts his hands on his hips.

"You have no idea—" She kicks at a stone on the ground. "He wasn't the only one who made sacrifices, you idiot."

Lucy turns away and takes a step toward her car. Greggory grabs her arm. "Don't you dare walk away—"

She yanks her arm from his grip and pushes him. "Don't touch me, you jerk."

"Bitch," he yells and storms off in the other direction. Lucy watches him, her body shaking.

CHAPTER 11

A horn startles me from behind. I turn and catch sight of Nico watching me. He tilts his head like he's caught me shoplifting. Or caught me eavesdropping, which he did. He closes the distance between us. "I won't tell if you don't," he says, taking off his sunglasses and winking.

"Nothing to tell," I reply, even though we both know that's not true. But if he caught me listening to Lucy's fight, then he was listening too.

"If you say so." He puts his sunglasses back on and takes a sip of the coffee in his hand, with the label from Mac-n-Cheesy, an odd choice for coffee when there is a gourmet beanery farther down the block.

"Until next time." He bows, turns his back on me, and walks toward Lucy.

Embarrassed, I wait as Lucy and Nico get into their car and shut the doors. Three toddlers in karate uniforms rush in front of me as I make my way to my car, causing me to stop in my tracks.

"Sorry," a man yells as he jogs after them. "Can't slow them down when fudge is involved."

Oh, to be a kid. I laugh to myself and walk to my car. Behind me, I hear Lucy curse. I turn and spot her standing at the back of the SUV, Nico next to her on his knees by the rear tire.

"What's going on?" I walk toward them.

"I can't believe this," Lucy mumbles as Nico lowers himself onto his back to study the wheel. He runs his hand along the tread and announces there's a nail stuck in the tire.

"Damn." Lucy rubs her temples with her fingers. "This day keeps getting better. I need to get home." The pitch of Lucy's voice rises. She probably has a nighttime ritual she follows before matches. Or, at the very least, a desire to rest, versus standing in the heat dealing with a flat tire in a town she hates.

A truck pulls into the lot and approaches the back of the pharmacy. The brakes grind to a halt, and a deliveryman gets out and walks around to the back of his vehicle.

"This town. Only bad things happen here," Lucy grumbles.

"Take an Uber, and I'll wait for AAA." Nico pushes himself up to stand, then wipes his hands on his pants.

"I'd be happy to give you a lift," I offer.

"Really?" She brightens, explaining they rented a house in Oyster Bay, about twenty minutes from here.

"I don't mind," I tell Lucy. "And we'll make everything off the record so Conrad can't get mad."

Nico glares at me but doesn't say anything. Is he worried I'll mention the fight I oversaw? That he also witnessed?

The deliveryman emerges, wheeling a hand trolley loaded with large boxes, and disappears inside the pharmacy as the kids in the karate uniforms reappear. They're walking slower, chocolate in their hands and on their faces.

"You sure?" Lucy moves her eyes back to me.

"I'm sure," I reply and smile.

"Don't mind me," Nico calls because Lucy seems to have already forgotten him.

"Thanks, Nico." She gives him a wave and follows me to my car.

I turn the air conditioner up and back out of the lot, pulling onto Main Street. In the rearview mirror I see Nico on his phone, arms flailing as he speaks.

"You mentioned the girls from the country club grew up in a nicer area—what section of town did they live in?" I ask as we pass the empty storefronts I walked by earlier.

"I can show you," she says, telling me it's in the direction of the highway. She directs me past old homes and then tells me to turn at a sign that reads **Glenport Landing.**

"This is the fancy part of town," she says. The two-story clapboard homes with stone chimneys look like mirror images of one another, except for different shades of paint. "The country club sits at the end of the road." She points to the bottom of the hill, where I see a gold-and-blue plaque that says **Glenport Country Club** in front of a closed gate.

Lucy sighs, staring out the window. "Looking at the homes now, they don't seem so special," she says, her voice miles away. "But back then, they felt so out of reach they might as well have been on the moon." I think back to my childhood, growing up in Berkeley, California, with my mom, stepfather, and brother. Our home was modest, but I never felt deprived of anything. And I was never aware of others in my community who lived an outlandish type of life, even though they probably did.

The closest I came to mansions and glamour was on television. Now in Greenwich, Connecticut, I still live a modest life compared to all the mega mansions and estates. But I prefer that. It's where I'm comfortable.

"Do you like where you live now?" I ask Lucy as I turn around in front of the country club. "I read you split your time between Florida and Greece."

"Nico and I love Greece. It's beautiful there. And peaceful. We have a small villa near his family's apartment. It has expansive terraces looking down at the ocean. I'd say that's my favorite spot." She stares out the window as she talks.

"How often do you get there?" I ask, following the GPS toward the Long Island Expressway.

"Only about a month a year," Lucy says. "It seems like a great extravagance, but Nico's brother stays there when we aren't around."

She lets the words hang in the air, and I wonder if Nico's brother is doing them a favor by keeping an eye on the villa or if Lucy is part of the gravy train for Nico's family. I know Nico must make some money from his commercials, but there's no way he has Lucy-level money. She may not be a favorite with sponsors, but she gets enough endorsements to make a nice amount of cash on top of all her success on the tour.

It's just after 6:00 p.m., and the traffic on the Long Island Expressway proves predictably brutal. "I don't know how people live here," Lucy says. "I couldn't stand driving in this every day."

"It's pretty bad where I live too," I reply. "But not like this." I reach for the radio and flip it on, the New York sports station coming through the speakers. The radio hosts discuss the latest on the battle between the Yankees and Red Sox. Then they switch to the US Open and immediately bring up Lucy. I reach to turn the station off, but she tells me to leave it.

"What do you make of this whole Lucy Bosco 2.0 stuff?" the woman asks.

"She's just trying to make herself more likable to win over endorsements. It's purely transactional."

"Agreed. Do you think she has a shot to win at the Open?"

"I would never count her out. But she is getting old," the cohost replies. I glance at Lucy and see her wince.

Again, I reach to turn it off. This time she doesn't stop me.

"Don't let it get to you," I say, trying to fill the silence.

"Are you bothered by what the radio host said?" Lucy turns to me. "She suggested I'm only doing this interview to change my image for endorsements."

I hit the brakes as the car in front screeches to a halt. Then press the gas as the car inches up and goes faster.

"Are endorsements the reason you are doing this story with me?" I ask, moving into the left lane.

"I think endorsements are the reason Conrad wants me to do the story. And it certainly would be nice to get more interest on that front. I'm not gonna lie," she says. "But my main motivation is that I'm tired of being misunderstood. Everyone thinks I have it so easy. The truth is I've struggled like all the other people out there. I just don't whine about it."

I glance at her as I take the exit for Oyster Bay. As a former athlete, I feel for Lucy. It's not fun to be vilified by the media—I know that. I've lived that. And isn't reporting also transactional? If she portrays herself well, then she helps her cause with sponsors. But landing an interview with Lucy helps my cause. She's a big name, and everyone wants to hear what she has to say. People love to watch villains. My story will capture the attention of viewers. Should I care what Lucy's motivation is?

I hear myself sigh. This side of the business makes me squirm. Like I need to take a few extra showers to wash the slime off. All I can do is focus on my story and do the most honest and accurate job possible.

I push the rest of it from my head and turn north toward Oyster Bay, one of the wealthier sections of Long Island. Unlike the rolling hills of Greenwich, Connecticut, the land here is flat, and the palatial mansions can easily be viewed from the main road. We wind our way toward the water and drive up a road lined with lush trees.

Lucy tells me to turn down a gravel road marked by pink and purple impatiens set in massive clay pots. Here the homes appear more secluded, hidden behind large manicured shrubbery.

"Turn there." She points to a dirt driveway with a sign that says **RESIDENTS ONLY.**

"You're really isolated back here," I say, turning down the hidden road.

"It's what I love about this house. I've rented it for the last ten years," she says. We pass two turnoffs, which she explains are the entrances to the neighbors' homes. I see only their driveways, the rest hidden behind thick pine trees. "But this house"—she points straight at a home that sits on a plot overlooking the water—"this house has the best views."

I see why she loves this spot. The home reminds me of a ski chalet: a wooden A-frame structure, large windows, and a chimney with the promise of a welcoming fireplace, for the cooler months. But the views take my breath away. Through the windows, I see the Long Island Sound with sailboats dotting the water.

"This is gorgeous," I say, in awe.

"It's a special place. And looking out on the water calms me."

"Does the seclusion bother you?" I ask, aware of how far she is from her neighbors.

"Not at all. I like the peace and quiet. Thank you—" She's interrupted by her phone and puts her finger up to tell me to wait a second. Nico's booming voice comes through the phone as he explains he's going to accompany the tow truck and wait for the car.

"But three hours?" she complains. "Can't they rush it?"

Lucy scowls at whatever Nico's now saying.

"See if you can rush them. Please," Lucy replies. "No. I understand. I'll figure something out for dinner, it's fine." She hangs up without saying goodbye. "Nico is going with the tow truck to a tire store that's open late. Getting it taken care of tonight. We were supposed to have dinner at the local tavern. It's kind of a tradition before my matches at the Open."

"Want me to go with you?"

She lets out a breath as she stares in front of her. "It's not like I don't have food in the house," she says. "Nico stocked the fridge. It's just—"

"Part of your ritual." I finish her thought, understanding all too well about game-night rituals. I always ate the same meal—pasta and chicken.

"It's stupid, right?"

"Not only did I always eat the same meal," I reply. "I had my own strange customs. When I was a kid, my friend and I would jump off the bed every time the clock hit eleven eleven. As I got older, I'd wait for eleven eleven and jump for good luck." I laugh, hearing how silly I sound. "I've never told anyone that."

"I'm glad you shared," Lucy says, and I see relief in her smile. "I'd love to get dinner with you. Thanks for understanding."

I turn the car around, and Lucy directs me to the tavern, less than a mile away. The restaurant sits next to an old fire station and across the street from a small bookstore and gas station. I see why Lucy likes this place, with warm mahogany wood and black leather booths. The hostess greets Lucy with a smile. "Your table?" she asks. Lucy nods, and the hostess leads us past a full bar with stained glass shelves to a booth in the corner.

A Beatles song plays softly in the background as the hostess hands us two menus. "Shepherd's pie is tonight's special," she says to Lucy. "Chef thought it would be a good meal before your match tomorrow."

"You really are a regular." I smile, studying the rest of the options.

"It's usually a winter special, but the chef knows how much I love it." She leans back in her seat and seems to relax for the first time all day.

A waitress comes and asks for our drink order. Lucy orders a club soda, and I decide to do the same, given the drive ahead of me.

"I googled you after lunch," Lucy says as the waitress walks away. "I guess you do understand what I'm going through." She bites her lip. "With the media and the hate thrown my way."

"I do." I feel myself soften toward her. "It really sucks."

The waitress returns with our drinks and places them on the table.

"Do you think they'd go after me for being so tough if I were a guy?" Lucy asks. "I feel like *asshole* is a brand for male tennis players."

"Not just tennis," I respond. It's a question I often wonder about. Would the media have pounced on me for going after an NBA player on video if I were a man? Or maybe the better question is, Would the media have leaned into the story quite as strongly?

"I promise to be fair," I reply. "You have my word."

"I know." She pushes a few strands of hair off her forehead and tucks them behind her ear, "Conrad spent a lot of time thinking about who to approach for the story. He wanted someone fair and with integrity." She smiles at me. "Someone he thought would care."

I can't help feeling proud of that fact, but also aware she might just be buttering me up. The waitress returns and asks what we'd like. We both order the shepherd's pie.

"You a fan?" Lucy asks when the waitress leaves.

"I haven't had shepherd's pie in years. But if it's made special, how can I resist?" I say, opening my napkin and putting it on my lap. "It's nice that they care about you so much here."

"Do you remember that show—*Cheers*? The bar where everyone knew your name? That's what this tavern feels like for me."

"And it's nice in our line of work, to find a home away from home," I reply, thinking of the blur of hotels and crappy diners my teammates and I would travel to from match to match.

"Sometimes the places on the road feel more like a home than my actual one," she muses, staring out the window. A different side of Lucy emerging: vulnerable and sad.

"Everyone thinks being a professional athlete is so glamorous," I say. "Little do they know—"

She turns her gaze to me, and I'm surprised to see her eyes glassy, like she's fighting back tears. "It can be really lonely," she says. "And people are so mean—" Her lip trembles as she wipes her eyes with the back of her hand.

"Before I went to my first national camp, my stepfather warned me not to get too close to the other girls, because they were also my competition. It's a hard balance. I'm sure it's much worse for a tennis player."

"Everyone in tennis is your competition—and not just on the court but with sponsors, and the press, and friends." Lucy looks down at her arm and twists her tennis bracelet.

"That's pretty," I say, looking at the delicate diamonds and the platinum clasp.

"My mom gave it to me." She smiles. "It has my initials." She holds it out to show me the **L. B.** engraved into the oval clasp. Lucy looks outside; her mind seems miles away. "You know how kids have security blankets or stuffed animals? For me, this bracelet always gives me strength. And comfort."

"Going home must have been tough today—" I say.

"It was hard," she says as the music switches to a Johnny Cash song. "I don't like going to Glenport. So many memories . . ." She stares off into space. "Not all of them bad. But all of them painful."

"I keep thinking about the girls we ran into at lunch," I say. "What jerks."

She laughs, surprised by my bluntness. "I read you had your share of issues with some mean girls as a teenager."

"I did," I reply, then tell her about the bullying that happened at the national soccer camps I attended. "My biggest regret is that I didn't stand up against it. I was scared."

"You can't blame yourself for another person's bad behavior." She takes my hand in hers. "It's on them." She squeezes my fingers. While I don't agree that I'm innocent, I appreciate her effort to comfort me.

The waitress brings our food, setting steaming pies in front of us, the smell glorious. I take a bite, the meat and mashed potatoes melting in my mouth. "This is so good."

"I know," she says, smiling.

We eat for a few minutes in silence. I notice an older couple approach the bar, the bartender placing two wineglasses in front of them before they even order.

I take another bite and then ask her how she feels about tomorrow's match.

"You want the honest, off-the-record answer?" she asks, wiping her mouth with her napkin.

I nod. "Yes, please. Everything tonight is off the record."

"I'm not that worried. 'America's sweetheart'"—she pauses to put air quotes up in reference to the well-liked aging Jill Wallace—"she just isn't good anymore. And she's even older than me," Lucy says with a devious grin.

I take the last bite of my dinner and notice Lucy's only halfway through.

"I'm a slow eater," she says to me. "I used to gobble my food, but my trainer put a stop to that."

"Smart."

"Can I ask you something?" she says.

"Sure."

"What did that NBA player say to you that made you lose your temper?" she asks, referencing the infamous gotcha video that got me suspended two years ago.

"He called me a bad mother, days after my son nearly died from a drug overdose," I say, the image of Jackson lying in the hospital, his heart flatlining bursting into my brain.

"That's awful," Lucy says. "I'm sorry to bring it up. How is your son now?"

"I think he's good," I say, worry bubbling in my stomach. "He just started his freshman year of college, and I haven't heard that much from him. But he also asked me to give him space. Apparently, I can be overbearing."

"I imagine there's a thin line between overbearing and concern," Lucy muses, then takes another small bite of her food.

"Did you ever want kids?" I ask and then immediately apologize. "I'm so sorry—that's crossing a line." I feel my face redden.

"It's all right," Lucy says. "You're easy to talk to. I don't meet many people like that." She steeples her hands in front of her plate. "Sometimes I think about what my life would have looked like if I made different choices," she says. "But I'm too old for that now." I'm about to tell her that thirty-seven is not too old to think about having children, but I'm sure she knows that.

The waitress comes over, clears my plate, and asks if she can get me anything else.

"Coffee, please," I say. "I have a little bit of a confession," I say once the waitress leaves. "I was in the parking lot when the pharmacist, Greggory Reese, started yelling at you."

"You saw that?" Her lips tighten.

"I did," I reply as the waitress places the steaming coffee in front of me, and I wave away her offer of milk and sugar.

"Greggory seems to think I'm responsible for Ian's bad luck—" Lucy shakes her head. "He should gather all his facts before he spits out accusations," she says, pushing her plate away. "Well, I think I've eaten as much as I can." The waitress brings the bill, and I insist on paying.

We head outside. "What a beautiful night," Lucy says, taking in a big breath as she stretches in the cool summer evening. The smell of the ocean catches in the light breeze, and I understand why this place feels calming to her.

"I really enjoyed dinner." She leans over and gives me a hug.

"Me too," I reply, feeling like Lucy could be moving quickly into the friend category, which would be nice. I don't have a lot of athlete friends.

"Get in," I say. "I'll drive you home."

"You're going to think I'm crazy, but I'm going to walk. I want to stretch my legs, and it's a beautiful night."

"Really?" I ask, looking down the narrow country road, without sidewalks. Images of horror movies coming to mind.

"It's under a mile, and I could use a chance to move my legs and clear my head."

"If you're positive—" I say, figuring it's not my place to mother her. As if reading my mind, she assures me this is what she wants to do.

We say goodbye, and she starts down the quiet road, her image growing harder to see under the barely visible crescent moon, with no streetlights or stars to illuminate the road.

I get into my car as the vehicle next to me backs out of the lot, a silver sedan that heads in the same direction as Lucy. I stare at the car through my rearview mirror. Something about it strikes me as familiar. I noticed a similar car idling on Lucy's street when we went to visit her childhood home. I didn't really give it a second thought at the time. People have many reasons to sit in their cars. But I can't help wondering if this is more than a coincidence.

CHAPTER 12

I pull out of the lot and start in Lucy's direction, not seeing her at first. I eventually recognize her white top in the distance. There are no cars between Lucy and me. My anxiety got the better of me, I think, figuring the sedan must have driven down one of the side streets. *Turn around, Kate,* I say to myself. *Now you're a stalker.*

I pull my car into the next driveway and turn in the other direction, driving toward the Long Island Expressway. Lucy's words from dinner come back to me regarding the balance between overbearing and concern. Was I just doing that to her? What about the unease I'm feeling about Jackson—a spidey sense that something is up with him?

Jackson seemed ecstatic his first week at college. But recently, he's avoided all my calls, following them up with a blow-off text—Can't talk. All fine.

If he's fine, he'd pick up. He knows it. And I know it. What's more—he knows I know. So, does he want me to nag him or leave him alone? The gymnastics of these scenarios hurts my brain. In the past, Jackson's psychiatrist cautioned to give Jackson space. I merge onto the Long Island Expressway, deciding that tonight marks too much space.

"Siri, call Jackson." Straight to voicemail. I try another time. And another. *Hi, this is Jackson*—I hang up before getting to the end. Any minute his *don't worry* text will pop up. Sure enough—the same message comes through my speaker, telling me not to worry. Enough is enough. I call again. And again. And again.

"Jesus, Mom," he hisses. "It's late, and I said I'm fine."

"Eight twenty is late? And if you're fine, then why were you only texting?" I ask, my voice sharper than I intend.

"Hold on." He lets out a dramatic sigh. I hear footsteps and a door close. "You still there?"

"Always," I reply, switching into the middle lane.

"I'm having some issues with one of my roommates," Jackson says but doesn't elaborate, and I can already tell getting information out of him is going to be an ordeal.

"What kind of issues?" I ask, turning the volume louder against the sound of cars whooshing by.

"Do we really need to get into it?" he whines.

"I'd like to," I reply.

"One of them kind of sucks," Jackson mumbles. Then adds that he wants to handle it on his own. "I didn't want to get into this with you."

"I'm not planning to hop in the car and drive up there," I say as I pass a sign warning drivers not to drink and drive.

Kids' shouting comes through the phone, and Jackson tells me to hold on again. The voices subside and he returns. "Did Nikki say something?" he asks.

"No." I feel my fingers squeeze the steering wheel, agitated that my daughter knew something but didn't share the information with me. "Jackson, you know I'm not going to let this go, so just spill."

He gasps dramatically but doesn't speak. "Let me call you back in half an hour. I don't want to talk from here. Too many people around."

I agree but warn him he'd better call.

We hang up, and I focus on the cars ahead of me as my brain moves into high alert. Jackson's been through so much these past two years and faced his problems with courage and fortitude. In high school, he started taking unprescribed Adderall, which was apparently a somewhat common occurrence in our town. But I had no idea, until one night he took Adderall tainted with something and mixed it with alcohol at a party. Shame overcomes me as that fact bubbles up. The call came from his sister, Nikki, hysterical as she relayed the information that medics were transporting Jackson to the hospital in an ambulance.

Their father was out of town and didn't arrive until the next day. Nikki and I stood in the hospital hallway, the smell of Lysol stinging our noses, as we watched doctors and nurses rush into his room with a crash cart.

It took Jackson a while to get back on his feet, but with the help of his psychiatrist, he made great strides. Then, last year, he blossomed, enjoying school and extracurriculars. In fact, Jackson, along with Nikki, took care of me for a while as I recovered from my own near-death experience.

When I think back on his overdose, I remember the event was precipitated by him pulling away. It happened gradually; I hardly noticed. I chalked his moody behavior up to teenage angst and gave him space. But now, providing space sends me into a panic. I check the clock on my dashboard; forty minutes have passed since we hung up. *Give him a little longer,* I tell myself, mustering every fiber of self-control not to call.

I reach the Whitestone Bridge and see the Manhattan skyline sparkling in the distance.

The phone rings as I get onto the Hutchinson River Parkway, and I click answer on the first ring.

"I was getting worried," I say, slowing down to let a car merge.

"Please don't storm the campus," he says, no hint of amusement in his voice. I wait for him to continue, but he doesn't say anything. All I hear is breathing.

"You said your roommate was an issue . . ." I prod.

"I said he was a bit of a jerk," Jackson corrects me. *Tomato/to-mah-to,* I think.

"In what way?" I keep the irritation out of my voice.

"My other roommate is really nice, though. We hang out a lot." I'm starting to get a picture. One roommate is a jerk and the other nice, creating the question of whether to tolerate the jerk.

"When you say the first roommate is a jerk, are you talking about his personality?"

"Not really . . ." Jackson admits.

"He's into drugs?" I ask, already knowing I'm right.

"Not just into them," Jackson says, his voice no more than a whisper.

"He's dealing?" My voice is louder than I want. Shit. *Calm down, Kate.*

"It's just edibles and shrooms," Jackson says, knowing how ridiculous that statement sounds.

Just! I want to scream but remain calm. Music blasts through the phone, getting louder and then fading.

"Maybe you should ask for a new roommate?" I say, an obvious course of action in my mind.

"But I don't want to leave. Sean and I really connected. He's my closest friend here so far," Jackson says about the third roommate; a soulmate after two weeks. I get it. Having a comrade during those early days of college makes a big difference. I always had my teammates, but it's harder when you start a new school without having a built-in social group.

"Have you talked to Sean about this?" I say.

"Oh, yeah. Brilliant, Mom. Hey, Sean. I know we've been friends for about a minute, but I nearly died from drugs a few years ago. And, well, I don't think it's great for me to live with our drug-dealing roommate—want to leave our triple and go to a new room with me?"

"I mean, yeah?" I say, but I get why he's uncomfortable. "Have you talked to Dr. Michaelson?" I ask, referring to his psychiatrist.

"We have a call Thursday," Jackson says. "Look, I need to go. I told you everything. Now give me some space to figure it out. That was the deal."

I agree to stay out of it. For now. But I don't feel good about that decision. We hang up, and I continue my drive home. Not happy about all the implications of our conversation. I debate calling Nikki to ask her take, but I don't want to put her in the position of ratting out her brother. And I shouldn't pressure her to share what he tells her in confidence. Although I could just call and check in on her. See if she offers anything.

I tell Siri to call Niki. My daughter picks up on the first ring, her cheerful greeting lifting my spirits.

"You caught me on my way to dinner," she says, and I hear steps in the background.

"Living on California time," I reply. "Tell me everything."

She rattles on about her classes, especially Art and Modern Civilization. "I'm really enjoying it. More than I expected," she says, adding that she might investigate art history as a major.

"How are your friends?" I ask.

"Great! I *love* my friends," she replies. "We're going to the beach this weekend. The girls want to go camping. It should be amazing. And next weekend we might go rock climbing."

"Rock climbing!" I reply.

"At one of those indoor places." She laughs. "I'm not ready for prime time yet. Lol."

"Have you spoken to Jackson—" I say before I can stop myself.

"Yes. He's fine, Mom." Nikki sighs. "He texted me you just talked."

"Sorry," I reply.

"It's all right." She sounds very adult. "I understand why you would worry. But he's got this. He's not the same person as two years ago. If there's something to worry about, I'll let you know. But he's good."

"You're amazing." I smile at the phone. "I'm really proud of you."

"Barf." She laughs. "Love you too," she says and hangs up.

I pull into my driveway and walk into my dark home, once again feeling the emptiness of the place.

I get a glass of wine and wander into my dining room, which for the last two weeks has become my Liam Murphy–investigation space. I stare at my research spread across the table and attached to the multiple bulletin boards lining the back wall. On the first board is pinned a photocopy from the police blotter of the *New York Post* from thirty-eight years ago. I pick it up and read it again, as if this time I will glean something I haven't from my past hundred reads.

Two police officers responded to a domestic violence call in Washington Heights, NY. Emergency operators received a call at 11:48 p.m. from a woman crying that her boyfriend was beating her with a coffeepot. Officer Harley Butler and Officer Liam Murphy arrived on the scene to gunshots. Officer Butler died at the scene from a bullet to his head. Officer Murphy was rushed to New York Presbyterian Hospital, where he remains in critical condition.

I remember that night like it was yesterday—my mother waking my brother and me up in the early morning and rushing to the emergency room, where she was sure my father would die. It was the last straw for her. Liam would need to make a choice, our family or his job. I return the article to the board and unfasten the second one, also from the *NY Post* but dated the next day.

The NYPD Public Information Officer told a room full of reporters that Officer Butler died when he heroically tried to break up a sophisticated drug ring. Seven gunmen opened fire when the NYPD arrived on scene, killing Officer Butler and severely injuring his partner, Officer Liam Murphy. Murphy, despite his wounds, was able to apprehend one of the suspects, who now faces felony charges, including the murder of a police officer.

I take a sip of wine and reread the number *seven*. Not one gunman, not two. No mention of a coffeepot. How did such an egregious mistake occur? It's hard to imagine even an incompetent reporter getting that confused.

I stare out the window at my block, more a stub than a street, with the other historic Victorian houses. Under the streetlamp I can make out the **For Sale** sign in front of the pink-and-purple home at the end of the cul-de-sac. When the owners first chose those colors, the kids and I started referring to it as the Puke House. But the exterior has grown on me, and I'll feel a little sad if the new owners decide to change the paint colors.

I finish my wine and pour a second glass, moving to the papers I've collected regarding the 911 call. This issue remains at the crux of my investigation. If the 911 caller really claimed she was getting beaten by a coffeepot, it makes sense that Liam and his partner would enter the residence without waiting for additional police. If the caller reported an arsenal of guns was inside the home, Liam and Harley would have requested and waited for backup. The mysterious disappearance of evidence regarding the 911 call screams of a cover-up. The transcript of the 911 call went missing, and the recording vanished. At least any *official* copies.

I've been hoping that the box Nancy promised me contains a recording or transcript of the 911 call. The image of Nancy's tearstained face returns to me. We met a year ago at hospice a few days after her mother died.

"Mom had been threatened to keep quiet," Nancy told me as she packed up old photos of her mother. "She needed to get it off her chest before she died," Nancy explained. She said the night my father was shot and his partner was killed weighed heavily on her mother. "My mom was one hundred percent sure the caller said there were no guns at the apartment. My mom says she asked the question twice and the caller said there weren't."

Besides Nancy's mother's deathbed confession, I have no tangible proof. And without the evidence, Liam evades my attempts to discuss the incident. But he always avoids my gaze when he denies my theory that he was set up. And that is a Liam Murphy tell.

I wonder what happened to make Nancy sound spooked earlier.

Before I overthink it, I send a text: Looking forward to seeing you in the morning. I'll have coffee ready.

Three dots appear. I wait. And watch. They disappear. No message comes through.

CHAPTER 13

DAY OF THE KIDNAPPING

My alarm sounds, and I jump out of bed, anxious to get the morning going. Specifically, seeing Nancy in less than an hour. By 6:20 a.m., I'm dressed in a muted-gray silk tank and dark-gray cotton skirt. A lighter choice than my go-to black outfits, but today promises to be hot and humid. For fear of my makeup melting off my face, I pack my cosmetics and throw them in my tote along with a thermos of coffee.

I fill a flowered yellow mug with a second cup of coffee and move to the living room to keep an eye out for Nancy. A maroon Subaru pulls in front of my house at 6:29 a.m., and Nancy steps out of the car. She throws her purse over her shoulder but doesn't retrieve a box.

I unlock the door before she reaches my porch. "Hi," I say, holding the door open; she stops before entering. She looks more put together than last time—but that was just after her mother had passed away.

"I'm not going to come in, Kate," she says, her eyes darting everywhere but my face. "I can't give you the box."

"I don't understand," I reply, anger seeping into my voice. "You promised."

She forces her gaze to me, and I register fear in her brown eyes. "I know. And I'm sorry." She bites down on her lip. "I don't think you realize how bad things can get." She glances around my block and steps closer. "I've been getting prank calls. Someone's been following my husband."

"You don't know it's related—" I say.

"I don't know it isn't." Nancy cuts me off. "Listen, the box is gone. It's with the person it needs to be with. I wanted to tell you face to face." She straightens her shoulders. "I felt like I owed you that. But we're done. Don't contact me again, Kate. And if you're smart, let this go."

She turns and steps down the brick walkway and into her car, not once looking back. The disappointment crushes down on me, physically gutting my insides. I'm not sure I can blame Nancy—she seemed genuinely scared. But why? What spooked her after all this time? And if I can figure that out, can I learn the truth?

—

Traffic to the US Open should have its own category in the dictionary. Worse than any traffic in the tristate, including rush hour in Manhattan. It's traffic on speed. Or, rather, the opposite. Half a dozen officers stand at the exit off the Grand Central Parkway to direct the vehicles in a loop so we can enter another loop to pull onto the Flushing Meadows lawns.

Even with my press pass, I'm relegated to a back lot, requiring me to take a shuttle to the Tennis Center. It takes me the same amount of time to park as it did to drive here from Connecticut. By the time I find Bill, I'm sweating. But Bill appears unusually cool. And clean. "Don't you look fancy," I say to Bill, taking in his fresh button-down and pressed khakis.

"Because my clothes aren't wrinkled?" He grimaces, but I can tell he's pleased with the compliment.

"Yup." I laugh. "How was last night's barbecue?" I ask as a group of people strolls past us, wine sloshing from their cups.

"A bit early to drink. Don't you think?" Bill says, watching them giggle and sip.

I raise my mug in the air. "Unless it's an espresso martini, nothing but caffeine at this hour."

"Cheers to that." He holds out his coffee cup and clinks it against mine. Bill and I are coffee compatible, both never polluting our java with milks, creamers, or any sugars or syrups. I turn at the sound of laughter and see two women pointing at the tree by the entrance gate, where orange tennis balls hang from branches. One of them holds up her phone and motions the other to squeeze in for a selfie. I love the hoopla around this event, like the tennis balls on strings. Maybe I'll adopt that as a decoration this October and go for a sports-themed Halloween.

"You didn't answer." I turn back to Bill, who motions for us to start toward the outer courts to watch Brynn's match. "How was the barbecue?"

"Grilled tofu is disgusting," he says, but laughs. We walk past more people with alcohol in hand, others lined up at the Tito's vodka cart for Bloody Marys.

"Second question," I reply. "Why are you dressed up?"

"It's my anniversary," he says. "Taking the wife to dinner and a show tonight."

"Very nice." I smile, glad to see Bill prioritizing his family. We walk past yesterday's court and make our way to number ten, the largest of the outer courts and a step up from where Brynn played her first match.

Bill starts toward the front seats, but I stop him. "Over there." I point to the upper row and the man with a Yankee baseball cap and Ray-Bans.

"Who's he?" Bill asks, climbing the stairs behind me.

"Someone I've been trying to connect with." I turn and smile at Bill.

"Cryptic much?" He huffs but follows me to the top row, then slides in next to me.

Franklin Fielding turns to look at me as I settle next to him. "You're kidding," he says, shaking his long neck, which looks like it could snap from the weight of his head.

"Just a chat," I reply. "Completely off the record."

"You can sit here, but I ain't talking." He inches away from me just to try and make a point. But there's not much room on his other side, unless he wants to end up in someone's lap.

The players appear. Brynn still wears tie-dye, but she's traded in the blues and purples for pinks and greens. She also changed the color of the streaks in her hair to match.

"Since when did tennis turn into Fashion Week?" Franklin whispers under his breath, and I smile. Lucy Bosco's coach may not talk to me, but I knew he'd start mumbling to himself.

Brynn serves first and makes quick work of her opponent. "What do you think?" I lean over and ask Franklin as the players change sides.

"Everything's off the record," he says.

"Just background, Franklin. I want your perspective on the whole Lucy–Brynn thing."

He nods, as I knew he would, partially because he's incapable of not talking. But also, because he knows he can trust me. We've connected a few times over stories, and I've proven myself to him.

"I wanna see if Brynn is more than just hype," he says.

"She did beat Lucy a few months ago," I reply.

"Lucy was barely able to walk at that tournament. She should've gotten a medal for showing up."

The umpire asks for quiet, and we stop whispering. Brynn's opponent's first serve goes into the net. Then she double faults. Her next serve goes wide. She bounces her ball, then stops, saying something to the umpire.

"Already rattled," Franklin says. "Not a good sign."

"Ladies and gentlemen, please refrain from finding seats until the game is over," the umpire says into the microphone.

Brynn wins the first set, and Franklin gets up, stretches, and then takes out his phone. "Shit," he says, and everyone turns to stare. He doesn't notice the reaction, just starts typing furiously into the phone as if his fingers carry emphasis.

"What's going on?" I ask.

"Nothing," Franklin snaps, clearly lying as he steps over his seat, into the aisle behind him, and leapfrogs through the stands, winding his way out of sight. The wind shifts, blowing hot air across my face, and I notice the flags along the outer part of the stadium whip in a new direction.

Brynn notices too. Catching her toss in her hand and pausing for the breeze to die down.

I look over at Brynn's box and see Zane Cole whisper something to his wife, Alexis. Her round oversize sunglasses block any sign of response. Zane removes his bucket hat and mashes it between his hands as if it's pizza dough. Something's got him worried. Could it be the same thing that caused Franklin to make a quick exit?

I pull out my phone and check for news about the US Open. There's a bunch of drama on the men's side with the top seed out from an injury and an upset of the second seed. But nothing eyebrow raising on the women's side. Just lots of speculation about this afternoon's match between Lucy and her old rival, who's sunk in the rankings. It's just an attempt at girl drama—*cold Lucy Bosco faces former nemesis and everyone's sweetheart, Jill Wallace, blah blah.* I scroll through the photos and see pictures of Lucy's opponent arriving at the gate, two bodyguards rushing her past the cameras.

I assume there are similar shots of Lucy but can't find them. Did she sneak in another entrance? I check the scoreboard, which shows Brynn up four games to one in the second set. Above the score, the time reads 11:55 a.m. Lucy's match starts at 1:30 p.m. Surely, she's here somewhere.

"Brynn's impressive." Bill leans over. "Since you haven't been paying much attention—I thought you'd want to know." He bumps me with his shoulder, flashing a little grin.

"I appreciate the update."

"What's wrong?" he whispers as we watch Brynn serve another ace.

"I'm sure it's nothing," I reply as Brynn wins the fifth game of the second set, now one game away from taking the match.

Brynn finishes off her opponent, puts down her racquet, and does a cartwheel right in the middle of the court.

Young fans hoot and holler. The chair umpire looks horrified. Are there rules against cartwheels on the court? Certainly, Brynn needs to shake her opponent's hand first.

"Quiet please," the umpire calls as Brynn steps to the net and limply shakes her opponent's hand before retrieving her phone and holding it up for a selfie. "Smile everyone," Brynn calls to the crowd.

"Brynn, Brynn, Brynn," girls chant. She loves the attention and encourages them with her arms, as if conducting an orchestra.

A security guard approaches Brynn, whispering something about decorum, I imagine.

Bill stands and pops a piece of nicotine gum in his mouth. "Wanna grab a quick bite and go set up for the interview?"

"I think I should touch base with Brynn and her parents first. You go ahead," I say.

"Don't worry, I'll eat healthy." He gives me a wink.

I follow Bill and the other spectators as we funnel down the aluminum stairs to the main level. Coach Zane and his wife remain seated as fans leave the court, searching for more matches to watch. Chatter reaches me about a tiebreaker on Court 6. But I move against the tide toward the player boxes and the Cole family.

Coach Zane stands with his back toward me, phone pushed against his ear. Alexis remains seated, a scowl on her lips as she watches her daughter interacting with the fans.

"Excuse me," I say to Alexis, about to introduce myself. Before she can answer, Coach Zane spins around and sticks his hand toward me to shake.

"Ms. Green." He puts his other hand, with his phone, over mine. "It's wonderful to meet you. Brynn is thrilled to be featured in your story," he says, voice booming even though I'm just feet away.

I glance over at his wife, who doesn't show any emotion behind her sunglasses. I've heard her described as an ice princess. "Nice to meet you too," I reply, pulling my hand back.

"When do we start?" Zane asks, and I explain that we don't have access to the outdoor studio for forty minutes.

"It's a great spot for the interview. Right in front of Arthur Ashe Stadium," I say.

"Love it, love it," Zane replies, running his hand through thinning gray hair.

Alexis removes her sunglasses and stares at me from deep-set green eyes. She stands, her cream-color knee-length dress hugging her thin body.

"Well, how lucky, we have time to kill." She steps next to me. "Why don't you and I go have a little chat."

Both Coach Zane and I look at her, surprised by the suggestion.

"Are you sure that's a good idea?" he says, brow raised so high it looks painful.

Alexis returns her sunglasses to her face and takes my arm. "Of course it's a good idea," she says in a dismissive tone. And I wonder what she could possibly want to discuss with me before the interview. Whatever it is, I brace myself for the worst because her scowl suggests she's not a Kate Green fan.

CHAPTER 14

I sit across from Alexis on the balcony of Aces, the overpriced, fancy VIP restaurant with a breathtaking view of the tennis grounds. Vivid bursts of purple-and-yellow flowers hang from baskets across from us.

A waiter sets a Bloody Mary in front of Alexis and a coffee by me, with a silver-plated cream-and-sugar set even though I ordered my coffee black. I watch Alexis as she lifts her drink and takes a sip. Up close, I notice her attempts to cover up her aging skin—from thick foundation to Botox that's frozen her forehead. She's barely spoken since dragging me away, and I'm wondering what's in store. A warning to go easy on her daughter?

She wraps her manicured fingers around her glass and leans forward. "You know we have someone in common?" she says, and I notice her perfectly white teeth. Veneers?

Why so much work? I wonder, calculating that Alexis must only be in her early fifties. With high cheekbones and bright-green eyes, she moved beyond tennis magazines in her prime, appearing on the covers of *Vogue* and other fashion magazines.

"Who do we have in common?" I ask.

"It's what I want to talk to you about." She leans back in her chair, assessing me.

Is she holding out on the big reveal as part of a game? Toying with me? If she's not going to speak, I will. There are some questions I have for her. Although, I really want to wait and ask them on camera. During my research, I came across an article about the adoption. In it, Alexis holds baby Brynn and tells the reporter she hopes her daughter never plays tennis. Does Alexis still feel that way?

"Something's on your mind." I decide to hold my questions for our interview. "Why don't you tell me what it is."

She gives a slight smile. "Fine," she says, raising her chin. "I don't trust you." She draws each word out.

"Me or the media?" I ask, thinking of no reason why she'd personally be worried about my trustworthiness.

"You." She keeps her eyes on mine.

I feel like she's daring me to look away. Like this is a test. I maintain eye contact and ask her if this has to do with the person we have in common.

"Yes," she replies. "The person is a longtime friend of mine, David Lopez. He was supposed to interview Brynn."

I feel my shoulders tense but refuse to let her see the effect of her statement. What kind of garbage did my ex-boyfriend tell her? And why is he still trying to undermine me?

"First," I say, deciding to deal with the facts of the situation. "Our producer notified you over two weeks ago that I would be handling the story."

She's not wrong that David was initially assigned to cover the Open, but Conrad insisted I interview Lucy and not David. TRP wasn't going to pass on a Lucy Bosco exclusive, so the assignment changed. But Brynn's team knew that. And TRP wasn't going to waste two of us on the same event.

I wonder what's made Alexis so guarded. From my research, I remember her easy smile when she and Zane first got together. They were dubbed the "golden couple of tennis." She, a multi–Grand Slam doubles champion, and he a famous coach. In those early articles, she appeared carefree. Dare I think happy?

"If you didn't want Brynn speaking with me you could have canceled the interview," I continue with more bravado than I feel. I need this interview. And soon. With the new deadline, I can't afford to lose half my story.

She regards me with amusement, then looks over the balcony at the fans streaming across the walkways. "Brynn insisted."

I find it interesting she chose to say *Brynn insisted*, because I would bet Alexis's opinion trumps Brynn's. My guess is Zane insisted on keeping the interview. Maybe he is the boss, after all.

"What can I say to make you more comfortable?" I ask, eager to get this standoff behind us.

"Nothing," she replies, putting both palms down on the table. "Just know, I'm watching. And can pull the plug at any moment."

A shout comes from the table next to us; the men stare at one of the television screens where a doubles team just won a close match. Alexis looks over, too, and I wonder if she's remembering her days on the court. Again, my mind wanders to her comment about not wanting her daughter to play. A question at the top of my list for our interview.

Bill texts that he's ready for us. I relay the information and take a final sip of coffee.

"I'll meet you there," she says. "I need to make a call first." As if to prove she's not lying, she pulls her phone from her purse.

I put money on the table, hesitating. Sure, her people agreed that she and Zane would participate with their daughter. But is Alexis about to blow off the interview? Or worse, will she sabotage the whole thing? I take a final look at her before leaving. Alexis's back is toward me, and she's speaking animatedly into her phone. Another person out to make life difficult. This one I didn't see coming.

CHAPTER 15

If you throw a rock, you're bound to hit some type of media organization here at the Open. So many news outlets descend on this event—some for the tennis, others for the scene and spectacle. Many for the combination. If you aren't covering the matches, you might be reporting on the celebrities. The US Open is different from any other sport I've reported on. Or participated in. Maybe it's the proximity to Manhattan's elite? Or the excitement of the single-elimination structure of tennis tournaments? Maybe it's that tennis is an individual sport, which automatically raises the intensity and scrutiny of the players? I can't put my finger on it, but there's a sizzle in the air that I haven't experienced anywhere else.

"Kate." Bill waves at me from one of the three mini studios to the right of the famous fountain, with dozens of spigots jetting water into the air.

I walk in his direction, passing other network setups before reaching Bill, who stands under the red TRP tent secured to a platform a few feet above the ground. "Over here." Bill points to aluminum steps atop a tarp covering electric wires. He extends his hand to help me with the last step as I reach the throw rugs placed on the platform to provide a warm atmosphere and keep echoes to a minimum. I say hello to the rest of the crew, who came to help with the interview.

"I'll have you here." Bill points to the folding chair facing three others. "You'll have the World's Fair grounds behind," he says, indicating the New York World's Fair grounds, with the stainless steel globe and the observatory towers. I stare at the towers in the distance, portrayed in the movie *Men in Black* as interstellar spacecrafts. My kids and I watched that movie three times this summer during our family movie nights. A pang settles in my heart as I recall last night's conversation with Jackson.

"The setup looks great," I say to Bill.

He motions to my face. "Where's your makeup?"

I forgot I hadn't put any on this morning. I sit cross-legged on the rug, back toward the public, and pull my cosmetic bag from my tote. I open a small mirror, balancing it on my knees, and cover my face with foundation. Next, I line my eyes with black pencil, add mascara. I finish with blush and dab lip gloss over my lips.

"I'm here," Brynn announces, taking the steps two at a time. She sports a new outfit, a variation on her tie-dye theme. A pink-and-purple tie-dyed dress and matching sneakers. She's let her long, thick hair down, the pink-and-purple streaks, mostly in front, frame her heart-shaped face. I shove my cosmetic bag away and stand up to greet her.

"My parents should be here in a minute," she says, sitting in the middle seat. "You mind if I do a little video for my socials?" She asks but doesn't wait for my answer as she pulls out her phone and starts speaking into the camera.

"Hi, everyone!" She smiles into the phone, batting her fake lashes as she speaks. "It's time for my big interview. I'm speaking with Kate Green." She turns the phone to show me, and I give a little wave, then pretend to study my notes. "I'm really excited." Brynn stands. "Check out the studio. It's right in the middle of the action, so everyone who walks by can see me." To illustrate her point, she taps the screen to change the camera perspective, holding it out to show all the spectators. "Oh, there's Mom. I better go." She smiles into the camera, her sparkling lip gloss highlighting her smile. "You all know how much she hates that I overshare." She draws out the word *overshare* and laughs.

"Can't you take a break for one minute?" Alexis says to her daughter as she steps onto the platform and sits on the chair farthest from the edge. And, by extension, from the crowd.

"Howdy, howdy." Coach Zane forgoes the stairs, raises himself onto the platform to a sitting position, and then swings his legs up, shaking the setup. "Sorry. Sorry," he says and walks to the empty seat. "Ready, Brynnie?" He gives her a smile.

"Always." She smiles back.

"Before we start," I say. "A reminder that you should try to ignore the cameras and keep your gaze toward me. Otherwise, it looks a little odd when we are editing."

"It's not our first rodeo." Zane nudges his daughter.

"One more thing," I reply. "I'm not planning to cover every topic now. This will be a relatively quick interview since we are spending the day together tomorrow in the city."

"Glad you are giving Brynn the same amount of airtime as Lucy." He nods, and I wonder if he's going to count the seconds each appears on air. I can already tell the Cole parents are going to be difficult.

"Let's get started," I say and motion Bill to begin recording. "Brynn." I turn to her and smile. "Why do you like tennis?"

She opens her mouth to speak and then closes it. I'm always surprised how the simplest questions stump people. She adjusts her position on the seat, quickly regaining her composure. "I obviously don't just like it." She giggles. "I love tennis. I love the way my racquet feels when I hit the shot just right. I love the competition and especially the fact that I don't have to rely on anyone else to win. That's why I don't play doubles." She glances at her mom, but Alexis shows no sign of emotion. "I love how tennis demands you show your talent in lots of ways—you know." She smiles at me. "You've gotta be fast and agile, but you also have to be precise and sneaky." She giggles again. "And it doesn't hurt that I'm so good at it."

Talk about confidence, I think to myself. I always wonder at what point confidence transcends into arrogance. And when overconfidence is an attempt to hide doubts.

"Zane, Alexis—when did you realize your daughter had so much talent?"

"By the time she could walk." Zane jumps to answer first. "There was no question she was extremely athletic. Then, when she picked up a tennis racquet, well, it was clear she was a prodigy."

Sirens sound in the distance, fire engines. Bill puts up his hand, asking us to pause. As the siren dissipates, I turn to Alexis. "Did Brynn's talent surprise you?"

"You mean because Brynn is adopted?"

I nod, watching her as she takes a moment to gather her thoughts.

"Like my husband said, Brynn showed athletic prowess at an early age, but did I think she'd become a tennis star? No. In fact, if we weren't her adopted parents, she might have chosen a different sport."

"Mom." Brynn stares at Alexis.

Zane opens his mouth to speak, but I cut him off, wanting to ask Alexis about the magazine story that came out when Brynn was born. "When Brynn was a baby, you gave an interview saying that you hoped Brynn would never play tennis." I stare at Alexis.

Out of the corner of my eye, I see Brynn roll her eyes, as if this is a topic she's used to hearing about. And hates.

"I remember that interview." Alexis gracefully crosses one leg over the other. "At the time—I had just retired from my tennis career. I had mixed feelings back then." She pauses and looks down. "Tennis is a wonderful sport. But the attention can be stifling. I didn't want my daughter. Our daughter"—she corrects herself—"to have to endure that scrutiny. But ultimately, she chose her path. And I'm supportive of that but—"

"The truth is," Zane jumps in, cutting off his wife. "Alexis was just basking in new motherhood when she gave that interview. I couldn't pry Brynn out of her hands back then. Always holding on so tight." His voice fills with condescension. "But of course our child would play tennis."

Brynn looks bored, fidgeting in her seat. I turn back to her. "How does it feel to be a seeded player at the US Open?"

"Oh, yeah. It's exciting," she gushes, then glances at her dad. She clears her throat before continuing. "But my focus is on getting as far in the tournament as I can."

"She has a real chance to go all the way," Zane breaks in.

"Does a statement like that make you feel pressured?" I ask Brynn, genuinely curious. So much of sports is handling expectations. I always preferred overperforming to underperforming.

"Not at all." Brynn smiles. "It makes me feel like my dad—my coach—believes in me."

Zane nods approvingly, but I wonder how much of that answer was rehearsed.

I ask Brynn some basic questions about her routine. She plays tennis before school, after school, on weekends. "It's not a regular school, either," Brynn says. "I'm homeschooled. A teacher comes to our house in Florida and spends a few hours a day with me. I'm almost done with high school. One more year."

"Were you always homeschooled?" I ask, not completely surprised, since tennis takes up so much of her time.

"Since sixth grade," she says, looking from parent to parent.

"It wasn't an easy decision," Zane says, glancing at his wife.

I decide to switch gears and ask about Brynn's relationship with her father. "How is it having your father as a coach. Is it hard?" I lean forward, making eye contact with Brynn.

"Not at all," she says, a bit too chipper.

"What do you think of the dynamic, Coach?" I turn to Zane.

"When I'm the coach, I'm the coach and not Brynn's father." He pats his daughter on the shoulder. "There is one benefit, though." He pauses and rubs his chin. "I know Brynn so well that I know her faults and insecurities. And, therefore, I can help her overcome her weaknesses in a way a regular coach can't."

Brynn winces.

"I would imagine that must be hard," I say to Brynn.

Her expression says yes, but her words don't. "Anything that helps make my game better is a positive," Brynn replies. *If this girl gives up tennis, she would have a great career in politics,* I think, admiring the nonanswer answer.

"Does your mom do any coaching?" I ask.

"Absolutely not," Zane answers for her. "You'd have too many cooks in the kitchen."

Alexis gives him a sideways look, and I can't help feeling like there's a lot more going on under the surface.

Bill clears his throat, and I check my watch. "We need to wrap up here," I say, explaining the anchors need the studio back for the 1:30 p.m. sports roundup. "This was a great start. I look forward to our time together tomorrow."

Bill collects the microphones as Alexis excuses herself to make another call.

"I need to speak to your trainer," Zane says, telling Brynn to meet him in the players' lounge.

Brynn picks up her phone and starts recording. "Okay, friends." She smiles into her camera. "We just wrapped up our interview. Part one. LOL." I tune her out, noticing a commotion under the large LED screen diagonally in front of us. Something big is going on. I squint to make out the words on the ticker and hear myself gasp.

CHAPTER 16

On screen, the camera shows a static picture of an empty tennis court. The court at Arthur Ashe Stadium where Lucy is supposed to play at this moment. The chair umpire leans down, speaking to a woman in a blazer. Ball boys and girls, dressed in bright-green-and-navy polos, remain with their backs to the wall behind the baseline.

But it's the words on the ticker that make me choke: **LUCY BOSCO FORFEITS MATCH AND PULLS OUT OF TOURNAMENT.**

"Coward," a voice from the crowd calls out.

"They better give me my money back," another voice calls.

I keep my eyes glued to the screen. This doesn't make sense. Lucy was fine last night. No injuries. No complaints. The sedan. I remember the silver car I thought was following her. Did something happen? My heart falls, and I feel sweat break out on my neck.

"Why would she drop out?" Brynn steps over to me, hands on hips. "Did she seem injured yesterday?"

"No," I reply, thinking how Lucy said she still had a lot to prove. I pull out my phone to search for more details. A statement pops up from her coach.

> "Due to personal reasons, Lucy Bosco informed me today that she can't continue at the US Open and is

pulling out immediately. She apologizes to her fans and requests that her privacy be respected."

—Franklin Fielding, Lucy Bosco's Coach.

Is this the news that freaked Franklin out when we were watching Brynn's match? I think back to that—he got a message on his phone and bolted. He acted surprised. He must not have seen this coming either. And to inform him hours before her match? It doesn't make sense. I dial Lucy's number. Nothing. I text. I call Conrad. Straight to voicemail. I begin dialing Nico when my phone rings.

"I don't have any information yet," I say to my boss, Charlie, before he even speaks.

"Get it. ASAP!" he barks over noise in the sports room.

Whatever, I think to myself as Charlie hangs up. At this point, I'm more concerned about Lucy than worried about the story.

I dial Nico. Nothing. I dial Conrad again.

This time he picks up. "Off the record," he says before even saying hello.

"Yes. Off the record. I'm worried," I reply.

"What's going on is that my sister is a selfish bitch." Conrad sounds unhinged. "I spent three months on this public relations campaign and then she sends a text saying she's decided to take a break."

"What do you mean?" I cup my hand over my ear to block out the noise of the crowd. "Is Lucy injured?"

"Nothing she hasn't fought through before. Personally, I think she's a coward and just decided she didn't want to deal. I'm done. And, hell, you can quote me on that. I'm done—"

"Wait," I yell, wanting to ask him exactly what Lucy messaged him, but he's already hung up the phone.

"Check this out." Bill calls me over and, by extension, Brynn. We turn to the monitor Bill is pointing to and see Jill Wallace, Lucy's opponent for this match, speaking in the pressroom.

"I can't say I'm surprised Lucy forfeited," Jill says, her blonde ponytail bobbing up and down. "I really wanted to play her. Gosh, I think it would have been a great match. Epic."

"Oh please." Brynn makes a barfing face. "Lucy would have destroyed her."

I keep watching the screen as Jill continues to describe what a historic match they would have had.

"What do you think happened?" a reporter asks Jill.

"Her coach said she forfeited for 'personal reasons.'" Jill shrugs. "Who am I to question whether they're because of a physical injury? Or loss of confidence." She pauses to let that word sink in, smiling in a vicious Barbie-doll way. "Or something more serious." She takes another pause, letting the words linger in the air. "Tennis is a mentally taxing sport."

Charlie pings my phone again, demanding to know what I've learned. I ignore him, continuing to watch Jill spew cotton candy–laced hate.

I hear a bang and feel something hit my foot. Looking down I see Brynn's phone bounce against my toe and tumble onto the top stair. I look up and see the color drain from her face.

I bend down to get it. "It's not broken," I say, noticing she's still ashen. Kids these days can't live a second without their devices. I extend the phone toward her, but she shakes, refusing to even touch it. I look at the screen and see why. Staring back at me is a photo of Lucy—bound and gagged. Underneath, the words—Don't call the police or she dies.

CHAPTER 17

My pulse quickens as I stare at the image of Lucy Bosco slumped on a cement floor, hands bound to a pipe. A piece of electrical tape covers her mouth. Dried blood is caked on her cheek, and her eyes seem open wide in terror.

"Could it be fake?" Brynn whispers, hope in her eyes. "Like AI or something? A terrible prank."

"I don't know," I reply. "See if you recognize the phone number." I hand the phone back to her.

She takes it with trembling hands and looks. "There's no caller ID." She shakes her head, pushing the device back at me as if the sender could reach through the phone and grab her.

"Kate." Bill taps my arm, and I jump, nearly dropping the phone. "Easy. Jeez," he says. "I'm going to stay and help with the live report. But we need to clear the podium," he says, indicating that Brynn and I must leave.

"Got it," I say.

"Are you all right?" He takes another look at me. "You look like you've seen a ghost."

"I'm okay." I force a smile on my face. "Just a little hungry. You know how I get—"

He laughs and tells me to get some food. Pronto. I bend down to retrieve my tote from the corner and quickly hold my phone over

Brynn's to take a photo of the image on Brynn's phone, along with the message.

My brain is already spinning with next steps; first and foremost, we need to determine if the photo is real. I know the sender said no police, but I need to contact someone. Discreetly. The obvious choice being Liam, my biological father and NYPD detective extraordinaire. I text him the photo and a quick message.

Sent to Brynn Cole. Real? No police, please. I'm glad he follows professional tennis and won't need further explanation about the identities of Brynn and Lucy.

"Kate." Brynn's voice squeaks. "What should we do?"

I shove my phone into my skirt pocket and throw my tote over my shoulder as I stand. "You need to call your parents," I tell her, forcing her phone back into her hands. "They should know what's going on."

"Kate!" Bill calls again, pointing to a pretend watch on his wrist. I put up my hands, indicating we are leaving, and lead Brynn down the steps and onto the plaza. The odor of sizzling meats mixed with wine makes me nauseous.

"Hey—that's Brynn Cole."

"Lucky break, Brynn." A middle-aged man with a big gut laughs through his popcorn.

The fans no longer seem charming or interesting but aggressive, like parts of an accordion pushing in on us. Is one of them involved in Lucy's situation?

"Tell your parents to meet us behind Court 13, by the ice cream concession stand. It's quiet there."

A gaggle of young girls runs up to Brynn, pens extended, begging for autographs. I remain next to Brynn, worried she might be a target. She signs a few balls with a shaking hand, hardly able to write her name.

"Sorry, everyone." I step between Brynn and the fans. "But Brynn is late for an interview. She'll sign more autographs later."

They moan but listen, and I hurry Brynn away from the crowd and down the path, passing a clothing vendor with large square prints of this year's US Open designs hanging in the back.

"Look over there." A reporter points at Brynn, rushing in our direction with a camera and microphone. "How do you feel about Lucy Bosco dropping out?" He pushes the microphone in front of Brynn's face, so close it touches her lip. "Makes it easier for you."

"I didn't think about—"

I take Brynn's arm. "She has no comment," I say and guide her away and down the path.

"Hey, Kate," the reporter yells. "You can't hog her. She's going to need to talk."

I ignore him and continue past the beverage carts and around the back of the food court to the patio furniture that Bill and I scoped out a couple of days ago.

"Let's sit," I say to Brynn, coaxing her onto the couch under the court. She drops into the cushion, and I sit catty corner, pulling my chair as close as I can. The sun appears from behind a cloud, its rays scorching my back.

"Are your parents coming?" I ask Brynn as softly as I can.

She pulls her phone from her pocket and fumbles to open it. "Mom is on her way," she says, her lips quivering.

I put my hands over Brynn's to try and calm her down. "We'll get to the bottom of this. Okay?"

She looks up at me, and I see the child beneath the bravado. My heart goes out to her, and I squeeze her fingers, hoping to give her reassurance.

"Brynn!" Alexis yells her daughter's name while shooting me a nasty look. "Did you do something to her?" she says, sliding onto the couch next to Brynn.

"No, Mom. Kate's been helping me." Brynn pulls her hands from under mine and covers her face, starting to whimper.

"What the hell is going on?" Alexis turns to me since Brynn is too choked up to answer. "Tell. Me. Now."

I glance around at the people nearby. The couple on the couch across from us sit whispering together. Two men leaning against a pole, eyeing us as they eat ice cream. Or are they just staring in front of them? To my right, a man transporting a large refrigerator by hand trolley. *Large enough to hide a body,* I think, my imagination running wild.

I keep my voice a whisper, leaning toward Alexis. "Brynn received a disturbing photo," I begin. "It's of Lucy Bosco. And it shows Lucy being held against her will."

"Is this a joke?" Alexis looks from me back at her daughter.

Brynn moves her hands from her face, her eyes blotchy, makeup smeared on her cheeks. With trembling fingers, Brynn retrieves her phone and hands it over to Alexis.

"You're serious?" Alexis takes the device and types in a password. Brynn looks at me; then we both watch Alexis. Her anger melts to shock. "Oh my God." Alexis's hand goes to cover her mouth.

"The photo just appeared," Brynn whimpers. "I don't know anything about this. The number's blocked."

"Maybe this is just a prank?" Alexis says, her disdain replaced, for a moment, with hope. "Photoshopped or something? A sick joke."

"I had the same thought," I say. "But with Lucy disappearing from the tournament . . ." I let the words sit in the air. "Listen, I already sent the photo to my father. He's an NYPD detective. And won't say a word."

"It says no police!" Alexis raises her voice.

"Shhh. Mom." Brynn looks around as people stare at us.

Alexis takes a deep breath and lowers her volume to a hostile whisper. "It should be our decision to make."

"With all due respect," I reply. "Lucy's life could be at stake. And the phone literally fell at my feet. So, no, I couldn't leave the decision to you. A serious crime might have occurred, and Lucy could be in danger. Brynn could be in danger."

Alexis puts her hands to her temples. "This is happening too fast. I . . . I need a second." She looks around.

Brynn's phone pings, and we all stare at her. She looks down slowly. "It's Dad. He says he's in a meeting and can't come."

Alexis grabs the phone—

"Wait." I put my hand on her wrist. "Don't say anything about the situation, just in case . . ." I let the words hang in the air, but she's not stupid. She gets my meaning. If someone was able to text Brynn's phone, can they read her messages? Or Alexis's?

She lowers the phone to her lap. "I need a minute. I need to think."

My phone pings, and I read the text from Liam. What hotel r they at? Mae and I will be there as friends.

"Who's that from?" Alexis demands.

I show her the text and the benign message. "This is my father. He'll meet us at the hotel. Mae is with the FBI. I promise they'll be discreet."

"Absolutely not!" Alexis says.

"Mom." Brynn looks at her. "We need to know if this is real—"

"And you can't walk into a precinct or contact the police yourself," I add. Alexis appears to be considering the situation. "Look, I know you don't completely trust me. But I'm also a mom. Trust that. This is what I'd do if it was my child."

Alexis looks from her daughter to me back to her daughter. "Tell him we're staying at the Ritz-Carlton Central Park," she says, putting her arm around Brynn's shoulder. "And for the record—this doesn't mean I trust you."

CHAPTER 18

We walk past the Court of Champions, with plaques commemorating the best US Open players of all time. I stare at the image of John McEnroe, his famous headband around his forehead, the image frozen as he reaches for a ground shot.

"Here." Alexis takes her sunglasses off and hands them to her daughter. Brynn puts them on, covering her red eyes and runny makeup. "Now keep going," Alexis says to Brynn, who seems a little woozy as the crowd grows.

Alexis leads us into the lobby of the players' tennis hub, which buzzes with activity. In front of us, players and their staff line up at the transportation desk. The air-conditioning should be a welcome reprieve from the heat; instead I feel a chill.

"Brynn, try your father again while I get us a car," Alexis orders before getting in line at the transportation desk.

I stay with Brynn, worried she might collapse if left alone. She doesn't move.

"Take out your phone," I urge her. She gives a shake of her head, obviously scared to even touch it, like the device is kryptonite.

A rush of voices makes her jump, and we turn to see Jill Wallace enter with her coach and other members of her staff. "Hi, Brynn." She smiles. "Hope to play you later in the tournament." She giggles and continues down the hall toward the dining area, her entourage following.

"Let's get some water," I suggest, walking with Brynn to a refrigerator with a glass door. "Or maybe some juice?"

She doesn't answer, and I take out the healthiest sugary drink I can find—orange juice. I open it for her and place it in her hands. She takes a sip, then lowers it.

"Better?" I ask, glancing at Alexis, who is next in line.

"A little." She shrugs.

"Okay." I keep my voice as soft as possible. "Take your phone out and dial your dad. See if he can come with us to the hotel."

She nods, teeth chattering, and removes the device, hitting his contact and then holding the phone to her ear. She looks at me and shakes her head. "Voicemail." She clicks off from the call.

I think for a minute. We can't tell him what's going on in case Brynn's phone is being monitored. But Brynn needs to tell Zane something.

"Text your dad that your mom has a headache and the two of you are heading back to the hotel."

She nods again and does what I suggested.

Her phone pings with a message. She holds it up for me to read. Meeting with Nike. See you later at the hotel.

"Is Nike your sponsor?" I ask, looking at her Fila sneakers.

"He wants them to be." She shrugs.

Alexis walks toward us, her heels clicking against the checkered floor. She's putting up a good front; except for a furrowed brow, she looks unshaken. I wonder if this is her game face.

We catch her up on Zane. "Whatever," she replies and tells us the car will arrive in ten minutes, suggesting we wait outside. We exit to the private area maintained for players and their staff to wait for transportation. Brynn collapses onto a wooden bench against the brick wall of the stadium. Above her I see a blue-and-gold plaque containing one of Arthur Ashe's famous quotes: "Start where you are. Use what you have. Do what you can."

Those words can apply to our situation, I think to myself. *Start where you are*—we're at the US Open, and someone might have kidnapped Lucy and seems to be threatening Brynn. *Use what you have*—I take as a message for me. I have police contacts that can work under the radar. *Do what you can*—and I will do whatever I can to help find Lucy. As I recommit myself to the task, a black Mercedes SUV pulls around a grass circle and a valet signals our car has arrived.

"Before we go." I stop them on the brick sidewalk. "Remember not to say anything about all this in front of the driver."

"We're not stupid," Alexis snaps, but Brynn gives me a quick nod as she follows her mother into the car.

I walk around the vehicle and enter from the other door.

"Why don't you go into the back row?" Alexis says, even though there's plenty of room next to them.

"No problem," I reply, not minding a little privacy—a chance to process what's happened. It feels like days since Lucy's photo appeared on Brynn's phone.

The valet closes the door behind me, and I lean against the cool leather seat. The SUV smells of deodorized pine. Soft elevator music plays through the speakers.

"Can you turn that off," Alexis demands. The music stops as the driver pulls away from the curb, and I turn my focus to the last hour.

The first question running through my mind is when Lucy's absence was first noticed. I remember Lucy's coach, Franklin Fielding, sitting next to me at Brynn's match when he seemed agitated by the text he received around noon. For now, I'm going to assume it was about Lucy. At 1:30 p.m., she didn't appear for her match. According to Franklin's press release, Lucy told him she decided to forfeit, and he relayed that information to the officials at the tournament. Did Franklin call Lucy and speak to her or receive a text? I take out my phone and find Franklin in my contacts and shoot him a message. I'm not going to hold my breath that he'll answer, but it's worth a try.

When I spoke to Conrad on the phone, he did say Lucy sent him a text. Did he also speak to her? And if so, when? I message him too.

The biggest question mark in my mind is Nico—I haven't heard back from him. I'm not Nico's go-to person. I get that. It most likely means nothing. But I am anxious to hear from him. I send Nico another text—Checking in. Wondering if you've heard from Lucy.

Three dots appear. Then disappear. I stare at the screen, trying to will a response from Nico. But my mind meld doesn't seem to be working at the moment.

The blinker sounds from the front as our bodies shift to the side, the driver cutting off another car to change lanes. Brynn startles, her head bobbing up. Even from the back, she looks a mess; her hair is matted with a single pink strand jutting in the air.

I glance again at the back of her head and shudder. If the image of Lucy is real, why did the kidnapper involve Brynn? Is she the next target? She's only seventeen years old, just a year younger than my kids.

I pull up the photograph of Lucy, ready to review it with a more analytical eye. I start with the background. The wall behind Lucy appears to be concrete blocks, like something you'd find in a basement or cellar. Gray and dirty. I don't see any windows, but a dim light shines from the upper left area, suggesting either a high window or an overhead light. On the right side of the photo, against the wall, rests a locker with writing on the bottom. I enlarge that section, hoping to make out the words, but the picture is too grainy. Maybe the authorities can identify something. I move my eyes to the floor, which appears to be a concrete slab with cracks running through it.

I take a breath and glance out the window, watching the cars drive by, just another warm summer day in New York. We pass a patch of grass where teens are kicking a soccer ball. My mind returns to Lucy, locked in a dark space, alone and scared. I return to the photo, now studying Lucy's face.

Her gaze is caught on something slightly to her right—like she sees the locomotive about to crush her as she's lashed to the train tracks.

She sees the danger, but I can only guess at it. I study Lucy's clothing. She's wearing a T-shirt and sweats. A different outfit from what I saw her in last night.

I zoom in, avoiding her eyes, to examine the red liquid covering her cheek. Her lower lip is split, like someone punched her. I study Lucy's arms, contorted at the shoulders and forced forward by the thick rope tied around her wrists. Her knees are pulled into her chest and crammed against the pole. The photo cuts off at her calves, and I wonder if her ankles are also bound.

I put the phone back in my tote and close my eyes. The first thing Liam needs to do is verify the authenticity of the image. Maybe—hopefully—this is a sick joke, and Lucy is on her way to Key West to soak up some sun. Although, my gut tells me that's not the case. I don't believe Lucy would willingly drop out of the tournament.

The car shakes as we bounce across a pothole. Someone behind us honks.

"I hate New York," Brynn moans from the seat in front of me as the driver abruptly hits the breaks.

"Damn bicycles," he mutters. Outside, a couple on Citi Bikes crosses in front of us. The man can't quite gain his balance and keeps putting his foot down and then starting again.

We wind our way to 59th Street, coming to a stop by the Ritz-Carlton awning, where a valet, dressed in a black suit and top hat, opens the door for us. "Welcome to the Ritz-Carlton," the young man says. "Great match, Ms. Cole." He smiles at Brynn, eyes sparkling.

"Thanks, Hank," Brynn says, blushing. We step onto the steaming sidewalk as a horse and buggy stops behind the SUV. I remember when Liam took my brother and me on one of those through Central Park—it was around Christmas, and we had cups of hot chocolate with us.

A doorman holds open the door for us, and we step into the cool, rich lobby, which makes me feel like I've been transported back to the days of the Rockefellers and Morgans. The lobby boasts dark wood with intricate carving, deep plush chairs, marble floors, and chandeliers diffusing a warm, soft light.

"Ready?" I say to Alexis and Brynn.

"Actually, I don't know," Alexis says, her hard demeanor melting into confusion. "I'm having second thoughts."

Of course you are, I think to myself, desperately scanning the lobby for Liam and Mae. At this point, I need reinforcements. But, to my surprise, they're not here.

CHAPTER 19

I slowly examine each person in the lobby, hoping I missed Liam and Mae when I first scanned the area.

There's a couple sitting together on a blue velvet love seat, but they are much older than Liam and Mae. Behind them, I see two young women sipping from champagne glasses.

"Kate," a familiar raspy voice calls from behind, and I turn to see Liam, dressed in a sports jacket and jeans, carrying two large shopping bags. He gives his half smile and half hug.

"Alexis, Brynn," I say, "I'd like you to meet my father. A big tennis fan. And this is his friend Mae Flynn." I point to Mae, who wears leggings and a sweatshirt, her frizzy hair pulled into a messy ponytail as if she's just been jogging.

"I'm so glad we get a chance to meet you," Liam says, and I watch Alexis size my father up, her eyes lingering on the scar stretching along his cheek. Liam looks like a modern art sculpture, everything a bit out of whack, especially his nose, which was broken at least three times. Still, he's got those gruff good looks that often have older women hounding him.

"If you don't mind, I'd love to drop these bags in your room, before lunch," he says as if we are friends about to grab a bite.

Alexis hesitates, and I see her mind weighing options. She looks from me to her daughter, then tells us to follow her.

We march across the marble floor, passing bountiful bouquets of lilies, the strong fragrance rich in the air. Mae sidles up to me, linking arms, and I fight the urge to pull away. Last year, Mae made no bones about how much she distrusted me when I helped her and my dad track down the person who'd murdered my former teammate.

"I'm so glad you got in touch." She smiles, pouring on the act.

"Ms. Cole." A bellman approaches from behind, his voice low. Decorum being an important part of their service here. We stop and turn; Brynn removes the sunglasses from her face. The bellman winces slightly at the sight of her red eyes and smeared makeup before regaining his composure. "Ms. Cole, this package was dropped off for you."

He extends his white-gloved hand, giving her a glossy yellow gift bag with white tissue paper. The first thing I notice about the package is that it doesn't have any logos.

"How lovely," Mae says. "Let me carry it for you." She takes the bag. "Did you notice who dropped it off?"

"Umm, sorry. I just came on duty," he replies, turning on his heels.

"Whatever it is, Brynn," Mae says, "it doesn't weigh much." She makes eye contact with Liam; I imagine she thinks the package is too light to be a bomb.

"Well then," Liam says, nodding to Mae. "Let's get upstairs."

Mae holds the bag with the tips of her fingers, as if the handle burns. We are all desperate to know if this is a real gift or someone toying with Brynn.

Alexis leads us into their penthouse suite; I nearly faint at how fancy it is. And that's just the entrance, an expansive square space with high ceilings, a thick black-lacquered round table with an ornate pedestal and orange roses in a crystal vase.

"Nice digs," Liam says, shutting the door behind us and then locking the bolt. "Where's the best place to talk?" he asks. Alexis leads us through a well-appointed sitting area with a fancy chessboard on display to an open dining area with a large rectangular walnut table in front of expansive windows overlooking Central Park.

"Let's sit," he says, and we all oblige. Alexis at the head of the table, Liam to her left and Brynn to her right. I slide next to Brynn while Mae takes the empty seat next to Liam.

"First things first," Liam says, turning to Mae. "Let's take a look inside that bag."

Liam retrieves rubber gloves from one of his shopping bags and puts them on. He slowly removes the tissue paper, placing it into an evidence bag Mae holds open.

"Is that really necessary?" Alexis sighs, her chin resting on her hands.

"I certainly hope not," Liam replies, pulling a jewelry box from the bag. "No label," he reports to the group. "Were you expecting anything?" Liam looks at Brynn, who shakes her head.

The box is square and thick and looks like something that would contain a fancy piece of jewelry. He lifts the lid slowly, then stops. His blue eyes, the same eyes that I have, cloud over with concern.

"What is it?" Alexis demands.

He opens the lid completely and holds the box from the bottom, turning it for us to see. "A tennis bracelet—that looks like it's splattered with blood." We stare at the sparkling diamonds. At first, I don't see the red substance; it's toward the bottom, by the clasp. But once I spot it, I can't pull my eyes away. Brynn lets out a squeal, pulling her legs onto the chair, wrapping her arms around them.

I stand and walk around the table to get a closer look at the bracelet.

"Are those initials on the clasp?" I ask. "Here, let me take a photo, and we can enlarge it," I say, holding my phone close to the bracelet and snapping a picture. I study the image and recognize the clasp from Lucy's tennis bracelet. "That's Lucy's," I say. "And she was wearing this bracelet last night at dinner."

"Zane needs to get back here right away. Damn him!" Alexis says, her eyes wide, like it's finally sinking in that we are in the middle of a serious situation. She shoots up; her chair rocks and then falls back on the rug with a loud thump. "Oh, no," she says, reaching down and picking the chair up. "I need to call Zane."

"Don't tell him anything about this," Mae warns. "Only that you need him to get back to the hotel. We don't know if anyone's monitoring your devices."

Alexis puts up her hands, "I know, I know." She leaves the room, disappearing into the kitchen.

"There's more items in the bag," Liam says, pulling out a device. "It's a burner phone. And there's a note."

"Hold on," Mae says, digging in one of the shopping bags Liam brought. "Let me get another evidence bag."

Mae opens another clear evidence bag, and Liam drops a thick white card with a thin gold border into the bag. "Okay, let's see what it says."

He places the card, now protected by plastic, on the table, and Mae, Liam, and I peer at the words, written in block letters.

> Dear Brynn,
> I did this for you. Now you must do something for me.
> Remember, no police or Lucy will be the <u>first</u> to die.
> Keep your new phone close

"I reached Zane—he's on his way back." Alexis returns to the room, carrying a glass of water. She stops and studies us.

"Mom," Brynn says, lips trembling. "The person sent a note." Brynn moves her gaze to the plastic bag on the table as the hum of the air conditioner kicks in.

"A note? What does it say?" Alexis walks behind Liam and starts reading the block letter words out loud. "Dear Brynn, I did this for you. Now you must do something for me. Remember, no police or Lucy will be the <u>first</u> to die."

Alexis clutches her throat as she stares out the window at Central Park, the tops of the trees fully in bloom. She shivers and walks to the window, then pulls the curtains closed, as if that can keep the danger out.

"There's more," Mae says. "The person also sent a burner phone."

Alexis moves into the living area, where she repeats her action, closing those blinds too. I make eye contact with Liam; we're both thinking the same thing. Whoever it is won't come at the Coles through windows on the thirty-third floor of the Ritz-Carlton. We remain quiet, letting Alexis do something to make her feel safer.

Liam takes a small black box out of his shopping bag and pulls out a container with white powder. He dusts the phone, looking for prints. "It's clean. Damn."

"And the serial number?" Mae asks.

Liam turns the phone over, shaking his head. "Scratched off." Liam opens the back cover and places it on the table; then he pops out the SIM card. "Quick, take a photo," he says to Mae.

She snaps a picture of both sides. "Got it," she says. "We have a serial number on the SIM card."

He nods and reassembles the phone.

Alexis, watching from the doorway, steps back into the room. "Can you track down the kidnapper with that number?"

"We should be able to trace where the SIM card was manufactured and possibly sold. It's something," Mae says, texting the photo to an agent.

"What now?" I ask.

"Now we wait for the kidnapper to contact us," Liam replies, and I hear gasps around the room.

CHAPTER 20

"Will Brynn need to talk?" Alexis yells. "That's crazy."

"Hopefully, the kidnapper will choose to text," Liam replies. "We need proof of life. Even if the original image of Lucy is real, we don't know when the photo was taken."

"But you are going to check the image sent to Brynn's phone, right?" Alexis replies.

"Of course," Liam says as the doorbell rings, a classical tune. Liam stands, turning his body to Alexis and Brynn. "From now on only an agent answers your door. Understood?" he says, his tone authoritative.

They agree, and Liam disappears to get the door while Mae suggests Brynn and Alexis rest. "Mrs. Cole, will you give us permission to download the cell data from Brynn's phone?"

Alexis nods.

"What about that one?" Brynn points to the burner phone.

"We need to keep that one around—" The implication clear. For when the person makes contact. "Okay?"

"Yes." Brynn stands, running her hand through her matted hair. "Mom, I want to take a shower."

Alexis doesn't seem to hear her daughter.

"Mom." Brynn kicks at the floor with her heel. "I don't want to be alone."

Alexis gets up. "Right. Of course," she says, all pretense of superiority gone. In fact, she looks like she's been hit by a freight train.

She walks over to her daughter and places a hand on her back. "If you need us"—she turns to Mae—"we'll be in there."

"Thank you," Mae says. "Go ahead. Get some rest where you can."

Alexis hesitates, then leads Brynn out of the room. We hear their steps on the marble floor, and then a door quietly closing.

"This is quite the situation." Mae turns to me, putting her fingers on her temples. "I need some coffee."

"I couldn't agree more—on both accounts." I follow her into the kitchen, sneaking a peek at Liam in conversation with another officer by the front door. I return my focus to the kitchen appliances, hoping there's some kind of coffee maker. We spot a Nespresso machine and pods next to it.

"Lovely," Mae says, giving me a smile. I consider telling her to give it a rest—no one is watching at the moment—but I let it go. "Now hopefully there's some cream and sugar."

I walk to the machine and pop a pod inside, then turn it on.

"I forgot, you consider it sinful to put milk or sugar in coffee," she says, opening the fridge.

"*Sin* is a strong word," I reply, adding that I also take offense to artificial sweeteners and nondairy milks.

"At least you are an equal-opportunity coffee snob," she says, closing the fridge and then leaning her body against the Sub-Zero stainless steel door. "Nothing but juice inside."

I look around the white marble counters, not spotting any creamers. "Maybe in one of these cabinets." I open the one above the coffee maker and spot a wire basket with creamers and sugar. "Here you go." I pull it down.

"You may be a snob, but you're also a nice person." Mae takes a few creamers and dumps them into a mug.

"That's a big jump from your opinion of me last year," I reply.

"That wasn't personal, Kate." She sighs. "I had a job to do. Let's put it behind us. We have a serious situation to address."

"Agreed," I say, appreciating her directness.

She walks next to me and starts brewing her cup of coffee.

"I have so many questions." I take another sip from my mug. "First and foremost, what connects Brynn with Lucy."

"Mm-hmm," Mae replies, dumping a third sugar in her coffee.

The sound of footsteps and voices gets closer; Liam steps into the kitchen with an officer. "This is our NYPD task force officer," he says, introducing the thin man before us. "He's going to check Brynn's phone to see if the photo of Lucy is even real. And see if there are any traces of prints or DNA on the *gifts*." Liam claps a hand on the man's back. "Especially on the bracelet," Liam adds, and my mind goes to what looked like dried blood.

"One other thing," I say to them. "I noticed a suspicious car outside the tavern where I had dinner with Lucy last night," I say. "And I think I saw the same car outside Lucy's childhood home earlier in the day." I look at the ground. "I thought something was wrong. I followed her for a minute, but the car disappeared. I figured I was being paranoid."

"Did you notice a make or model?" Mae asks.

I think back to the car. It was dark outside, but it looked to me like a basic midsize sedan. "I think it was either a Toyota or Honda—maybe a Camry or Accord? Something that looks like that," I reply. "And I'm pretty sure the license plate was yellow and white—maybe a New Jersey plate."

Mae pulls up a photo of a New Jersey license plate and shows it to me. "Did the license look like this?"

I study the photo of the plate, with a gradient of yellows and beiges and the words **Garden State** written in black. "Yes. That's it."

"Thanks, Kate. Your information is very helpful," Mae says, telling the officer to make sure someone on the task force looks into the vehicle.

The officer leaves with the evidence inside one of Liam's shopping bags as Mae and I return to our seats.

I notice my father watching Mae over the screen of his laptop and sense some tension between them.

"What?" I ask.

"For the record," Liam says, leaning forward, his hands locked together. "I don't agree with what Mae is about to ask of you."

I turn to Mae as she sighs. "Kate's a big girl Liam, not a child." She shakes her head. "We'd"—she clears her throat—"I, on behalf of the FBI Violent Crime Task Force, would like to ask for your help on this case. You have access to all the potential suspects. Lucy's husband, brother, the Coles, whatever the hell their involvement is. I spoke to my supervisor, and we'd like you to go undercover with one of our agents. He'd accompany you as your producer."

"I'm going to say it again. This is a ridiculous plan. I don't want Kate in the middle of this investigation. And with him?" Liam reiterates.

"Jeez, Liam, chill," Mae says. "You wouldn't be alone. You'd primarily just be providing access. The other agent will do the heavy lifting."

Liam slaps his hands against the table, shaking his head.

Mae turns to him. "It's not like she's never helped with an investigation."

Liam glares at her but doesn't speak.

"Kate, it's your decision. We'll have eyes on you the whole time," Mae says, turning to me.

"Absolutely I'll help. It makes a lot of sense to me," I respond, refusing to make eye contact with Liam.

"Okay," Mae says. "Our undercover agent will be here in twenty minutes. In the meantime, we need you to get him credentials as a TRP producer."

CHAPTER 21

Mae gives me the man's name, and I call Charlie at TRP. "What the hell, Kate?" he barks into the phone, yelling about the dozens of messages he left me.

"I'm sorry," I say, trying to sound contrite instead of angry. "I was following up on a lead and couldn't call," I reply, which is technically not a lie, since I didn't claim to be following up on a lead for my story.

"I'm not sure how important this story is anyway." He sighs, telling me an NFL player got knocked into a coma at a restaurant an hour ago in Florida.

"What?" I gasp. "Is he all right?"

"Touch and go." Charlie explains that some players went out for a late lunch after training ended. "A teammate attacked him after the meal. Crazy stuff," he says. "Sounds like it was over a girl." Charlie sighs. "Let's get back to you." He changes the subject. "Do you still have a story?"

This is my opportunity to get that press credential. "Yes," I say. "Brynn is still around, and her story is very interesting. And I got great material yesterday from Lucy. In fact, I ran into a producer who covered Lucy quite a lot. He might be able to help track her down. Could we hire him for a few days as a freelancer? I could really use the help," I add, trying to keep desperation out of my voice.

Through the phone, I hear the television volume increase and some words about the football player.

"Charlie?"

"Wait," he orders as someone starts speaking to him. A voice I recognize, David Lopez, my ex. And he's lobbying to push my story out a week in favor of the football-training-camp incident. *Yes! Please move the date,* I think to myself.

"Kate." Charlie's voice sounds muffled and the ambient noise more distinguished. "You're on speaker. David's here with me. In light of this latest situation in Florida, David's suggesting we move your story back a week. I tend to agree."

I take a moment to respond. If I agree too quickly, they'll know something is up. But the extra week would let me focus on finding Lucy. "If you make me delay my story, the least you can do is let me hire that freelance producer."

"Fine," Charlie says. "For two days."

"Since my story is this week, I would like Bill to come with me to Florida," David says through the speaker.

"What?!" I yell, even though having Bill away from this dangerous situation would be good for Bill. And me. It's just so irritating that David always tries to steal Bill from me.

"Kate," Charlie says. "It seems reasonable. And if you need a camera operator, we can send you someone or borrow someone at the Open."

"Fine," I reply. "But I'm not happy about it."

I can see David grin through the phone as we hang up. But really, it's safer for Bill to be away from me anyway. I make another call to TRP and ask if they can rush a media credential for Wade Flanders and leave it with security. Then I tell Mae she can send Wade to TRP to pick it up. "They'll just need to see his driver's license," I say.

"Great job," Mae says.

"Was the photo real?" I ask, watching the two of them from across the table.

"It seems so," Liam says. "But that doesn't mean she's still alive—"

The weight of his words hits me. I squeeze my eyes shut against the current of fear I'm feeling on behalf of Lucy.

Just then a message buzzes from the burner phone—got my present?

Liam picks up the phone and types in a message—yes.

We watch the screen, waiting for a response. It comes quickly. Like it?

"What a psycho," Mae huffs. "Let's think about this response. We need to sound like a teenage girl." Mae takes the phone and types. Not rly. How do I know u rly have Lucy anyway?

A photo shows up—Lucy with a tablet set against her stomach with the headline about the fight at the football training camp.

"That story just broke," I tell them. "She must still be alive."

The phone vibrates again—I'll be in touch soon.

My body shudders as the reality of the situation sets in. Lucy Bosco is at the mercy of a maniac. And Brynn Cole, a teenager, could be next.

CHAPTER 22

Alexis rushes toward us, banging into a small coffee table and knocking over a pile of corporate-looking gifts.

"Zane will be here any minute," she says, bending to pick up the items. She's wearing black leggings, a tank top, and a zip-up Lululemon sweatshirt. She looks freshly showered, wet hair pulled into a ponytail. But the strain around her eyes remains prominent.

I walk over to help her as she lifts up a jewelry box, shaking her head.

"What's that?" I ask.

"Every year the sponsors give Brynn a gold bracelet, even though they know she's allergic to gold," Alexis says, tossing the box into the garbage. If we weren't in the middle of a crisis, I'd retrieve the box and suggest she donate it to someone. But at this point, Alexis looks so forlorn I don't want to stress her.

We hear someone try to open the door, then a knock.

"I put the door chain on," Liam reminds us, starting to the door. Alexis follows him. Mae and I hear footsteps and Liam introduce himself to Zane before quickly leading him into the living area.

"What's going on?" he says, looking from Alexis to Liam to Mae to me.

"Please, sit down, Mr. Cole," Mae says. "We have a lot to catch you up on."

Zane takes his bucket hat off, scrunching it in his hand, and walks to sit next to his wife. "Where's Brynn?" Zane turns to Alexis.

"Resting. She's fine—" Alexis says, looking at the ground, not finishing her thought, which I imagine is that Brynn is fine *for now*.

I tune out as Liam catches Zane up on the situation, recounting the image sent to Brynn and then the *gift bag* waiting at the hotel.

"They said no police?" Zane's voice sounds shaky as he tries to digest all the information. He turns to Alexis, eyes wide. "Our baby," he whispers.

Alexis puts her hand on top of her husband's in a gesture of comfort. "We don't have a choice. It's too dangerous. Someone's threatening her."

"You're right," he says. "Of course." He takes both hands and laces them around the back of his head, leaning down. "I just don't know what to even say—"

"We're aware this is a lot to take in, but we need to ask you some questions. Questions that could help us," Mae says.

He removes his hands and looks up, eyes finding me. "Why are you here?"

"She's helping us," Mae replies, offering no further explanation. The air conditioner kicks on, and I hear the hum from the vents.

Zane studies me for another second and then turns back to Mae. "What do you need to know?"

"Let's start with your connection with Lucy Bosco," Mae says, voice calm. Zane jiggles his foot, the back of his sneaker hitting against the rug, but doesn't speak.

"You coached Lucy when she was Brynn's age," Mae says, looking at Zane.

"I did," he replies. "It was so long ago." He rubs his temples. "I just don't understand how it connects to Brynn."

"That's what we're trying to figure out." Liam leans forward in his seat, across from Zane. "Because the person responsible for this sees a connection."

The weight of those words hangs in the room. This beautiful room with leather chairs, silk curtains, and gold-framed mirrors; an ivory tower meant for luxury.

"What was Lucy like?" Liam breaks the silence.

"Stubborn," Zane blurts out, irritation bubbling up. Alexis puts a hand on his shoulder, and he takes a deep breath. "She was young. Headstrong. But I don't really know her as an older player, except to say hello."

"You seemed excited that Brynn could be facing her—there was a little trash-talking going on at the press conference," Liam says, something I mentioned to him when we had a moment earlier.

"You can't take that stuff seriously," Zane replies and stands. "Listen, I bet that photo comes back as fake and that tennis bracelet is a sick joke. Maybe Lucy orchestrated this whole thing because she's scared."

"Scared?" I can't help but say. They all turn to me, as if they forgot I was here. I can tell by Liam's glare I should have kept quiet.

"Yes," Zane says, sitting back down. "Lucy might have won today's match. She probably would have. But after that, the competition would get tough. She's not who she was."

Mae's phone buzzes; she stands and looks at me. "Kate and I need to meet someone, but we have a few agents on their way to keep your family safe. And Detective Murphy will remain here too. Mr. Cole"—she turns to face him—"let me be clear. The Evidence Response Team already confirmed the photo of Lucy is real. And half an hour ago, we received proof of life. So, this isn't a joke. And you and your family need to take the threat seriously. Very seriously."

CHAPTER 23

Liam stands up and asks to speak with me in private before I leave. We walk to the entranceway of the suite, Mae agreeing to wait in the hall just outside. "One minute," she says to Liam, putting up a single finger to emphasize the number.

The door shuts, and Liam turns to me. "I don't want you going undercover. It's a terrible idea."

"It's a great idea," I reply, refusing to back down even though I always feel myself melting into my childlike self around Liam. I straighten my shoulders and keep my tone strong even as I look up at him. "It makes sense for me to be involved."

"I don't like it." Liam rubs the scar on his cheek. I can't believe we're here again. The Liam Murphy roller coaster.

"This whole situation with Lucy could be my fault," I say to Liam, my voice softer. "I saw that silver sedan and left her even though I had a feeling something was off. I didn't follow my gut."

Liam's features soften. "This isn't your fault, Kate."

"It might be," I say. "Please, let's not fight."

Liam leans down, lowering his voice to a whisper. "This guy the FBI is hooking you up with—he doesn't have a lot of experience," Liam says. "It's not you I don't trust. He's too green."

"If Mae thinks it's the right call, then I'm all for it," I say. Despite our past differences, Mae is a good agent, and I trust her.

"He only joined the bureau a few years ago. He's too new," Liam says again.

"I appreciate your concern," I reply, not sure I mean it. "But at some point, you need to start trusting me." I keep my gaze on his, wondering if he feels the weight behind my words. Does he know I'm not just speaking about this situation but the information he's keeping from me about his shooting decades ago? My words hang over us. But we have no time for that issue. Even if he were inclined to discuss it.

"Fine." He sighs, leaning down to give me a full hug. "Please be careful. Don't do anything risky," he whispers. "They'll give you a device so we can hear you—and if I need to reach you, I'll text. Keep your phone close."

"I promise," I say and hug him back.

Liam opens the door for me, and I step into the hallway where Mae waits. "He try to talk you out of it?"

"He tried," I say, giving her a shrug.

Mae and I head for the elevator as she informs me that Wade Flanders is new to the task force, "but he's whip smart, a rising star."

She explains that she wants Wade and me to head to Lucy's house. "We need to get a beat on Nico. An undercover just spotted him pulling up to the home he and Lucy are renting. We want to gauge his reaction with you before we officially approach him. He might be more open with what he shares."

"That makes a lot of sense," I tell her as we step out of the elevator into the lobby, which is busier than before, patrons perched on velvet couches in front of large oil paintings of Central Park.

"Wade's outside in a green Ford waiting for you," she says, reminding me not to introduce myself until we're alone. "You are supposed to already know one another."

"Got it," I tell her and walk off across the marble checkerboard floor, my heels clicking against the brown and beige squares.

The doorman opens the door for me, tipping his hat as another hotel employee steps in front to open the passenger door to the green Ford.

"Thanks," I reply, sliding into the leather seat as the door shuts, and I turn to look at the man next to me. Wade Flanders appears to be in his late forties, with a touch of gray sprinkled into brown hair. He gives me an easy smile, his hazel eyes warm.

"Nice to meet you, Kate," he says, pulling away from the curb. "I appreciate how quickly you were able to get me the TRP credentials."

"Happy to do anything I can to help," I reply, still wrapping my head around the fact that Lucy's been kidnapped and Brynn's been threatened. *Lucy will be the first to die.*

"Do you know Lucy well?" Wade asks, as if he can tell where my mind went.

"No. But I really like her. We had dinner together last night, and I felt a strong connection," I say, then recap my time with Lucy over the last few days. I appreciate how he listens without interrupting, appearing to take in all the information.

Wade pulls onto the RFK Bridge toward Queens as I finish telling him about the silver sedan I spotted outside the tavern.

"You know you can't blame yourself for that, right?" He turns to look at me. I shrug, not wanting an additional person to tell me what I know in my brain but don't feel in my heart. Cars slow, and I steady myself for another traffic-filled trip.

"What's up between you and my father?" I ask as Wade merges onto the parkway.

"You mean, your father doesn't like me?" Wade raises a brow.

"Well, if you haven't figured that out, then I really should be worried about your investigative skills."

"Touché," Wade gives a little laugh. "I think it's less about disliking me and more that he doesn't trust me to protect you. Though, I imagine you can protect yourself."

"I appreciate you saying that." I feel my cheeks flush. Liam Murphy definitely struggles to view me as a capable adult. Although, dear ole Dad is getting better at it. In the past, he would have tried to forbid me, a grown-ass woman, from taking on this task. I decide to change the subject and ask Wade what he did before joining the FBI.

"I was a documentary producer." He replies over the growl of a diesel truck.

"Ahhh, the perfect cover," I say, marveling over his decision to undertake such a drastic career change at this stage in his life. "What prompted you to switch jobs?"

Wade slows down, stuck behind one of those trucks that hauls vehicles, in this case, bright, shiny sports cars. I hate driving behind these trucks, always imagining one of the cars coming loose and crashing into the windshield. Wade must not like it, either, because he changes lanes, accelerates, and moves ahead of the vehicle.

"I got tired of being an observer," he says, exiting the highway and turning toward Oyster Bay. "Many of the films I made focused on crime. I'd tell the story, but I didn't feel like I made a difference. Not really. I wanted to do more." He glances at me. "Does that sound dumb?"

"It sounds admirable," I respond, and he smiles. Wade turns onto the main country road, and I study the surroundings. The street looks different in the afternoon light compared to the darkness of yesterday. We pass manicured hedges, a gated country club with a gold plaque before approaching the tavern. "This is where Lucy and I ate last night." I point to the quaint Tudor-style building with a warm, welcoming feel, then scan the parking spots in front, as if the sedan might have returned.

Wade glances at me before returning his eyes to the road, telling me that agents are pulling footage from local traffic cameras to search for the silver sedan.

I nod but don't speak.

"Meanwhile," he continues, "a few agents already spoke to people inside the tavern. A waitress remembers seeing both of you but didn't notice anything unusual. She did confirm Lucy was a regular—"

A regular, I knew that. But the implication hits me. If Lucy was known to frequent the tavern, it wouldn't be hard to track her whereabouts. "Someone could have been waiting for her here," I say, my mind again moving to the sedan.

"Or at the house," Wade says, explaining Lucy has been renting the same place for the last ten years. "All the locals know where she rents. It's an open secret. We even found a few posts online, showing the Lucy Bosco–US Open rental."

"So basically, anyone with a phone could figure out where she was staying."

"Yup," Wade says, turning onto the dirt driveway to the *not so private* private rental of Lucy and Nico.

In the daylight, I can make out the other two homes on the driveway. On the right sits a colonial with columns on either side of the front entrance. Wade tells me an elderly couple lives there and they don't remember hearing or seeing anything.

Across from the colonial is a ranch, set back behind thick trees. A couple with two teenage kids resides at that home. "Agents spoke to the parents, who heard a car in the driveway last night around 9:00 p.m. But there's no way to tell whether the vehicle went to Lucy's home or the other house. Or whether the driver was just lost."

Again, I feel an overwhelming sense of guilt, imagining the vehicle the couple heard was the silver sedan. Something felt off—my gut told me to go after Lucy. Maybe this never would have happened. What if they kill her?

"Don't do that," Wade says, looking at me with concern in his eyes.

"How do you know what I'm thinking?"

"We all blame ourselves. That's what caring people do. But it's not your fault. You can't storm after every person just because a car pulled out of a lot. This is no one's fault but the perpetrator's. The only thing you can do now is help us find Lucy."

I nod. Liam might not like Wade, but so far, I do. He strikes me as a good guy.

Wade parks the car behind a black SUV that I recognize as Lucy's car.

"Before we go." He takes out a silver necklace with a turquoise stone heart on it. "Mind wearing this? It has a microphone and video camera so the task force and I can hear and see what you do."

I take the *jewelry* and put it around my neck. "Does it have an off switch?" I ask, thinking I might have a private conversation at one point.

"Yes—on the back of the pendant," Wade says. "You ready?"

"Ready, producer," I say. As Wade steps out of the car, I see how tall he is—at least six foot three. Maybe six four. He bends forward, not in a hunch, but more a slight curve as if trying not to emphasize his height.

Together we step onto the flagstone path, walking toward the chalet-style home, which looks even more substantial in the light. The honey scent of the lush hydrangeas in front of the house lingers in the warm air. The large flowers sit like lavender pom-poms on either side of the front door. I press the antique brass bell, which looks out of place for the clean-lined, open-window structure of the home.

No one answers, but we know from the task force that Nico went inside. I peek through the glass panels flanking the door and spot two suitcases in the hallway. Wade rings the bell and knocks. Still nothing.

"Nico," I yell. "It's Kate. I came to check on Lucy."

We ring the bell again. Finally, I see Nico appear in the large hallway, his long hair loose against his shoulders.

"Kate," he says through the door. "It's not a good time."

"Nico, please open the door," I reply. "It's important."

We hear loud movement inside the house. Wade and I stand quietly waiting. Finally, a bolt turns and the door swings open. The first thing I notice is that the suitcases are no longer in view. The second is a large deer head mounted over a stone fireplace.

"Like I said, Lucy's not here." Nico puts his body between us and the house. He turns to Wade, "Who are you?"

"This is my producer, Wade," I say. "Maybe you met earlier in the week?" I add.

"Ohh, ummm—" Nico opens his mouth to speak but stops as I slide past him.

"Kate, it's not a good time." He tries to get in front of me, but I'm swift and stride into the living area, where more mounted dead animals hang on walls.

"The owners enjoy hunting," Nico says by way of explanation. "Personally, I find the interior creepy. But Lucy likes it—she used to hunt sometimes with Conrad."

"Are you going somewhere?" I point to the luggage pushed behind a wet bar along the far side of the wall.

"Look, Kate," he says, taking a band from around his wrist and pulling his hair into a ponytail. "The truth is Lucy didn't just quit the tournament. She quit me." He slumps down into a maroon couch and puts his hands over his face. I sit next to him, while Wade remains across the room.

"What do you mean?" I ask, trying to muster my most sympathetic tone.

"Hell." He reaches into his pocket, fishing out his phone. "See for yourself. She sent it after she dropped out of the tournament. Didn't even have the decency to tell me in person." He hands me his device—pointing to a text that reads—**We're done. We have been for a long time. You and I both know it. Don't try to find me, I need space.**

I can't believe Nico handed me his phone. One of my jobs was to get Wade the phone so he could extract data, which the task force just obtained a warrant for. Not only that, but Nico also unlocked the phone.

I start to cough, then stand and bend over in a full state of choking.

"Do you want some water?" Nico jumps up.

I nod, eyes on Wade, who walks toward me as Nico rushes to the kitchen. I give Wade the phone.

"I've got to take a call," Wade yells and disappears outside as Nico returns and hands me a cup of water. I start to sip. Slowly.

"Thank you," I say. "Can you point me to the bathroom?" I motion to the tears in my eyes that formed during my coughing fit.

"Around that corner," he says. Thankfully he forgets about his phone for a minute. I lock the door and flip on the lights. The powder room is small and dark with grasscloth wallpaper and a few nature photos of birds. Given what I know about the owners, I wonder if these photos show an appreciation of nature or are a species they like to kill and mount.

The lightest of knocks indicates that Wade finished. "You're doing great," Wade whispers as I take the phone from him. I head back to find Nico. My next job is to distract him so Wade can take a look around.

I put Nico's phone down on the glass dining room table and walk over to the window where Nico stares out at a well-maintained hard court, in front of a gorgeous view of the Long Island Sound. "Feeling better?" He turns to me. I nod as I take in the dark circles sketched into his tan skin.

"I'm not surprised Lucy left me." Nico rubs his neck. "But I can't believe she'd quit the tournament. Tennis means more to her than anything in the world," he says, and I hear bitterness in the last sentence. "Did she cancel the story with you?" he asks, turning to me. I search his eyes for insincerity and don't spot anything. But he strikes me as someone who can put up a good front.

"I need to show you something," I say, suggesting we return to the couch. He follows, sitting a little too close to me for comfort. Keeping my eyes on his, I tell him that I think Lucy has been kidnapped.

"Very funny." He rolls his eyes, as if I told him an alien had landed on Earth and taken her away. Why would his first reaction be disbelief?

I retrieve a paper copy of the photo of Lucy from the picture sent to Brynn and hand it to him. "This photo surfaced a few hours ago," I say.

He takes the paper in both hands and stares at it, lips tightening. "If you got this, why didn't I see it on your station?" A smart question, one I didn't expect from him.

"Reporting on it would put Lucy in jeopardy," I reply.

"How do you know this image hasn't been photoshopped?" he says, touching his fingers to the bruise on Lucy's face.

I'm prepared for this question. "My station has all kinds of technology to determine what's a real image and what isn't."

"So you are putting this on television?" He looks triumphant.

"Not while Lucy is in danger," I reply. "But I'm worried about her. We had dinner together last night at the local tavern. She seemed fine. Good in fact."

"Did you tell the police?" Nico asks.

I don't answer that question but pivot. "The sender messaged the image to another tennis player," I say, keeping my eyes on him.

"Another player?" he says, returning his gaze to the image.

"Brynn Cole," I reply. "Does Lucy have a relationship with her?"

"With the kid? Brynn?" Nico says, rubbing his chin.

"Can you think of any connection between Lucy and Brynn?" I repeat.

"They played one another a few times," he says. "If Lucy was kidnapped, who texted me?" Nico asks, seeming to piece the information together. "Do you think it was the person who took her?" His eyes go wide. It's a good question; the kidnapper used a blocked number to contact Brynn. But it appears the person used Lucy's phone to text Nico the breakup message. That might explain how the kidnapper got Brynn's phone number. Lucy probably has contact information for all the players on the tour.

I shiver, realizing the kidnapper would also have my address and phone number.

"I'm scared for her, Nico," I say, my eyes spotting a magazine on the side table, an old issue of *Tennis Today*. The headline—THE TEN BEST-LOOKING MEN ON THE CIRCUIT. I wonder if Nico enjoyed that distinction. Or whether he capitalized on it only because he never made it further on talent.

"Did you see or hear from Lucy last night after my dinner with her?" I ask, then tell him I parted ways with Lucy around 8:00 p.m.

"You sound like you're asking for an alibi." He folds his arms across his chest.

"I'm concerned for the safety of your wife," I answer. "Besides I'm sure the police will ask you the same question."

"I'm sorry," Nico says, not seeming sorry at all. "I didn't mean to question your motives." He looks at his sneakers, bright and shiny and designer.

"Lucy said you took the SUV to a tire shop?" I try another way, recounting what I know of his timeline last night.

"A local tire place in Glenport. It took about an hour."

"When you finished, did you come back here?"

He stands and walks across the room to the corner where a grand piano rests, his movements making me dizzy. He slams his hand against the keys, sending a jarring dissonant sound through the room. "If only I had come back," he yells. "Maybe I could have protected her." He sniffs, either genuinely upset or making a good show of it. "I stayed in the city last night," he says to me. "I needed some time alone."

"Why?" I ask, leaning against the piano.

"I was so tired of how I'd become an afterthought in her life," he mumbles, more to himself than me. "There's only so much humiliation a person can take." He pauses and looks up at me, and I notice wrinkles around his eyes. The years showing on his pretty-boy face.

"I also thought a break would be good for *her*," he adds, trying to spin his comment.

How very noble, I want to snap. Instead, I keep the judgment from my face and my tone benign. "Where did you go?" I ask. "Because when the police get involved, they're going to want an alibi."

"A friend of mine from Greece owns an apartment in SoHo," he says without looking at me. "He gave me a key for when I want to get away. He barely uses it. I stayed there last night."

"Was there a doorman or anyone who can vouch for you?" I feel like I'm in a bad cop movie.

"No doorman. I don't know if anyone saw me." He shrugs. "Knock yourself out, Kate. The address is three five five eight MacDougal Street, apartment three Q."

"What did you do today?" I ask Nico.

"Came back here just before Lucy's match. Was going to watch this one on television," he says.

"Why?" I reply.

He gets up and tells me he's tired of playing twenty questions.

"The cops are going to want to know," I reply, pushing him for an answer.

"Then I'll tell them," he says. "If you don't mind—" He stops midsentence, looking around the space. "Where did your producer go?"

"He's outside on a call—" I say as the front door flies open. But it's not Wade who storms inside but Lucy's brother Conrad. And he looks furious.

CHAPTER 24

Face red, fists clenched, Conrad runs at his brother-in-law, grabs Nico by his shirt, and shakes him. "Where is she? Where is my sister? I need to talk to her. Now!" Conrad yells.

Nico puts his hands over his face in a defensive move. Wade reaches Conrad in seconds, leans down, and yanks both arms away, holding them behind Conrad's back.

"Let go of me." Conrad tries to free himself, bobbing back and forth. But Wade restrains him without effort. "Who the hell are you?" Conrad cranes his neck, glaring up to examine Wade.

"I'm with Kate," Wade says. "Her producer."

"I don't remember you," Conrad replies. "I dealt with Leah Fulton."

"She's at the station. Wade is the field producer," I explain as Conrad keeps fighting against Wade, reminding me of a caged bull, ironic in this house full of mounted animals.

"You and your sister are crazy," Nico gasps, panting. "I can't wait to be rid of your sick family." Nico puffs his chest now that Conrad's restrained.

"Why did she drop out? Why won't she answer my calls?" Conrad continues to demand answers from Nico, but he stops pulling against Wade, who releases Conrad but remains inches away in case he needs to grab him again.

"Conrad—Lucy didn't run off. She's been kidnapped," Nico blurts out. So much for telling Conrad on our terms. Nico couldn't keep his mouth shut for two minutes.

The setting sun dips behind clouds, casting dark shadows across the hardwood floor, making the mounted animals around the room appear as if they might jump from their perches. What secrets have they borne witness to? I wonder, staring at the large deer, whose black eyes seem to watch the scene.

"What the hell are you talking about?" Conrad looks from Nico to me, disbelief replacing anger. Or so he projects.

"It's true, Conrad," I say. "Let's go outside and speak in private." I put my hand lightly on his back to guide him from the living room, Wade following.

The wind picks up, rustling through the trees. A warning of a summer storm.

"Happy to get away from this asshole," Conrad mumbles, stomping across the driveway, passing his blue Mercedes, where I notice his assistant in the driver's seat.

"Does he go everywhere with you?" I ask Conrad, staring at the kid.

"Pretty much." Conrad continues along the driveway as I think back to yesterday in Glenport.

The minion wasn't with him. "Why didn't he join us yesterday?"

"I had some stuff he needed to take care of at the office," Conrad replies, rounding the house to the side lawn where four Adirondack chairs surround a stone firepit.

"Nico was just messing with me back there, right?" Conrad looks at me, eyes filled with worry. "Lucy wasn't really kidnapped. Right?" He removes his phone from his pocket. "She texted me earlier. Surely, she's just run off—"

"What did she text?" I ask.

Conrad unlocks his phone and scrolls. I'm done with tennis. Need space.

"When did you get the message?" I ask.

"About a half hour after the forfeit was announced. I kept calling and calling. Every time it went straight to voicemail. She sent this note instead."

Wade and I exchange glances. Seems the kidnapper decided to send a bunch of messages from Lucy's phone about a half hour after sending the encrypted message to Brynn. I hope the authorities can track Lucy's device.

"What's going on?" Conrad yells, bringing me back to the moment. Once again, I take out the photo of Lucy gagged and bound and pass it to Conrad. Wade and I watch as Conrad grips the paper, holding it in both hands. "She looks hurt." His voice cracks. "How did you get this? What did the police say?"

Thunder claps in the distance, and I see the lightning across the sky.

Conrad asks a lot of questions but not the one everyone else has—are you sure the photo is real?

"Kate." He looks at me. "How did you get this?"

"The photo was sent to another tennis player—that person showed it to me," I tell him.

"What?" He squints, as if trying to digest what I'm saying.

"It was sent to Brynn Cole," Wade adds.

Another crack of thunder sounds, this time louder. Closer. The air grows heavier, an invisible force squeezing against our skin.

"The daughter of Lucy's former coach?" Conrad perches on the arm of the chair closest to him. "Why?"

"That's the million-dollar question," I say.

"What do the kidnappers want? Money?" Conrad asks. "How come I'm just hearing about this now? Where are the police?" The questions come in rapid fire.

I lower myself into a chair hoping to put Conrad at ease. My body slides uncomfortably back, much too casual a position for the situation. I readjust, pushing myself to the edge of the chair, leaning forward.

I never understood the appeal of Adirondack chairs. Wade remains standing, his full height looming over us.

"Did you talk to Lucy or see her after we said goodbye to you yesterday in Glenport? I'm asking because I drove her home." A truck rumbles from the street, and I lean closer to hear Conrad's response over the noise.

"I met a friend for dinner in the city," he says. "It was a Hinge date." He looks down, seeming embarrassed. "I didn't tell Lucy, because she'd have been annoyed that I left her for that. But, well, I wish I had stayed."

A Hinge date should be easy enough for the task force to confirm. I imagine Mae already assigning someone to the job.

Conrad turns his head to look at me. "Why are you involved?"

The question I hoped to avoid. "I may have been the last person to see her," I respond.

"What about Nico?" Wade demands, color once again rising as he looks back at the house.

"Nico says he stayed in the city last night," Wade replies.

"Good-for-nothing jerk." A crash comes from the beach, and I stand, peering across the darkening estate, past the tennis court to the sandy shore. Kayaks lie scattered on the ground, a rack fallen on its side.

"Nico must have done this," Conrad says. "I'm sure it's him."

"Why do you say that?" I ask as another clap of thunder sounds above.

"Nico's a leech—just hanging on to Lucy for money. And the moron agreed to an ironclad prenup when they got married, so he'll be broke when they split."

"What do you mean *when* they split?" I interject, my voice drowned out by the wind. "When I interviewed Lucy, she said she and Nico patched things up."

"That's not true," Conrad says, then adds, "off the record." I almost laugh that given the dire situation, he's still worried about television.

"We're way past a news story," Wade says to him.

Conrad stares in the direction of the water as he speaks. "You're not going to like what I'm about to say."

"It doesn't matter," I reply. "Finding Lucy is the only thing that's important. And whatever you know, you're going to need to tell the police."

Conrad takes in a big breath and blows the air out slowly. "I made a deal with Nico—"

My body tenses, but I will myself to remain calm. And quiet, waiting to hear what diabolical plan these two men conjured up.

"I offered to pay Nico $100,000 to stay with Lucy through the tournament."

"Why?" Wade asks. But I'm guessing it had to do with me and my story. Conrad probably thought it would be bad for Lucy's image to be in the middle of another divorce.

"Because of my story. Right?" Conrad nods, and I feel repulsed by his duplicitousness. Not only manipulating me. But Lucy.

"That's outrageous," I snap.

"I know." He hangs his head. "But I did it for my sister. Really. I didn't want your interviews to focus on her latest personal baggage. That would have overshadowed everything."

I ignore his outrageous rationalization, focusing on Lucy. At the tavern she spoke about how lonely she finds the life of a professional athlete. But on top of those challenges, she's been surrounded by an unscrupulous husband and brother scheming and dealmaking behind her back.

"How could you do that to your own sister?" I say to Conrad, unable to keep the disgust from my voice.

"Nico's scum. Lucy deserves better," Conrad pushes back, as if what he did was for Lucy's benefit. A selfless act to protect a sister. If Conrad were capable of such an evil lie, what else could he have done? Kidnapped his sibling?

"And yet you pimped her out for the story—" I reply. Wade shoots me a glance—the intention clear—calm down.

Conrad doesn't answer, the only sound a foghorn on the water. A raindrop hits my head, a deluge minutes or seconds away.

"There's one other thing," Conrad says, then stops as if reconsidering his words.

"What is it?" I ask as a few more drops fall to the ground.

"You know." He stands up and takes a step toward the driveway. "I'm going to wait and tell it to the police."

I'm about to argue, but Wade gives a shake of his head. As long as Conrad shares the information with agents, and quickly, he doesn't need to tell us. I'd think it's a positive sign Conrad wants to speak directly with authorities. But I don't trust Conrad for a second.

The clouds open—rain pounds down on us. We rush to our cars, and Conrad gets into the passenger seat of his Mercedes. I slide into Wade's Ford, the dampness soaking through my clothing and onto my skin.

The rain beats against the windshield, trees mere shadows in the now dark sky. Wade reaches into the back seat, grabs a small towel, and holds it out.

"Thanks." I take it, dry my face, and squeeze some of the dampness from my hair before returning it to him. "What now?" I ask as lightning flashes behind the neighbor's ranch.

"I'm sure the task force is already coming up with a plan," he says, and I remember my necklace is still broadcasting. I reach behind the heart-shaped device and flip the switch to off.

The lights of Conrad's Mercedes illuminate the driveway as the vehicle slowly drives away.

"Agents will pull Conrad over by the tavern," Wade assures me. "We'll know much more soon."

"What about Nico?"

He gives a little smile and juts his chin forward. Low beams move closer toward us and pull along the side of the driveway.

"They're already here." I squint at the vehicle, blurred by the pounding rain.

Wade nods. A man and woman emerge from the vehicle, dressed in dark suits, large umbrellas protecting them from the rain. I wonder if it's raining where Lucy is being held. Is she alone at this moment? Is the monster who took her Nico or Conrad?

The agents walk right by us, then knock on the front door; Nico opens it as they flash what must be badges, before heading inside.

I think about how quickly Nico deserted Lucy last night. I remember when Lucy spoke to him on the phone, sitting in this very driveway less than twenty-four hours ago. She seemed so disappointed that Nico wouldn't be back for their tavern dinner.

"Guess now or never." Wade flashes a weary smile, puts the car in drive, and pulls onto the street. His body leans close to the steering wheel as he squints to see the road in front of him. A million questions swirl around my brain, but I keep quiet, not wanting to distract Wade.

As we reach the RFK Bridge, the phone rings.

"Hi, Mae," Wade says, relaxing his grip on the steering wheel as the rain eases to a drizzle.

"You guys did great," she says, and I squirm at this positive, friendly version of her.

"Agents spoke to Conrad," she says. I hear shouting through the phone and the voice of a woman I don't recognize. Mae gets back on the line, telling us a few more agents have arrived at the hotel suite. "What's your ETA?" she asks.

"About twenty minutes," I reply, glancing at the GPS.

"Good," she says. "We'll catch up on everything then. Conrad's claiming Nico tried to extort him last night. I'll give you the details when you get here," she says. "One more thing—the original text sent to Brynn's phone is a dead end. We can't trace the message app."

"What about the messages sent to Nico and Conrad?" I ask, hoping they're traceable since they originated from Lucy's phone.

"We were able to track them," Liam jumps in. "You'll never guess what cell tower picked those up." He doesn't wait for us to answer. "The one at Flushing Meadows."

"The kidnapper was at the Tennis Center?" I reply; a chill moves up my spine.

"If not there, very close," Liam replies.

The kidnapper was right under my nose, I think. Did I see the person in the crowd as I rushed Brynn through the Tennis Center? Was the person watching us? A chill breaks out across my whole body as my mind spins at the awful possibilities.

CHAPTER 25

By the time Wade pulls up to the hotel, the rain has stopped. We step inside, and I feel conspicuous among the laughing, lounging patrons settled on rich velvet couches, sipping their drinks. A man holding a crystal tumbler seems to have his eyes trained on us. Is he wondering why we look like drowned rats? Or is something more sinister afoot?

The man has shoe-polish-black hair, greased back from his tanned skin. He nods at me as I walk by. "Is he an agent?" I whisper to Wade.

Wade refrains from looking over his shoulder, waiting until we reach the elevators to glance over. But all we can see is the back of the man's head as he strides toward the hotel exit.

"I'm probably just a little spooked," I say.

"You can never be too careful," Wade replies as the elevator opens. "I'll have someone check him out."

We get off at the thirty-third floor and walk past the Coles' suite to an adjoining room now occupied by the joint task force.

The smell of oil and cheese drifts into the vestibule. "Pizza," I say to Wade as we knock softly on the door.

"Expect it to be cold," Wade replies, reminding me it's past 8:00 p.m. and they probably ate hours ago.

"Anything will be fine," I say, absolutely starving. An agent I don't recognize opens the door and ushers us into a smaller version of the Coles' suite. Instead of a grand entranceway, we step directly into a sitting area with the same sand-colored couch and decorative zebra pillows that were in the Coles' suite. There's no fancy chessboard on the smaller coffee table, but there is a tasteful bouquet in a small vase.

"Kate?" Liam comes over to me, his sports coat gone, and shirt sleeves rolled up. "You did great." He gives me his half smile and half hug. He looks at Wade but doesn't say anything.

I roll my eyes. It's as if I'm a teenager out on a date and not a grown woman partnering with another grown adult.

"Where's the food?" I ask Liam. He points to pizza boxes resting on the white marble counter of a compact kitchenette. Mae appears through a hallway, still dressed in her jogging outfit. She looks like she's run a marathon, with her hair a mess. "Grab a few slices and join us in the dining room," she says. "We're about to review all the new information."

It's like a scavenger hunt finding leftover slices. The meatball and pepperoni pies are gone. One vegetable slice remains. Wade asks if I mind if he grabs it. Which I don't.

"Here's two mushrooms," I call, feeling like I hit the jackpot. "Want one?"

"You take those," he replies, saying he found a slice of plain. "Unless you'd rather have this one."

"Nah." I open the microwave and put my two slices inside. "But we are going to need some real food after this."

"Agreed." He smiles, grabbing us two waters from the mini fridge.

Wade doesn't bother heating his food, and we walk into the dining room, where two new agents have joined our group. I sit next to Liam as Wade takes the seat on the other side of me. Mae makes quick introductions, explaining the heavyset male agent with tortoiseshell glasses is a special agent with expertise in tech. And the young woman with shaved diamonds in the back of her head is the staff operations specialist. "Our SOS. She basically coordinates all our information. And she's the best at the bureau," Mae says.

I nod hello to the two agents and take a big bite of my pizza.

Behind Mae stands a smart board with the word **Suspects** on top, four names written underneath, photos next to the names.

- Conrad Bosco (Lucy's brother)
- Nico Pappas (Lucy's husband)
- Zane Cole (Lucy's former coach / Brynn's father)
- Alexis Cole (Brynn's mother)

"Okay." Mae stands and points to the first name. "Let's start with Conrad. He claims that Nico called him last night and demanded $200,000 to remain with Lucy during the Open."

"So, double the original agreement," I say, stating the obvious.

"Correct," Liam responds. "There's no way to confirm the information, but we do know that Nico placed a call to Conrad last night. And the two spoke for a few minutes."

"As for Conrad's alibi—" Mae continues. "Conrad did, in fact, have a Hinge date. Security footage from a midtown restaurant shows him and a woman dining from 7:00 p.m. until 10:00 p.m." Mae hits something on her iPad, and a video pops on the smart board showing Conrad with an attractive middle-aged woman, holding hands and kissing.

"The woman works at an ad agency. She says Conrad came back to her apartment, had a 'good time,' and that Conrad left in the morning. Around 9:00 a.m." Mae explains that the camera across the street from the woman's apartment confirmed this information. "He could have always gone out the back or something, but the doorman didn't see anything."

"We also placed Conrad's phone at the apartment for the duration," the tech agent adds.

"Where did he go after that?" Wade asks.

Mae explains that Conrad went to his apartment for half an hour. "Probably to change." Then back to his midtown office before heading to Flushing Meadows.

"So, basically that rules Conrad out, unless someone else did his dirty work," Wade says as Mae nods.

"What about Conrad's minion?" I ask, my mouth full of mushroom pizza.

"Who?" Mae turns to me.

I put my finger up as I finish swallowing my food. "Conrad has an assistant who's always at his side. Except yesterday. I don't know his actual name; I call him Conrad's minion."

Mae gives me a side-glance and tells the SOS to find out the identity of the minion. And his whereabouts yesterday.

"One other thing," I say and tell them how Conrad seemed to orchestrate a spontaneous meeting between Lucy and her father during my interview with Lucy yesterday.

Sorry, Conrad whispered to his father. I repeat the story for the group, suggesting the authorities look into Victor Bosco.

"We'll check him out," the SOS says.

A siren sounds from the street, muted but audible. "Conrad certainly is shady," Wade says. "Even with an alibi. Where is he now?"

Mae tells us that agents have eyes on Conrad, who is currently at his apartment.

Mae moves to the next name on the list—Nico Pappas. "There's no security footage at the SoHo apartment Nico mentioned to Kate. But we have agents checking for cameras in the area. Hopefully, we'll get something."

From all accounts, Nico is motivated by money and believed he and Lucy were heading toward divorce. But one thing is bothering me about this story. "Here's where I'm confused." I push my plate away and stand up. "If Nico was only motivated by money, why wouldn't he just stay with Lucy? She has money, and she didn't seem to want a divorce."

"Maybe *Nico* wanted out of the relationship?" Wade suggests.

"That would mean there was something Nico wanted even more than money—" I say.

"Maybe he was looking for love? Or respect?" Liam suggests.

"Could be." I shrug.

"Let's move on to the Cole family," Mae says. "What connects the Coles to Lucy? There's the obvious—Zane was Lucy's coach nearly twenty years ago. I want to know everything about their relationship."

Mae looks at the two new agents. They tell Mae they are working on it.

"Work faster," Mae says. "A woman's life depends on it. Anything else?"

"Yes," I reply, standing up and walking over to the smart board. I take the stylus from Mae and write two names down.

- Ian Reese (Lucy's high school boyfriend)
- Greggory Reese (Ian's brother / argued with Lucy).

"Explain," Mae says, and I tell them everything I learned yesterday about the Reese brothers from Ian's time as Lucy's high school sweetheart, to his apparent accident and descent onto hard times, to Greggory's outburst at the pharmacy. And the fight I witnessed between Lucy and Greggory in the pharmacy parking lot.

"Greggory accused Lucy of ruining his family," I add.

"Okay," Mae says, looking at the SOS. "We need to find out everything we can about Greggory and Ian Reese. Kate"—Mae turns her tired gaze to me—"can you remember anything else?"

I close my eyes, trying to visualize the fight I witnessed in the lot, my brain feeling foggy from an overload of information and the long day. "There is one thing." I open my eyes, looking at them. "When Greggory blamed Lucy for everything going wrong in his family, she told him that he didn't understand the sacrifices *she* made. I assumed she meant tennis . . . but." I shrug.

"All right, it's getting late." Mae looks at the clock over the dinette, which shows 9:00 p.m., and starts talking about sleep shifts and schedules when Liam stands and asks me to come with him. I follow Liam into the kitchenette, noticing the stack of dirty cups in the sink.

Liam looks exhausted, but I know he's about to start talking about my need for sleep. "Why don't you go stay at my place tonight?" he begins.

"What about you?" I ask, but I already know he'll insist on working through the night. The first twenty-four hours of a kidnapping being the most crucial.

"I'll catch a little sleep here," he says, running a hand through his salt-and-pepper hair. "Just let me have an agent escort you to the apartment. Okay?"

"Fine," I answer, too tired to argue. But I make him promise to wake me if anything happens.

"And if you think of anything from your time with Lucy, even if it feels small, call me," he says. "The littlest thing could prove essential."

I promise, and he gives me a half hug good night. As I head downstairs in the elevator, a memory from yesterday flickers in the recesses of my brain—something about Lucy and her time in Glenport. It feels important, but I can't access it, despite how hard I try.

CHAPTER 26

I immediately scan the lobby for the man with the shoe-polish-black hair but don't spot him. The lobby is emptier than before, with only a handful of guests sitting around, enjoying a late-night drink and conversation. Two receptionists whisper together at the front desk.

An agent meets me outside the hotel, and I climb into the seat next to him. He nods but doesn't engage in conversation, which is fine by me. I lean my head back and close my eyes, unable to fight against the exhaustion seeping through my bones.

What was I trying to remember about Lucy? I still can't reach it. I know the best strategy is to let my mind wander toward a different thought and the memory will pop up when it's ready. But Lucy doesn't have the luxury of time. Nor does Brynn. I know Brynn is being watched and guarded, but that doesn't change the fact that a maniac is targeting her. *Lucy will be the first to die.*

The agent finds a spot a block from Liam's apartment, and we walk down the avenue toward Liam's street. Until last year, I didn't even realize Liam stayed in the neighborhood where I had spent my first years on this earth. Our apartment just a few blocks from here.

We pass a small playground, the equipment empty at this late hour.

An image flashes in my mind of coming to this park with Liam and my mom. Liam would push me on the swing, and I'd demand to go higher and higher. Liam would laugh and laugh, saying I'd touch the sky. We turn onto Liam's street, stopping at his modest brick building, a yellowish light glowing from the small lobby.

"I promised your father I'd walk you in," the agent says, sounding apologetic.

"Figured," I reply, fishing out the key chain Liam gave me last year, with the silly little soccer ball. It felt like such a thoughtful gesture at the time. Still does, despite my irritation with Liam. The agent follows me into the small, cool lobby with brass mailboxes and a single slender cactus resting on the windowsill, something new. Or fairly new? When was the last time I visited here anyway?

Four months ago? Five? Liam and I aren't estranged, exactly—but things are strained. He's so stubborn. The familiar anger resurfaces as the agent and I walk through the small lobby. Doesn't Liam understand that our relationship would be so much better if he explained himself? The not knowing eats at me. My brother would insist I just want to view our dad as a good guy. But Liam shows signs of evading. He breaks eye contact when I ask about the past. And last year, two different women shared stories suggesting my theories are correct.

Every time I get close to securing irrefutable proof, it evaporates, though. Like this morning when Nancy had promised to hand over the box to me and then reneged.

Last year Nancy admitted her mother, a 911 operator, took money after the shooting to remain quiet about the call. Frustratingly, I can't corroborate this information. My mind returns to Nancy's visit this morning—there was something else about her demeanor. She seemed scared.

I turn from the cactus and lead the agent to the elevator, then push the button for the third floor. The elevator rattles to a stop, the door opens, and we step into an empty hall, the smell of garlic and sautéed tomatoes filling the vestibule. The woman who lives across from Liam must have had a visit from her grandkids. She always makes a big pasta dinner for them and then brings my dad the leftovers.

I unlock Liam's door and hold it open, knowing the agent will insist on looking around. He does a sweep of the apartment as I dump my things on the small square dining room table.

"All clear," the agent reports, walking to the door. I let him out, lock the bolt, and add the chain. The first thing I want to do is take a shower. A long, hot, steaming shower. I go into the study with the pullout couch and shed my clothing from the day, then grab a towel from the closet. I close my eyes under the hot spray, letting the water beat against my body. What a terrible day. Poor Lucy alone in a basement or cellar, held against her will. What monster took her? Please let the monster keep her alive.

Brynn enters my mind, her tie-dyed outfits and streaked hair. Today I saw the child behind the persona—scared and timid. I'm glad she and her parents agreed to protection. I hope they remain safe.

Done with the shower, I pull on a pair of sweatpants and a T-shirt from the stash I keep here and head into the kitchen. The sound of *Jeopardy!* seeps through the thin walls as I pick a bottle of wine from Liam's small collection of chardonnay. I pour myself a glass and sit at the table, wondering again what ties Brynn and Lucy together. Obviously, Zane, who coached them both. There must be something else, though. Unless a random crazed fan or stalker wants to mess with them.

A light knock comes from the door, and I look out the peephole to see Liam's neighbor from across the hall.

"Hi there, Kate," she says as I open the door. "I thought I heard someone walking around." She extends the container, with the heavenly smell of pasta, sauce, and cheese. I suddenly realize I'm still famished and grateful I don't have to wait on takeout. "I saved some for your father." She peeks behind me. "Is he here?"

"He'll be back soon," I say, not sure why I'm uncomfortable telling her I'm alone. Fear playing tricks with me.

"Oh." She tries to look past me again. "When do you think? It's so late already."

"I'm surprised you're still up." I laugh, moving my hip against the door ever so slightly; she's not usually nosy.

"I hardly sleep these days," she says. "Well, there's enough for both of you."

"Thank you." I take the warm container from her. "Sorry to rush, I'm just really tired."

"Let me know if your father enjoys it," she says.

"Thanks again." I give her a big smile and ease the door closed, wondering if she has a little crush on my dad.

Fork in hand, not even bothering to put the pasta on a plate, I sit back down at the table and eat. The sauce and cheese taste divine.

Done with my meal, I stifle a yawn as I move into the living room and sink into the leather recliner. Through the window, lights twinkle from the apartments across the street, and I wonder what kind of day the residents within those buildings experienced today. I hope better than mine. Certainly, better than Lucy's.

My eyelids get heavy, but I'm not ready to sleep yet. There's something I want to take another look at here. I push myself from the chair and move to Liam's bookcase, running my finger along the spines of the memoirs and biographies until I find the book—*My Father Was a Bad Man*, written by New York City's former mayor, Marsha Compton.

I take the heavy hardcover with me to the recliner and open to the worn inscription I know by heart.

> Dearest Liam,
> I wouldn't have gotten here without you.
> All my love,
> Marsha

I turn the book over and reread the description.

In this revealing story, the daughter of Mayor Tony Compton tells the harrowing tale of how she helped bring down her own father when she learned of his betrayal of New York City. After graduating from Brown

University, the young, bright Marsha Compton worked her way quickly up the ladder of city government, discovering the true corruption of her father and his administration. Putting love of city over her own family, Marsha helped with an extensive undercover operation that brought down her father, multiple commissioners, and the mob. For the first time ever, Marsha shares what made her choose duty over her father and the toll it took on her and her family.

My eyes move to the face of the young Marsha Compton, so much more glamorous in this photo than the woman I met last year at the Olympics. There's no doubt in my mind her involvement in the investigation into *her* father somehow connects to the shooting of *my* father. But how?

I get up, taking the book with me as I walk into the guest room. Maybe I'll reread a chapter before going to sleep. I set up the bed, get under the covers, stifling a big yawn. Who am I kidding? I'm bone tired—how could I possibly read a word? As I drift off, my mind hangs on the mayor, and I remember the tension between the mayor of Glenport and Lucy. That's what I've been trying to recall. The mayor of Glenport and Lucy used to be best buddies. Their high school coach showed me photos of the two of them laughing and smiling.

But Lucy barely acknowledged the mayor, Heather Liu, at the ribbon-cutting ceremony, and she made a comment at the high school about not really knowing Heather's true nature.

I grab my phone and send a text to Liam detailing the interaction between Lucy and Heather. Relieved that I remembered, I allow my eyes to close and my mind to drift off—settling into a deep, welcome sleep.

Images of Lucy float into my brain—she's playing tennis, her forehand strong and disarming. Her opponent, a shadow of a figure, can't return a single shot. The figure grows, still obscured but looming closer.

It grabs my arm. I pull against it. But I'm caught. My scream wakes me, and I bolt up in bed. My arm. I tug. Why can't I free my arm? I flick on the light with my free hand and see my other arm, tangled in the sheets.

Calm down, Kate, I order myself, the jolt of adrenaline coursing through my veins as I untangle the sheet.

I swing my feet over the edge of the bed, knocking something onto the ground. It lands with a thud. The mayor's book. Next to it is a piece of paper folded in half.

I pick up the paper and open it, blinking hard at the one word written in my father's handwriting. A deep sense of betrayal floods my body as I read the name—*Nancy*. Next to it is a phone number.

Please don't let this be my Nancy. The one who promised to give me the box about Liam. The one who told me she decided to give it to the *right* person. Was that person Liam? A dog barks in the night as I take out my phone and scroll to find Nancy's contact. I take a deep breath—*please don't let the numbers match,* I think to myself.

But they do. Of course they do.

CHAPTER 27

DAY AFTER THE KIDNAPPING

The more I try to will myself asleep, the more awake I feel. And angry. So angry. Hours pass, my eyelids slowly getting heavy, and I finally feel myself drift off. Images of Nancy, Liam, and Mayor Marsha Compton haunt me—they laugh, pointing at me, as they whisper among themselves. *What are you saying?* I yell at them. *Tell me, please.* My gaze finds Liam's kind blue eyes. He beckons me forward. I walk in his direction, getting closer and closer. He continues to wave me toward him. A few feet between us, I hear his voice—soft at first and then scolding. Loud. Angry. The floor evaporates; I fall, faster and faster, spinning into an abyss as his laughter echoes around me.

I shoot up, sweating. Still feeling like I'm falling. I blink my eyes hard and grope around for the mattress, my hands landing on solid material. *It was a nightmare,* I tell myself, slowing my breath, trying to ground myself. My mind snaps back to last night—and the note. I search the floor, the bed, then the nightstand. A small piece of lined paper sits folded on the table. Slowly, I pick it up and open it. Maybe this was a dream too? Before I even look, I know in my gut this part is real. My eyes read the name—*Nancy*, with her phone number. My heart falls—once again Liam is working to stifle my efforts. To deceive me. I stuff the paper inside my wallet. The betrayal is real. Very real.

A pallid light bleeds through the window, the sun slowly rising on the city. It's early, but I know there's no use trying to fall back to sleep.

After pushing myself out of bed, I head into the kitchen and retrieve the gourmet dark roast Liam keeps in the cabinet for me, as he is more of a Dunkin' Donuts kind of guy. The image of Liam from my dreams rushes into my brain, and I drop the bag of grounds on the floor, deep rich coffee spilling onto the worn wooden planks. Suddenly his sweet gestures of coffee and wine and key chains fill me with a deep sense of sadness and rage.

I pick up the package and clean the mess, using the remaining grounds to start a pot of coffee. The rich aroma fills the small room and makes me feel more awake and grounded.

A key sounds in the lock, turning. From my spot, I watch the door push forward, blocked by the chain. For a moment, I wonder if someone is trying to break in. Then I hear a familiar raspy voice.

"Kate," Liam calls. "Are you awake?"

The anger bubbles up—I swallow it down and go to open the door for him, reminding myself of the peril Lucy and Brynn still face. My issues with Liam need to wait until both women are safe. Liam looks exhausted, deep circles under his eyes, hair askew, clothing rumpled. "I came back to take a quick shower and change." He gives me a weary smile. "Coffee smells good, even if it's yours."

He waits for me to return his smile. When I don't, he moves to the kitchen.

"What's the latest with the case? Are you any closer to finding Lucy?" I ask, keeping my voice neutral. Even if he hears an undertone, he'll chalk it up to the kidnapping.

He pours himself coffee, adds milk and sugar, and lumbers over to me. "There's a lot to catch you up on," he says. "Mae's holding a briefing in an hour at the hotel. But there's one thing we need to discuss first," he says, and I wonder if he knows I know about the note. "Let me shower and get changed, and then we can have a quick chat."

I take my coffee into the guest room and grab a clean outfit from the closet—a black cotton skirt and brown tank, along with a light blazer. Through the door, I hear the shower running. I fold the bed, straighten the room, and return the mayor's book to the shelf in the living room, wondering what Liam will think when he discovers the paper missing.

The shower turns off, and I hear footsteps from his room. Changing my mind, I take a piece of paper and pen and scribble a new note for Liam, then put it inside the book. How I'd love to see his face when he finds it.

"Ready in a minute," Liam calls. He walks into the living room wearing jeans and a light-blue button-down; his appearance is neat, but his face remains tired. "Why don't you take a seat?" He points to the couch. I perch on the edge of the cushion as he sits across from me.

"We tracked down the silver sedan," he says, expression serious. "The gas station across from the tavern has security cameras, and we ran the license."

The soft murmur of morning traffic reaches the room from outside. Through the window, I see people scurry onto a bus across the street.

I turn back to Liam, who's waiting to continue. "The car belongs to a thirty-year-old named Oliver Milton. He has a record," Liam says, leaning close. "Two charges of domestic abuse, and his former girlfriend has a restraining order against him."

My mind races back to the night at the tavern. The silver sedan did follow Lucy after our dinner. Where did it go when I turned in their direction? He probably saw my headlights and hid on a side street.

"Do you know if Oliver's sedan was also the silver car I saw outside Lucy's family's house in Glenport?"

"Oliver's car was outside the Bosco home in Glenport." Liam answers my question, then explains a neighbor's security camera captured the vehicle. "Here's a photo of him." Liam pulls up a picture of a wiry man with greasy long hair and a smug smile. "Does he look familiar?"

I shake my head.

"Officers are on their way to his home in New Jersey," Liam says, standing. "We should have an update by the time we get to the hotel."

I stand and follow Liam—the mayor and Nancy a distant memory as my worst fear appears to be coming true: The driver of the sedan might actually be Lucy's kidnapper. Oliver Milton has a record for domestic abuse and a restraining order against him. And he may also have Lucy locked in a basement or cellar. *Please let the agents act quickly,* I repeat to myself as we leave Liam's apartment to get briefed on the raid of Oliver's home.

CHAPTER 28

The friendly demeanor of the doorman at the Ritz-Carlton feels offensive, given the dire situation. But how could he possibly know what's going on? He just sees a beautiful early-morning sun, rising over Central Park as he greets his guests, including Liam and me.

"What a wonderful morning," he says to us as he opens the door.

"Thank you," Liam manages, while I can't even force out a grunt. We rush across the marble floor, passing the impeccably dressed staff at the reception desk with big smiles across their faces. A few tourists walk leisurely past us, talking about visiting the sights of New York.

The elevator feels like it takes forever to arrive. I'm aware of impatiently tapping my foot. As the doors open, I step to get in, only to pause as a family lingers as they exit.

Hurry up, I scream in my head. We rush inside and hit the button for the thirty-third floor.

Housekeeping staff push a trolley past us as we speed walk down the hall. Liam swipes a key card over the electronic pad to the suite. The smell of stale pizza and coffee hits me at the door as Mae calls for us from the dining area.

"Units are ten minutes out from Oliver Milton's home," she says as we rush through the sitting area to the group gathered around the black lacquered table, where empty coffee cups and paper plates litter the surface.

"Are there signs of Lucy?" I ask.

"Agents spoke to neighbors. They describe Oliver as creepy, but no one noticed anything specific," Mae says, still dressed in the same leggings and warm-up top as yesterday. "Meanwhile, the kidnapper made contact a few minutes ago."

My heart pounds as I digest that information. I stare at Liam, who also seems to be hearing that news for the first time.

"The kidnapper sent a rhyme to the burner phone given to Brynn yesterday," Mae continues, moving something on her tablet, which puts the message onto the smart screen. "It's really bizarre."

Go about your day like nothing's new

Otherwise, the next one taken will be you

At 9PM you must pay 2 million to me

Or Lucy is dead, and your parents' secret set free

"Did the kidnapper send proof of life?" Liam asks, running his hand through his hair. No one speaks, the only sound the SOS typing on her computer.

"We requested it—" Mae replies, explaining they fashioned a response that would sound like a teenager. "Still waiting."

I turn my gaze to the ransom demand and study it line by line; my eyes stop at the second half of the last line. A threat to Zane and Alexis Cole. your parents' secret set free

"What secret?" I turn to the others in the room. "Do we have any idea?"

"That's the million-dollar—" Mae stops herself. "*Two*-million-dollar question."

A collective groan resonates around the table. Zane remains the obvious connection between the two players. But that's not a secret. Did something happen between them? Something Zane wants to keep hidden so badly he might pay $2 million for it? Then again, the line says *parents*—not *Zane*.

I glance at diamond-shaved-head girl and tortoiseshell-glasses guy—both have their eyes down, typing furiously on their keyboards. I imagine scouring their databases for links.

I reread the first line—Go about your day like nothing's new.

The kidnapper wants Brynn to participate in her off-day activities, which likely means training, stretching, etc.

Brynn is scheduled to practice at the Tennis Center today, I think, remembering her schedule since I planned to spend the day with her.

"She's supposed to be there at noon," Mae says. "We're going to talk to the Coles to discuss logistics," Mae continues, then explains Brynn has a practice court, followed by a mobility workout. Poor Brynn—she finally gets the break she's worked her whole life for and now finds herself in a dangerous pressure cooker. And she's a kid.

"We just got proof of life," tech guy yells out, throwing a photo onto the smart board. I gasp at the image showing Lucy with fresh bruises. She's propped up against the pipe, a newspaper positioned on her lap. It's the morning edition of *USA Today*. In a sick twist, the kidnapper picked the sports section with today's featured article about Lucy. The article shows a photo from Lucy's only match at this Open. Above it, the large headline—LUCY BOSCO PULLS OUT OF US OPEN FOR PERSONAL REASONS.

My eyes land on Lucy's cheeks, puffed and newly injured. But her defiant gaze remains the same. She's a fighter. And, so far, she's hanging on.

Mae presses a finger against her earpiece, her features tight and focused. She holds up her hand, indicating something is going on. I take a seat next to the tech agent, his glasses low on his nose. Liam pulls up a chair next to the SOS.

Wade enters from the kitchen and sits in the empty seat on my left, a large cup of coffee in his hand. He's freshly shaved and showered and looks fit in his jeans and a T-shirt. As he sips his coffee, I see there's no milk lightening the brew. I wonder if he adds sweeteners.

"They arrested Oliver," Mae reports to the group, her voice a staccato recap of what she seems to be hearing from the field. "They're searching his house now for Lucy."

I stand, too anxious to remain seated, and go to the window to stare across at Central Park, where the canopy of trees is thick and lush, hiding my view of the people in the park—like Lucy hidden from our view.

Seconds tick by as I use every fiber of my being to wish Lucy found and this nightmare over. But as I turn and look at Mae's face, I know the news is bad.

"No sign of Lucy," she reports, folding her arms across her chest. "They're searching for clues—"

I move into the kitchen to get away from everyone else, feeling a roller coaster of emotions—optimism that Lucy would be found, then crushing disappointment that she wasn't. It's surreal how vested I've become. We only knew each other a few days, but I felt a connection with her I haven't experienced in a long time. I guess I've been on guard with friends the last few years. Not that anyone could blame me after what happened with my last bestie. My phone rings, and for some reason, I think maybe it's Lucy, which is silly.

Jackson's name appears on the screen, and a whole different part of my brain starts to spin. "You're up very early," I say, heading down the hall to find some privacy in a bedroom. I knock before entering, in case someone is taking a nap. The room is empty.

"Not by choice." Jackson sounds anxious. "The residence counselor came by to speak with me this morning."

"What about?" I ask him.

"He said there have been complaints that someone is selling drugs out of our room. He asked what I knew about it."

"That's a good thing. Don't you think?" I ask him.

"I don't know. I have a record. What if they don't believe me and think I'm involved?" Jackson's voice trembles.

"Your record is sealed, Jackson," I reply, wondering if somehow the school could take a peek.

"He's a really manipulative kid," Jackson replies. "I'm worried he's going to try and pin this on me."

"Maybe I should come down," I suggest.

"No," Jackson snaps. "Not yet at least. Someone's at the door," Jackson says. "I'll call you right back."

"Wait—" I say, but he's already gone. My heart says to get into the car, but restraint wins for now. I'll give him half an hour. I return to the dining room as everyone else files in.

Mae is busy on her tablet, then looks up at me and frowns. "Agents found some disturbing photos scattered on Oliver's desk," she says. "They've uploaded the images."

She hits something on her screen, and images appear of Lucy jogging in daylight, Lucy getting into her car, Lucy at the ribbon-cutting ceremony for the tennis dome in Glenport.

"Brace yourself." Mae looks from Liam to me. And I immediately understand why. The next batch of photos are of Lucy and me. The two of us walking down Main Street. The two of us eating dinner at the tavern. Then the photos switch to just me.

A chill travels up my spine as I stare at an image of me getting out of my car in front of my house in Connecticut, over fifty miles from the tavern. Me through my living room window, me drinking wine, me closing the blinds in my bedroom, me leaving in the morning to drive to the US Open the day Lucy never showed.

"Stop," Liam says. "We get the idea."

Mae hits something again, and the photos disappear. I feel dizzy at the realization that this man, Oliver, was stalking me. Wade puts a hand on my arm as I work to regulate my breathing. "My kids," I say, worried if Oliver followed me, would he follow them? Or worse.

"We're trying to figure out Oliver's actions after he left your block," Mae says. The air conditioner kicks on, and I hear the hum across the room.

Then something else dawns on me. If Oliver was stalking me the whole night, would he have had time to kidnap Lucy? "Was he at my house all night?" I look up at everyone.

"You have Blink cameras. Let's see," Liam says. I attempt to pull up the app, but my fingers are shaking. I can't get Oliver's smug face out of my brain, the image Liam showed me this morning. What was Oliver doing while I slept? Peeking through the windows? Thank God Liam made me fix my alarm system last year. And that I turned it on. But my biggest fear is that this freak might go after my kids.

"Let me have your phone." Liam reaches his weathered hand out and gently takes the device from my hands. My anger from this morning has evaporated, and I welcome his protection and help.

Liam puts the video from my phone onto the smart board. We see the silver sedan pull in front of my house five minutes after I arrived home from dinner at the tavern. Liam fast-forwards through the footage, but the silver sedan never moves.

I feel so exposed watching. I know our small group at this hotel is only the tip of the iceberg of agents and officers working the case. Most of Mae's task force is operating out of Federal Plaza, and all of them will view these images.

At 3:00 a.m. the driver's door opens, and Liam slows the video, playing it at regular speed. We watch Oliver close the door, push his greasy long hair back from his forehead, and walk across my lawn to my living room window. He peers inside, then walks to the front entrance and looks through the glass pane on the side of the front door.

My whole body trembles, remembering that I was upstairs asleep while he peered into my home. What was he looking for? Did he plan to break inside?

My eyes find Liam, who's seething with anger, his hands clenched in fists.

"Kate," Mae says, and I jerk my head in her direction. "Where is your alarm panel?"

"By the front door," I reply, realizing that's what Oliver was probably looking for. "Do you think he would have tried to come inside if I hadn't set my alarm?" My mind goes to the alarm panel and the light that turns red when the system is armed.

Mae doesn't respond. She doesn't have to—we all know the answer. Liam continues to fast-forward through the video, stopping again at 5:15 a.m. This time we watch Oliver step from his car, walk to my lawn, and pee on the grass.

"Gross," I mumble under my breath.

Liam fast-forwards again, and I realize he's about to spot Nancy at my house. Sure enough, Liam slows the video at 6:30 a.m., when the Subaru pulls up and Oliver moves his car in front of my neighbor's lawn.

"I had a visitor that morning," I say, telling them they can forward through that video. Liam looks at me, but I avoid his eyes.

My mind returns to Nancy, who seemed nervous at my house. Had she noticed Oliver? Had she been worried about him?

Once again, Liam fast-forwards, this time stopping at video of me leaving my house and getting into my car. As I drive my black BMW to the edge of the street, Oliver's sedan pulls right behind.

"How did I not notice him?" I stand up so quickly the chair starts to fall, only to be caught by Wade before it crashes to the ground.

"We need to know where he went next," Mae says as I return to my seat.

Tortoiseshell-glasses agent interjects. "I just tracked Oliver's car on traffic cams that show he followed Kate to the US Open." He pauses a minute, tapping away at his keyboard. "And then he's seen watching Brynn's match, a few rows below you," he says to me.

My mind races with the implication of this—and the possible danger I didn't even register.

"Right now, we don't know if this creep is also the kidnapper," Mae says. "Even if he didn't physically abduct Lucy, he could be working with someone else. Give me a minute." She gets up and leaves the room, motioning for Liam to follow her.

I walk back into the kitchen to get some coffee. The smell of the espresso pod steadies me. I take the cup and bring the rim to my lips, wanting a few sips despite how hot the liquid feels, as if the burning will distract my mind. Liam and Mae reappear in the hallway and cross into the kitchen. Both of them look at me with concern.

"We spoke to headquarters; other agents will handle Oliver."

"Because of me?" I ask.

"Partly." Mae nods. "But also, you're here to help give us insight into the people you have interacted with, and Oliver's not someone you have firsthand knowledge of."

If I hadn't set my alarm. "Will you be able to hold him in custody?" I ask, still worried about Nikki and Jackson. Mae looks from me to Liam and promises to do her best. "But as you know it depends on the judge he gets at the arraignment."

"Either way, we will make sure you, Nikki, and Jackson are safe," Liam says and promises to have officers watch us if necessary. Somehow that doesn't make me feel better, as the image of Oliver peering through my window returns to my brain.

CHAPTER 29

Despite the respite Charlie granted me yesterday regarding my feature story, my phone buzzes with a call from him. I pick up on the first ring.

"Are you at the Tennis Center yet?" he asks.

"No," I reply, noting it's only 9:00 a.m. and all the big matches are later in the day—not that I'm even covering those. "My plan today is to watch Brynn practice," I say, feeling the need to prove I'm not slacking off, which is crazy since I pull so many long shifts.

Through the speaker, I hear shouting.

"What's going on, Charlie?" I ask, raising my voice against the noise.

"That player I told you about in Florida—he just died," Charlie says. "The other player is about to surrender to police. We'll run this story on Sunday, yours the following Sunday," he says, telling me the same information he already shared yesterday. "Let's talk later." He hangs up as if I called and bothered him instead of the other way around. And so goes the world of sports reporting.

Mae and Liam leave to speak with the Cole family, hoping to get insight into the "secret" mentioned in the ransom demand. I hear them walk down the hall and knock on the door next to this suite.

My phone rings again. Jackson is calling back, and immediately my brain rushes to the stalker. But Oliver is in custody—at least for now.

"Mom," Jackson says. "Good news." He sounds relieved. "The RA said my other roommate gave him the same information I did."

"That should make you feel better," I say, glad for some positive information. "Is the school going to do anything?"

"The school has to investigate," Jackson says, and I can hear him rolling his eyes. "But they have a policy where my roommate and I can move to another dorm right away, if we want."

"Are you going to do that?" I ask, hoping he will.

"Definitely," Jackson says, explaining it would be one of two dorms, and both have rec rooms in the basement. "You know, I should have listened to you when you suggested talking to my other roommate."

"Wait? Can you say that again?" I laugh. "You're saying I was right?"

"Once in a century," he responds. "By the way—both rec rooms have Ping-Pong tables and a large-screen television. What do you think?"

"I think that's great," I reply. "And I'm proud of you for working this out on your own."

"Thanks," Jackson says.

Should I warn Jackson to watch out for strangers? Not yet, I tell myself. Hopefully, I won't have to at all.

"Mom?" Jackson says. "Are you there?"

"Sorry," I reply. "Yes. I'm really happy it worked out. Love you."

"You too."

My shoulders release a bit, knowing at least Jackson has navigated his situation and found a great solution. Heck, he even told me I was right about something. And I can't worry about Oliver until and unless he's released. One problem at a time.

I return to the dining room and find Wade standing next to the smart board, bending to look down at the list of suspects.

"We could use your help," Wade says, explaining that they're reviewing the latest information dug up on each person. I take a seat and study the board, noticing some names crossed off.

- ~~Conrad Bosco (Lucy's brother)~~
- ~~Victor Bosco (Lucy's father)~~
- Oliver Milton

- Nico Pappas (Lucy's husband)
- Zane Cole (Lucy's former coach / Brynn's father)
- Alexis Cole (Brynn's mother)
- Brynn Cole
- Ian Reese (Lucy's high school boyfriend)
- Greggory Reese (Ian's brother / argued with Lucy).
- Glenport mayor

"I'm assuming you crossed off people who have alibis?" I ask, leaning against my chair.

"Exactly," Wade says, starting with Conrad. "Everything he told us panned out, from the Hinge date, to the overnight at the woman's apartment, to returning to his building and then heading to Flushing Meadows."

"And the father, Victor?" I ask.

"Victor was playing poker that night. His friend said Victor was too drunk to walk home alone and he needed to accompany him. It's hard to imagine Victor was in any condition to pull something like this off. And street cameras don't show his car leaving the house. And he is her father."

"I mean, he is," I say. "But their argument was pretty heated. Did anyone check Lucy's uncle? She didn't seem to hold him in high esteem," I say, remembering how Lucy described his cruel behavior toward her as a kid.

"He has dementia. Lives in a nursing home in California," Wade replies.

I look back at the list, my eyes stopping at the last name, the Glenport mayor. "What did you find about the mayor, Heather Liu?"

"Busy with town events most of the night, but she had a few hours unaccounted for in the morning. Agents are working to pin down that timeline. Do we know what transpired between Lucy and Heather?"

"No. But someone must," I say, thinking Conrad and S.J. would have the information, assuming we can get them to share.

Wade suggests we review the rest of the suspects. There's a fifteen-hour and thirty-minutes window we are looking at. We know Lucy disappeared sometime after I finished dinner with her on Tuesday at 8:00 p.m. Agents confirmed that Franklin Fielding received a message from Lucy's phone at 11:30 the next morning. So, agents assume she was taken some time during that period.

Wade shows the relevant timeline for the Coles.

6:00 p.m.—Zane, Alexis, and Brynn dropped off at Ritz-Carlton.

7:00 p.m.—Zane and Alexis left hotel in an Uber.

7:30 p.m.–9:45 p.m.—Zane and Alexis attended a Wilson dinner in lower Manhattan at a private club.

8:00 p.m.—Room service delivered food to Cole suite. Door was left open. Shower was heard.

8:30 p.m.—Alexis left dinner (walked to clear head).

10:15 p.m.–midnight—Alexis & Zane arrived together for cocktails at Stardust Manhattan for a USTA sponsored celebration.

12:30 a.m.—Uber dropped both off at Ritz.

7:00 a.m.—Room service delivered breakfast to suite/confirmed seeing Zane and Alexis.

7:45 a.m.—Family picked up by a USTA car and taken to the Billie Jean King Facility.

Brynn has the most time unaccounted for according to the chart. No one saw her from the moment she got dropped off at the Ritz-Carlton at 6:00 p.m. through the time she left the next morning at 7:45 a.m. That's over twelve hours of time by herself. Even when room service delivered food—they left it in the dining area, hearing the shower from the bathroom.

"What does video surveillance from the Ritz-Carlton show?" I ask the tech guy.

"No signs of Brynn coming or going during those hours," he says. "And Alexis says she checked on Brynn when she got home around twelve thirty in the morning and that her daughter was asleep. If Brynn did go somewhere," he continues, pushing his glasses higher on his nose. "She was smart enough to leave her phone at the hotel. We were able to triangulate its location."

I look at Wade, who tilts his head back as he takes a big gulp of coffee; his Adam's apple rises as he swallows. "My gut tells me Brynn wasn't involved," he says, looking at me. "Not that my gut is evidence." He gives me a smile. "But it's hard to imagine a teenager pulling something like this off. And why? I'm more interested in where Alexis went from 8:30 p.m. to 10:00 p.m.," he says, then explains Alexis claims to have just walked around downtown to clear her head.

"You don't buy that?" I ask as the sound of raised voices reaches us from the Coles' suite.

"Not sure," Wade replies, taking a few steps into the sitting area and closer to the wall between us and the adjoining suite.

I stand and move next to him, Liam's raspy voice rising above the others. Straining to listen, I can only make out a few words—*hiding something* from Liam. And *leave us alone* from Zane.

Wade and I stand inches apart, and I can smell the spice of his aftershave. We stare at the wall that divides our suite from the Coles' as if facing that direction will reveal information. The opposite occurs, with the volume dying down to barely a murmur.

Wade turns to me, voice low. "Doesn't sound like they're having luck," he says. "My money is on Alexis opening up to you."

"Me?" I ask, surprised. Yesterday Alexis made it clear she doesn't trust me.

"You're easy to talk to," he says. I feel myself flush at the compliment, my eyes finding the ground, embarrassed by my reaction. I consider what he says. My relationship with Alexis did improve after the kidnapping. But I'm guessing that was more necessity than trust.

Raised voices get my attention, and once again we stare at the wall. "The agent that spent the night in the Coles' suite said the parents have been bickering about everything."

“Like what?” I ask, noticing golden specks in Wade’s hazel eyes. He holds my gaze for a second. I break eye contact, looking at the wall, as the shouting continues.

“Meaningless stuff,” Wade says. “Leaving a dish in the sink, talking too loud on the phone. It’s less about the topic and more that they’re breaking apart under the stress.”

“Unless they always fight,” I reply.

“That’s true. You never know how people handle anxiety. My parents never argued,” Wade says. “They kept everything inside and stuck smiles on their faces.” I feel like he’s waiting for me to share, but it certainly wouldn’t be appropriate to say anything about Liam. Or anyone frankly. It’s not his business. He coughs and suggests we return to the dining room. I follow him, glancing over my shoulder at the wall, hoping Liam and Mae get the Coles to talk. Because if I’m their last resort, we could all be in trouble.

CHAPTER 30

Before Wade can continue, Liam and Mae burst through the door. We all turn as they enter with their heads down. They speak in hushed tones, and only Liam joins us in the dining area, after retrieving a slice of cold pizza, one Wade and I must have missed when we were scavenging last night. "I convinced Mae to lie down for a half hour," he says while chewing. "She hasn't stopped since yesterday morning."

"How'd it go with the Coles?" I ask, although the answer is written all over Liam's face.

"Not well." He sits, refusing to expand on what happened or why we heard so much yelling through the walls. Wade and I exchange a glance but don't say anything.

I return my focus to the board—studying the photos next to Ian and Greggory, which look like driver's license pictures. Ian appears nothing like the smiling kid from the yearbook. His face is too thin and his eyes vacant. Greggory's photo resembles the man I saw at the pharmacy, except his beard lacks the pointed end.

"Let's move to the Reese brothers," Wade says, standing by the smart board. "Greggory left the pharmacy at 9:00 p.m. and returned to the pharmacy the next morning at 7:00 a.m.," Wade says and explains there's a camera a block away from the store that caught his car. "We're lucky he drove north. There's no camera on the south end of Main Street."

"And the time between?" I ask.

"We don't know," Wade says and adds that Greggory lives alone and says he went straight home, had dinner, watched some television. "Greggory's neighbors didn't notice anything, and there aren't a lot of cameras in his section of Glenport. As you know, the only camera near Lucy is the one across from the tavern. We can't say either way. Ian's a bit more complicated," Wade says. "His *official* address is his parents' home a short distance from Greggory," Wade explains, the last part drowned out by a roar from the street—a drill or some piece of construction equipment.

"Meaning?" I ask.

"Ian is a drug addict and often disappears for days. He's in and out of rehab, methadone clinics, mental hospitals—"

"And he wasn't at his parents' house at the time in question?"

"He was not," Wade confirms as the drill switches to a thudding machine. Even on the top floor of one of the fanciest hotels in Manhattan, the clamor of the city seeps inside. "We have a record of him leaving a clinic around the same time you and Lucy had dinner at the tavern. After that—nothing."

Great, I think to myself, wondering what, after all these decades, might spark Ian to turn on his high school sweetheart.

"Are there any therapists willing to talk about Ian?" I ask.

"One spoke in general terms," the SOS chimes in. "He said Ian is a gentle guy who lost his way. But he did do a stint in prison. Ian seriously injured someone during a DUI."

The SOS puts an article up on the smart board from the fall of 2007 from the *Glenport Weekly News.*

I move closer to the board so I can read the small print.

> 20-year-old Ian Reese is charged with a DUI after he was found driving under the influence. Reese is also charged with vehicular assault for crashing into the car of another local resident who sustained multiple injuries and remains in the County Hospital.

> The accident occurred just after 10PM on Main Street after Reese spent the night with friends at the Mac-n-Cheesy where witnesses say he was intoxicated and belligerent. Ian Reese is the oldest son of the owners of the Reese Pharmacy. His parents and brother declined to comment for this story.

I remember Lucy and Conrad's gym teacher, S.J., talking about a car accident. She said Ian was never the same following it. S.J. also said it happened about a year after Lucy and Ian graduated from high school. This accident must be the one she meant.

"Was Ian injured in the accident?" I ask.

The SOS says no, "but check this out." She puts some photos up on the screen of Lucy and Ian posing in front of tennis courts. They're smiling and holding hands. In one photo, Ian is caught kissing Lucy on the cheek. She's grinning into the camera. I hardly recognize this Lucy—she looks happy and carefree. "These photos were taken less than a week before the accident."

"They certainly seem happy there," Wade says.

"Or Ian and Lucy are good actors," I add.

"Are there more articles about the accident?" Liam chimes in from the back as he stuffs the last bit of pizza into his mouth.

Diamond girl nods and puts another article onto the smart board, the date two weeks after the story about the crash. The first thing that strikes me is Ian Reese's mug shot. In stark contrast to the smiling boy from the photos with Lucy, Ian's eyes look vacant, his skin sallow. He's aged years in those weeks. The headline reads: IAN REESE PLEADS GUILTY, SENTENCED TO PRISON.

I read the first paragraph of the article.

> Ian Reese pleads guilty to vehicular assault in the second degree and is sentenced to three years in prison.

Even more shocking than learning Ian went to prison for so many years is the revelation of who Ian injured in the crash. I reread the name of the victim a second time just to make sure I didn't get it wrong.

The article is clear. The victim in the crash was Sophia James—S.J. The woman I interviewed the day before Lucy went missing. There are so many conflicting thoughts swirling in my brain. Top among them—why didn't she tell me that she'd been the one hurt? She repeatedly mentioned the accident but never shared she'd been the victim. I read the full text, slowing down at the paragraph describing S.J.'s injuries as severe, including multiple broken ribs and a bruised lung.

Liam walks next to me and leans over my shoulder to see what I'm reading.

"I interviewed Sophia James," I tell him. "She mentioned the accident but never shared that she was the person injured. She said *he* had an accident. And that *he* was never the same since."

"You'd think she'd mention it," Liam says, rubbing the stubble on his chin.

"Maybe she didn't want to derail Lucy's story," Wade offers. "You were speaking to her as a reporter. She might not have wanted anything stirred up."

I think back to my interaction with S.J. and remember another thing—she pulled me aside as we were leaving and encouraged me to stay away from the Ian angle. I relay that information to Liam and Wade.

"Something's off there," Liam says. "I'm not sure how it relates to Lucy's kidnapping, but we should pursue it, nevertheless."

"Let me talk to her." I turn to Liam and register the skepticism in his eyes. But he doesn't try to interrupt me. "We have a rapport," I say.

"Yet she didn't tell you the truth in your first go-around," Liam counters.

"True," I admit. "But I didn't ask her who the victim of the accident was."

Liam shrugs but doesn't respond with more than that.

"I have something," tortoiseshell glasses says. "Agents just spoke to a few people in Glenport about Greggory. They describe him as a stand-up guy who stepped in to take care of his family when everything fell apart. But one person did mention that Greggory has a temper."

"I can vouch for that," I reply, remembering his confrontation with Lucy in the pharmacy parking lot. He was so angry, accusing Lucy of ruining his family. Did he mean the car accident? But that wouldn't make sense—Lucy was at a tennis facility hours away. At least that's what everything we are reading indicates.

The more we learn about the people in Glenport, the more questions and inconsistencies emerge, which makes me wonder what else they could be hiding.

CHAPTER 31

Something else happened around the time of Ian's accident, I think to myself. If I remember correctly, Lucy stepped away from tennis due to her own injury. That's a strange coincidence. And I'm not much of a believer in those.

I search the internet and find an article in *Tennis Weekly* from the winter of 2008 saying Lucy Bosco took time off to rehab a ligament sprain in her ankle. Another search shows Lucy back on the tour by mid-summer. Did her injury have anything to do with Ian's accident? The timing is a little off, but a public relations person could have massaged the story. I share the information with the group as we hear footsteps from the bedroom.

Mae comes in, hair wet and pulled away from her face, wearing a blouse and trousers. She looks more tired than before.

"Kate, can we talk?" Mae says to me, asking if I can speak in private with her and Liam. I follow them and perch on the edge of the cream couch, feeling as if I just got summoned into the principal's office.

"As you already figured out, our attempt at getting information from the Coles didn't go well," she says, motioning with her chin to the wall separating this suite from the one the Coles occupy.

Liam shakes his head, hands gripping one another. I can tell he's not happy about what Mae's going to propose.

"We"—she clears her throat—"*I'm* hoping you and Wade can accompany the Coles to the Tennis Center and see if you can find out what the parents are hiding. Maybe they'll confide in you. We'll have agents undercover around the entire grounds."

I open my mouth to speak, but Liam interrupts.

"For the record, and I know we've already been through this," Liam says, then takes a breath. "For the record, I don't think it's a good idea. But I'll respect whatever you decide."

I nearly fall onto the floor. Liam's never said that. *I'll respect whatever you decide.* Maybe he's maturing? Or knows I've already made up my mind? Or maybe there's more of a mind game–thing going on—something to do with what I found last night inside the mayor's book at Liam's house. Does he think I'll let my investigation into his past go if he treats me more like an adult? Whatever his motivation—Liam's concession, while appreciated, won't counteract the conversation we need to have once the present nightmare ends.

"It's ironic because I'm a reporter—you'd think I'd be the last person they'd want to talk to," I say as the mini fridge starts to hum.

"Except," Mae says. "You've known about this situation for nearly twenty-four hours, and not one word has been mentioned on your station. I'd argue you've proven that you're the most trustworthy of any of us."

"I hadn't thought of it that way," I reply, considering Mae's logic. "Of course I'll do it," I say. "I actually told my boss I planned to attend Brynn's practice, so it kind of works out perfectly."

Mae shoots Liam a *told you so* look as she explains that my attending gives Wade a reason to be close. "We'll have agents around the facility—but you and Wade can be with them."

"It makes perfect sense," I say.

Mae stands, telling us she's going to grab a cup of coffee.

The coffee maker hisses; then I hear cursing as the refrigerator opens and closes. I walk into the kitchen and open the cabinet above the Nespresso machine. "You looking for this?" I extend the wire basket with the creamers and sugar packets toward Mae.

"Yes, I am." She flashes a weary smile and takes three sugars and two creamers, then dumps them into her drink.

We return to the dining room; the soft murmur of conversation abruptly stops.

"Anything you want to share?" Mae asks, looking pointedly at each person sitting at the table.

"I got something on Nico." Tortoiseshell pushes his glasses up on his nose. "There weren't any cameras from the SoHo apartment Nico said he went to the night in question. But a security camera at the ATM across the street did catch this image at 9:00 p.m." He swipes on his iPad, and a grainy black-and-white photo appears on the smart board.

I stare at the image of Nico, wearing a dark-blue button-down, his hair pulled into a neat ponytail. What's troubling is that he's holding a woman's hand. A woman who most definitely is not Lucy.

Pretty much the only thing we can make out about the woman is that she's tall—taller than Lucy. She's wearing a raincoat that covers her outfit, a hood pulled over her head.

I'm not surprised to learn Nico is cheating on his wife—but I'm disheartened. Seeing Nico holding another woman's hand makes his betrayal feel visceral, and I feel desperately angry on Lucy's behalf. Especially since I experienced the same type of infidelity.

I push that emotion aside, needing to focus on what this new bit of information means to the kidnapping. Does it give Nico a greater motive to abduct his wife? Could the woman be in on it? Was Nico planning to leave Lucy for this woman but wanted to cash in first?

"Is there a better view of her?" Liam asks, walking close to the smart board to study the image.

"There weren't a lot of cameras near the SoHo apartment."

"So, Nico definitely went to his friend's apartment," I say, stating the obvious.

"He did," tortoiseshell says.

"Any other images from the bank? Do we know when they left?" Mae asks, holding her coffee mug against her lips.

"Something happened to the bank's camera shortly after this image was captured," he replies. "We don't know when Nico and the woman left the apartment. The bank's IT department says the camera has been on the fritz lately."

"All right, everyone, keep digging into Nico," Mae says. "The fact that it appears he's having an affair gives him an even stronger motive."

"Here's something else," the SOS states, putting an image of Nico and Lucy's SUV on screen. "We got this from a traffic cam on the Long Island Expressway Wednesday morning at 7:36 a.m. It's of Nico and Lucy's car, and it shows Nico pulling off at the Oyster Bay exit at 7:36 a.m., hours before he claimed to return to the house."

I think about that for a moment. It doesn't show Nico actually at the rental home, but it puts him in proximity. And it's caught him in a lie. He told agents he didn't return to Long Island until later that morning.

"So, Nico has motive and opportunity," Mae says.

"Has there been any movement from him at the house?" Liam asks.

"About two hours ago Nico went to the local coffee shop and picked up a few things; then he returned to the Oyster Bay rental," Mae says.

"There's more," the SOS says. "I found the prenup between Lucy and Nico to see if Conrad was right that Nico would receive nothing."

"Was he?" Mae asks.

"Not completely—Nico gets some money. Not enough to maintain the kind of lifestyle he seems to enjoy—a few hundred thousand. He has a modest amount of money saved up, but nothing that would accommodate what he's used to."

"So maybe $200K from Conrad wasn't enough. Maybe Nico got greedy and kidnapped Lucy to get more," Liam says.

"Any mention of a home in Greece in the prenup?" I ask.

"As a matter of fact, there is. It goes to Lucy. Why?" the SOS says.

"When Lucy and I had dinner, she mentioned that she and Nico only get to the house about one month each year, but that Nico's brother watches it for them."

"Let's also start brainstorming places Nico could hide Lucy," Liam chimes in.

I'm completely distracted by the new information concerning Nico, but I need to focus my attention on Brynn and her parents. For one, we might be wrong about Nico. And even if we're not, if Nico's working with someone else, Brynn remains in danger.

I gather my things and follow Wade to the elevator and into the lobby, where chandeliers of layered crystals cast a warm glow over the space. Wade stops at the coffee station, takes a paper cup, and fills it from the large stainless steel pot. I do the same, grab a napkin full of small pastries, and follow him across the marble floor and outside, where his sedan waits.

"We have a lot to mull over," he says, pulling away from the curb and following the Coles' SUV, driven by another agent.

"I'm trying to wrap my brain around Nico and the thought that he could have done this to a woman he supposedly loved," I say, strapping myself into the car.

Wade nods as he heads north. Manhattan looks so different from when Liam and I arrived this morning. The early sun shined bright over the buildings. Now, clouds hang across the city, covering the glass-and-steel skyscrapers in a dirty haze.

"I'm not surprised Nico has moved to the top of our suspect list," Wade says, glancing at me. "It usually turns out to be the person closest to the victim." Wade veers toward the bridge, taking us to Queens.

"I get that," I reply. "But what's the connection to Brynn? That's what's baffling me."

Wade merges onto the highway, and a sea of brake lights. Typical. Impatient drivers honk, despite the fact there's nowhere to go.

"That's what we're hoping you can find out." Wade lifts a brow. "The parents are hiding something. They must be. Why else would the kidnapper take such a risk involving them?"

"Unless the kidnapper is a sick scumbag," I reply.

"Well, we already know the kidnapper is that." Wade presses the gas as the traffic begins to move. "What do you make of the rhyme?" he asks.

I repeat the words out loud:

Go about your day like nothing's new

Otherwise, the next one taken will be you

At 9PM you must pay 2 million to me

Or Lucy is dead, and your parents' secret set free

"The kidnapper seems to be enjoying themselves," I say, noting the strange feeling of glee in the message. The kidnapper isn't just asking for an exchange of money for Lucy. He or she is playing puppeteer. Toying with the family.

"I agree," Wade says, pulling off the highway at the sign for the USTA Billie Jean King National Tennis Center and following the traffic toward the press lots.

"No FBI parking credentials?" I ask as we sit in line to reach the parking area.

"Can't blow my cover." He shrugs.

"Are you worried the kidnapper is at the Open waiting for Brynn?" I don't finish my thought—that she might get kidnapped too. Or worse.

"It's a possibility," Wade says, then adds that the FBI and NYPD are ready for that scenario with a mobile surveillance unit and agents on scene.

"Has there been any talk about paying the ransom?" I ask, noting we are just under ten hours until the 9:00 p.m. deadline set by the kidnapper.

"As a policy, the FBI and NYPD do not pay ransoms. The kidnapper seems to want the Cole family to pay, but so far, they don't appear inclined to comply. Lucy's brother is adamant that he will be ready to pay if necessary."

"Conrad has that kind of money?"

"He can put it together from a line of credit and some working capital from his company," Wade explains. Well, that's interesting. The man who wanted his sister to pay for lunch at the Mac-n-Cheesy plans to cobble together $2 million. Will wonders never cease?

CHAPTER 32

Brynn straightens her shoulders, raises her chin, and walks onto the court, phone facing the scattering of fans at the back of the practice courts. She waves and smiles, wearing another tie-dyed outfit with matching sneakers. She doesn't milk the moment, ending it quickly—a truncated version of a Brynn performance—but I admire her ability to remain in character.

A casual setting, coaches stand on the courts, conferring with their players. A few superfans lounge on the bleachers, while some lean against the fence surrounding the courts.

"Hey, Brynn," a middle-aged man yells as Brynn starts hitting volleys. He sticks his hand through the chain links. "Can you sign this?" He holds out a tennis ball. Brynn flinches as a security guard approaches the guy, telling him to back up. Normally, Brynn happily agrees to provide autographs, but I spot a flash of fear in her eyes. The man doesn't know what she's going through. And who knows if he's even a legit fan? Maybe he's the kidnapper. Or working with him or her. I imagine agents are checking his identity and background at this very moment.

Alexis watches the security officers walk the man back from the fence. One puts out an arm, suggesting he exit the area. He shakes his head, pulls away, and sits in the stands, eyes fixated on Brynn. I feel my jaw tighten as I watch him.

"That guy's making me nervous," Alexis says, peering over her sunglasses. "He should be removed."

"I feel the same way, but they can't," I say. "There are agents all around, though." Alexis keeps her gaze on the man, as the sound of racquets hitting tennis balls resonates in the background.

"Brynn's handling herself well," I say to Alexis, watching Brynn practice her serve and volley.

"My daughter can put up a good front, but I see the cracks," Alexis mumbles, turning her attention to Brynn, who smashes a volley into the net.

Jill Wallace enters the courts, all smiles and kisses; the aging Barbie-doll player who advanced when Lucy didn't show for their match. She gives Brynn a bright wave that makes a complete half circle.

"That woman is the one who benefited most from Lucy's disappearance," Alexis whispers. I nod. There's no way Barbie-doll Jill would have made it to the next round if she'd played Lucy. But Liam said her alibi was rock solid. Alibi or not she gives off bad energy, and I don't trust her at all.

Zane yells something at Brynn, and she slams her racquet against the ground. A collective gasp ripples through the stands. Brynn isn't known for bursts of temper. Alexis is right—her daughter is coming apart.

Brynn's hitting partner walks to the bench and grabs a new racquet for her.

My phone pings with a message from Mae. Ask her. On the court, Brynn hits another serve into the net. "C'mon, Brynn!" she yells to herself.

"Alexis, we really need to talk." I turn to her, but she keeps her gaze on her daughter. "There's some connection between your family and Lucy. You need to tell us—"

Alexis glances at the middle-aged man staring at her daughter. "I know. Are you sure the agents are watching him?" she says, motioning in the man's direction.

"Yes," I reply, pointing out a woman in a baseball hat, just behind him.

"All right." Alexis looks at me. "But not here." She stands, beckoning me to follow her. We walk past the chain-link fence as Brynn takes a water break, her eyes finding us. I flash a smile, hoping to reassure her that everything is all right, but her eyes stay on her mother, worry clouding her face.

"Brynn," Zane yells across the court. "Let's go," he says, his tone harsh.

Alexis flinches at the sound of Zane's voice but keeps her head forward, moving along the outdoor path to the main plaza. She stops near the famous gurgling fountains in front of Arthur Ashe Stadium. The spray of water mixes with the sounds of the crowds, making it a very noisy spot. Alexis sits on the slate edge.

"You want to speak here?" I ask. "It's so loud."

"No one can overhear us," she replies, head close to me, her breath rapid. "The connection between Lucy and Brynn is me." She blinks back tears. "It's all my fault," she adds, her lips trembling.

I place my hand over hers and ask her to explain.

"This is between us." She looks into my eyes. "Right?" Her words come out staccato against the rush of water behind us.

"Between us and the investigators," I add. "I promise not to report it on television if that's what you mean," I say, noticing a little girl and her mom sitting near us, the girl licking an ice cream cone.

"I don't want to embarrass Brynn," Alexis says. "She's been through enough. I hate myself for it."

"What do you mean?" I ask, keeping my voice low for fear of scaring her.

"I did something terrible." She covers her face with her hands. "I'm so ashamed of myself."

"You're doing the right thing telling us," I say. "It's the only way to help Lucy and keep Brynn safe. How are you the connection?" I ask.

"I kept racking my brain as to why, of all people, the ransom demand came to Brynn," she says. "Brynn hardly knows Lucy; she's only seen her in the locker rooms and during their few matches," she replies, breaking eye contact to stare at the rushing water, gurgling behind us.

"Your husband did coach Lucy."

"He did," she replies. "But that was so long ago." Alexis's lip quivers. "Zane isn't an easy man to be married to." She looks back at me. "He only cares about himself. And tennis. I hate to think that he just cares for Brynn because of tennis, but sometimes I wonder. Everything to him is tennis. Tennis. Tennis."

I don't interrupt, just let her continue.

"I want you to know the background. Even though it isn't an excuse for what I did."

"Okay," I say, trying to make her comfortable. "What did you do?"

"I had an affair." She hangs her head. "I was so lonely. Zane and I haven't had a real relationship in years. It's only about Brynn's tennis. I'm convinced he's cheated, too, not that that's a good excuse. Two wrongs and all," she says, looking lost.

"How does this connect Brynn to Lucy?" I ask.

"Because my affair is with Nico Pappas."

I let that information sink in. Alexis Cole is sleeping with Nico Pappas. I didn't see that coming. So many questions come to my mind. How does this impact Brynn? What does this mean for the kidnapper's motive? There must be more to it. I'm about to ask Alexis these questions when I spot a familiar figure, lurking in the background. Not the man from the tennis court but the man I could swear I saw last night at the hotel. The man with the shoe-polish-black hair gelled off his face. He removes his sunglasses and takes a step in our direction, his lips set in a sinister frown. I reach for my necklace and make sure it's pointed in the man's direction, then grab Alexis's arm.

"Let's talk somewhere else. That guy's making me nervous," I say as she shoots up. Alexis follows me past the food court to the back area with the patio furniture. The same spot I brought her and Brynn just yesterday when this whole nightmare began. More people have discovered this area, hanging around eating ice cream. But there's enough privacy for us to speak quietly without anyone overhearing.

"Do you know who he is?" Alexis says.

"No." I reach for my necklace, hoping someone on the other end can figure out his identity. I sit catty corner to her on the patio furniture, thinking about the video from the bank camera by Nico's SoHo apartment. Alexis is the same height as the woman in the images. It must have been her.

"When you told police you went for a walk two nights ago, did you really go to meet Nico?" I ask, wanting to confirm my hypothesis.

"Yes." She hangs her head, as if speaking to the concrete below. "Nico's friend lets him stay at a SoHo apartment."

"What time did you meet him, and what time did you leave?"

She tells me she met him around 9:00 p.m. "I never planned to see him this week. But he texted, and I just needed to be with someone who cared about me. Zane has been particularly difficult to be around this week." That all makes sense so far with the timeline the task force put together.

Alexis's phone rings, and she picks up—Brynn's voice is so loud, I can hear, too, and she sounds frightened.

"Mom, that man attacked me," she cries into the phone. "And he got away." She says something else, but we can't hear through her crying. There are loud shouts and movements. Brynn's crying stops, and the phone goes dead.

Alexis and I jump up and speed toward the practice courts. Alexis tries to call Brynn back as we walk, but the call goes to voicemail over and over again. My heart pounds at the thought that that man is the kidnapper. And he's still out here. Lurking and dangerous.

CHAPTER 33

Wade texts to say he's with Brynn in the players'-lounge lobby but doesn't provide more information. We know she's safe, for now, but nothing else. A man bumps into Alexis, and she startles. I grab her trembling hand and lead her through the throng of people, my eyes darting around, searching for the middle-aged man from the practice courts.

We make it into the players' area and spot Brynn sitting with Wade on a small couch by the transportation desk. I notice two women nearby, watching Brynn, and assume they are agents.

"Are you all right?" Alexis takes Brynn's hands in hers. Brynn blinks against the tears falling down her cheeks.

"That man grabbed her through the fence," Wade whispers. "Agents arrested him."

Alexis's face flushes red with anger, but she keeps her voice calm. "Brynn, you don't need to do this. Tennis isn't everything. This tournament isn't everything."

She looks at her mom, her shoulders hunched. "I have to follow *his* directions." She whispers the word *his*.

"Where is your father anyway?" Alexis looks around, registering Zane's absence.

"Daddy went to speak with the Nike people." Brynn sniffs. "It happened after he left."

A gush of air whooshes toward us as the sliding doors open and the air-conditioning blows stronger. Barbie-doll Jill rushes toward Brynn, fake concern plastered on her face. "Dear." She smiles as if feasting on Brynn. "I can't believe that man grabbed you. Fans can be so unpredictable. Are you up for this? It's important to take care of yourself." She glares at Alexis as if she were at fault.

Wade stands, putting himself between Brynn and Jill. "If you'll excuse us," he says, his tone stern. "We're discussing our feature of Brynn and would appreciate some privacy."

Jill's face turns pale. "If that's who you want to interview." She rolls her eyes. "Good luck with your ratings." She struts away.

"Agents should really check her again," I whisper to Wade.

"I agree," he responds and then turns to Brynn and Alexis. "The man is being taken in for questioning right now. We'll have more answers soon. Until then, we should operate under the theory he's a crazed fan and assume"—Wade looks around—"the *other* person is still out there."

My phone vibrates with a text from Mae. Finish your conversation with Alexis! I can imagine Mae pacing back and forth, wearing a hole in the carpeting. My hand reaches for my *necklace*, a reminder that the task force is still watching everything. If the middle-aged man is just a fanatical fan, then we still need to get to the bottom of the kidnapping and the connection between the Coles and Lucy.

"Alexis, let's take Brynn to the players' dining area and get her something to eat," I say, feeling terribly guilty about continuing with my task. But also rationalizing that food could do Brynn some good. Not to mention, catching the kidnapper will do wonders for Brynn's mental health.

Wade quickly agrees, and we usher Brynn and Alexis toward the private players' dining area. The cafeteria reminds me of one of those grand ballrooms at a country club. The place is brimming with options: make-your-own omelets and pasta stations. A smoothie bar, sushi station. Chopped salads. Large windows provide views of the practice courts where Brynn was just attacked. Media are only allowed into this dining hall after getting special permission and an invite from a player. And everything here is off the record. Always. Not that it matters since I'm not here for a story.

"What would you like, Brynn?" Alexis asks and offers her a hamburger, French fries, and a smoothie.

"Dad would have a heart attack if I ate that," Brynn says, her eyes wide.

"He doesn't need to know," Alexis replies.

"Why don't you ladies grab the food, and I'll wait with Brynn," Wade offers, asking me to bring him exactly what Brynn is having.

"That will make three of us." I smile, impressed how he quickly orchestrated an opportunity for me to finish my conversation with Alexis.

Alexis and I move to the grill line and place our orders. We're given a number and told to wait. I step back to provide us with privacy among the bustle.

"Can we return to our conversation?" I say in a soft voice.

"While we wait?" She looks at all the people around us.

"No one will hear," I say. "The more the task force knows, the better equipped they'll be to keep Brynn safe."

She doesn't argue with the logic and tells me again she never planned to meet with Nico this week. "But he reached out, and I just needed to see someone who cared about me." Her lips quiver, and I glimpse the vulnerable woman behind her usual tough exterior.

"Did he call you on your regular phone?" I ask, feeling like their correspondence would have been flagged by the FBI.

She reaches into her bag and pulls out a flip phone. "We have burners." She hands it to me, knowing the FBI will want to check through her correspondence.

I move her back to the timeline, wanting to hammer out those details. "You met Nico around 9:00 p.m. What time did you leave?"

"I stayed less than an hour." That correlates with the task force's information, which showed Alexis leaving a downtown dinner at 8:30 p.m. to go for a walk, then returning to the second event with Zane at 10:15 p.m.

"Where did Zane think you were?" I ask Alexis.

"He's much more into networking than I am. Always has been. For years, I'd disappear for an hour or so to walk around and clear my head. He just thought I was doing what I always do," she explains.

"How long have you and Nico been together?" I ask, watching the cafeteria staff flip burgers. "And how did it start?"

She looks into my eyes, and I see so much sadness in her expression. "It's been going on a long time," she says, stopping as a player walks by us to place his order at the counter. "Over a year—" she says once he's out of earshot. "It started out casual. We were both at the same Wimbledon party last summer, hanging around on the outskirts of the event. We commiserated about being tennis widows. One thing led to another, and we ended up sneaking out and, well—"

The player nods a hello, but neither of us responds. He seems to get the message and walks a few feet away, taking out his phone and scrolling.

"We'd usually meet up for a drink when our paths crossed," she continues. "Sometimes we just talked all night. Sometimes . . . more. Nico really understands me, and I really understand him."

"Did you talk about leaving your spouses?" I ask just as our number is called. We approach the counter and take trays, then carry them to the table and place them in front of Brynn and Wade so they can start eating.

"We'll go get the smoothies now," I say, noting that the color has returned to Brynn's cheeks.

"Thanks," Brynn replies, grabbing a few fries. "Wade is making me laugh. He tells the dumbest jokes."

"If they're so dumb, then why are you laughing?" He winks at her.

Alexis's shoulders ease, and we walk to the line for smoothies, which is longer than the grill line.

"Did you plan to leave your spouses?" I ask again, against the low chatter of the cafeteria.

"No, but for different reasons." Alexis leans over to whisper. "There's no love between me and Zane. But I won't leave Brynn alone with him. He's too hard on her. Maybe if she got another coach. Or when she starts her own family. But not now."

We get to the front and place our order over the whir of blenders.

"And for Nico?" I ask as we take a few steps back to wait.

"It was harder for Nico," she says. "He still loved Lucy. He really wanted it to work out."

"Loved? Or loves?"

"That night he said something he never did before. He said his marriage was over. That it had been for a long time, but he'd finally realized it."

"Did he say why?" I ask, my breath catching.

"He said he was tired of being in a loveless marriage and wanted out," she replies. "I asked him what made him finally decide to pull the trigger, but he didn't want to talk about it. And, well, we didn't do much talking after that." She blushes.

"Do you think Nico is capable of . . ." I don't finish the sentence. I don't need to.

"I mean, I never would have thought so, but . . ." she says.

"But?" I press.

"But I'm the only connection between Lucy and Brynn. I tried calling him," she admits. "He's not answering his phone."

"Even if Nico would kidnap Lucy, why bring Brynn into this?"

"Nico seemed very agitated at the apartment. He's usually charming and laid back. But he was really wound up." She pauses, looking around. "He was saying how we were victims of controlling spouses. That Zane shouldn't be able to wield so much power over me by holding me *hostage*."

"Wait," I stop her. "Did he use the word—*hostage*?"

Alexis nods. "He did. That exact word."

"It wasn't just emotionally hostage but financially." Alexis hangs her head. "I'm ashamed to admit that I let Zane handle all our money. When I was young, my father handled my winnings, and when I married Zane, I just let him continue. Finances overwhelm me. Nico hates Zane. I don't know if it's from when Zane coached Lucy or because of the things I've shared—"

"Did Nico have any kind of previous relationship with Zane?" I ask, trying to make sense of all this information.

"Not that I'm aware of," Alexis says. "But Nico and Lucy started on the adult circuit around the same time. And Zane was Lucy's coach. So, who knows?" Alexis shrugs. "It's not like I asked Zane if he happened to know the man I'm having an affair with," she adds, the first sign of irritation and maybe a hint into a more bitter part of her personality.

"So your theory is that Nico kidnapped Lucy to help you out but also extort $2 million since he wanted his marriage to end," I say. "And who was he extorting the money from? Did he think Zane would pay? Or was he thinking someone in Lucy's family would cough up $2 million?"

"I don't know," she says. "And it is twisted that he would think this would help me. But he did seem irrational that night—"

The player near us interrupts, and Alexis literally jumps. "Sorry—your order's ready." He motions in front of us, where the woman behind the counter placed four giant smoothies. We grab our drinks as I try to wrap my head around what Alexis just shared—especially Nico's use of the word *hostage*.

CHAPTER 34

The strawberry-banana smoothie tastes heavenly—and I don't even mind a dose of something healthy after all the pastries this morning. It also makes me feel less guilty about the greasy burger and fries waiting at the table.

Alexis and I slide into our seats and eat silently as Wade and Brynn chatter about a pop band I've never heard of. The scene feels shockingly normal. Then a rush of shame floods my body as I remember a man just attacked Brynn less than an hour ago.

I know the importance of eating, but the joy has left. I chew my burger and fries without tasting the food. I might as well have ordered a salad. Or a vegetarian burrito.

Wade's phone rings, and he picks up, nodding at whatever he's hearing. "It seems the guy who tried to grab you is just a fan. But he's being charged and brought to Federal Plaza for further questioning." *Some* fan, I think, recalling when a fan spit on me last year when I was covering the Olympics.

Brynn nods but doesn't say anything.

My phone pings next with a text from Mae. And I wonder if she literally hung up with Wade and texted me. Her message says that before the Coles leave, we need to speak with Zane—alone. Gauge his reaction to the affair. Are they thinking Zane would kidnap Lucy to punish Nico and his wife? But why involve Brynn? Unless somehow, he thought sending messages to his daughter allowed him to control the situation?

Is Zane that diabolical? I told Alexis I'd share the information only with investigators, but finding Lucy and protecting Brynn trumps everything. Even blowing up a loveless marriage.

As if reading my mind, Mae sends another text, saying they need the information ASAP and if an agent is seen talking with Zane, it will raise eyebrows, especially if the kidnapper is on the premises.

"Are you still planning to do your mobility workout?" Wade asks, looking at Brynn.

She gives a little smile. "I'm feeling calmer now, thanks. I think I should. I sort of have to." She shrugs, in reference to the kidnapper's demand. *Go about your day like nothing's new.*

"I'll come with you," Alexis says, smiling at her.

"Kate." Brynn looks at me. "Thanks for postponing our interview," she whispers.

"We'll get back to the interview as soon as this ordeal is over and everyone is safe," I say, patting her shoulder. "In the meantime, Wade and I have some stuff to take care of. See you later?"

"Yup," she says and goes back to drinking her smoothie.

Wade grabs our trays, tosses the garbage, and places the dirty trays on the stack above the trash. I text Zane and ask if we can talk in one of the private interview rooms, which I managed to get permission to use for half an hour *and no more.*

Wade and I walk toward the front of Arthur Ashe Stadium, and he asks if I think it's better for me to speak to Zane alone or with him.

"I think he's more likely to open up if it's just me," I tell Wade. "He won't feel like we're cornering him."

Wade agrees and reminds me the task force will be listening—he adjusts the charm on my necklace, and I feel a little spark from his hand grazing my skin. He seems to feel it, too, flashing a sheepish smile.

We approach the interview room; he opens the door for me and tells me he'll be down the hall. Nerves stir in my stomach. I'm not scared of Zane; I'm worried about messing up.

As if reading my mind, Wade tells me not to stress. "You've got this. You're a natural investigator."

I go inside and sit on an orange chair, staring at the same USTA wallpaper that was the backdrop for my initial interview with Lucy. This room's smaller than that one, which won't matter since I'm not going to record anything. The important feature is no windows.

Zane enters like a bull. "Kate, you know what's going on. I don't have time for anything. What could possibly be so important?"

I put my finger to my lips and motion for him to shut the door. He throws his hands up but listens.

"We just learned something important," I say. "It can't wait until we return to the hotel."

"Was that scumbag the kidnapper?" he asks, referring to the fan at the practice court.

"It doesn't seem so," I tell him and explain the man's been arrested but that authorities ruled him out as the kidnapper. "I found a second link between your family and Lucy's family."

"You did?" His jaw drops as if I'd punched him, and he sits in the chair across from mine. Is that fear I see in his eyes? "Well?" He leans forward.

"I have a theory," I say.

"A theory? We don't have time for theories," he says, crossing one leg over the other.

"Indulge me," I say. My plan is to first ask Zane about Nico. Then, after I see what he shares, I'll bring up the affair. Zane is cagey, and I can't help but wonder if there's another layer to all this that Alexis doesn't even know.

"Is it possible Nico Pappas might be behind this?"

Zane looks more relieved than surprised. "Lucy's good-for-nothing husband. I'm going to wring his neck—" Zane tightens his hands into fists. "Wait, why would he be involved with my family?" Zane seems genuinely confused.

"Do *you* have any history with him?" I ask.

Zane gets quiet, scratching the back of his head. "Decades ago, he wanted me to coach him. As if." Zane shakes his head and laughs. "He was never very talented. Obviously, I said no. You think this is retribution for not taking him on back then? I might have called him a talentless prick, or something like that. But it was decades ago—"

Zane seems proud of his insult, chuckling a little to himself.

"How about Brynn? Or your wife? Do they have a relationship with him?"

"Brynn is seventeen years old, for god's sake." He gasps.

"What about Alexis?" I watch carefully as he stares at me. His mind seems to process the implication of my question. Considering the idea. Weighing the information.

"What are you getting at?" he replies, lips twitching at the corners.

"How is your marriage?" I ask, and I see his brain working. Zane is not a dumb guy, and he knows where I'm heading with my questions. But he also seems confused.

"Certainly not perfect. But we both love our daughter and would never do anything to hurt her—"

"And each other?"

Zane stands up and leans forward, arms pressing against the table between us, like a cougar ready to pounce. "Are you telling me that my wife is having an affair with that empty-headed playboy, Nico?"

"Yes." I stand too.

He slams the table with his hands, sending it flying toward me. I jump to my right, narrowly avoiding the moving projectile.

"What the hell?" I shout.

"I'm sorry," he says, not sounding sorry at all. Still, he has the presence of mind to take a few steps back, putting distance between us. "It's just—you dropped a bomb on me. I mean what the hell did you expect?" he says, defending his outburst, like it's my fault he exploded.

"She's going to regret this," he mumbles under his breath. "Making me the fool."

"Is that a threat?" I ask.

He ignores my question and asks his own. "How long has the ungrateful bitch been cheating on me?"

"That's something for you and your wife to discuss," I reply. "Did you know about the affair?"

"Does it seem like I knew?" He sneers, face flushed.

My phone pings, and I look down at the message. It's from Liam, and he suggests Wade join me. I type back NO. Zane is just starting to talk; if someone else enters the room, our chance for new information will vanish. I put my phone away, hoping Liam respects my opinion.

I return my attention to Zane, deciding to appeal to his ego. "You're a smart guy," I say. "You must have noticed something—"

"I knew Alexis felt neglected. It's not that I think she's consciously jealous of Brynn, but I do give our daughter most of my attention," he replies, letting the accusation settle in the air. Instead of seeing Alexis's infidelity as an indictment of his marriage, he's spinning the affair as a reaction to his relationship with Brynn.

"I never would have imagined Alexis would fall for an empty-headed tool like Nico Pappas, though." He shakes his head. "If Nico is doing this, then Alexis brought a psycho into our lives and threatened our daughter with her actions." He stands up, seeming buoyed by the thought.

"Does that make you happy?" I ask, watching his mind put puzzle pieces together. He doesn't answer right away, pulling out his phone and then scrolling through something.

"Zane, does that make you happy?" I repeat the question.

He looks at me, his coach veneer returned. "*Happy* is the wrong word. Would I ever choose to put my daughter under this kind of stress, of course not. But as a father, it's also my job to protect her from anyone who threatens her safety. And I take that very seriously."

I watch him leave, confident he's already leapfrogged from the present crisis to strategizing how to break the bond between Brynn and Alexis. Or was that his plan from the beginning and he just needed us to present him with information he already knew?

About to follow, I'm blocked by Wade, who steps inside and shuts the door behind him. "The kidnapper just reached out," he says, leaning his back against the door as if to shield me from something on the other side. "This message was about you."

CHAPTER 35

Someone knocks on the door, and I flinch before remembering I promised to be out of the room in half an hour. "We should leave," I say.

Wade doesn't speak but goes to the door, opens it, and tells the person on the other side they need to wait five minutes. Raised voices follow, but Wade shuts and locks the door.

He walks over to me and holds his phone out. "This was sent to the burner the kidnapper gave to Brynn."

The words are jarring, and I hear myself gasp. Keep this nosy bitch reporter away before I do it 4 u.

But the photo is worse. The photo shows Alexis and me sitting on the bleachers at the practice courts. I'm next to Alexis, and my head's moving like an animated cartoon, falling off to the side with blood spurting out. As a reflex, I reach for my neck.

Multiple thoughts ping-pong through my mind. First among them, the kidnapper was close. Very close. We were focused on the middle-aged man, but where was the real perpetrator?

"We're reviewing all the footage of fans," Wade says, reading my mind. "But the kidnapper could just want us to think he or she is close. The person could have poached the photo from a feed." I don't know if Wade hopes his words are reassuring, but frankly, I find them more troubling. I want the bastard to be close so we can catch the sicko.

A loud knock pounds against the door and doesn't let up. "We should go," I say to Wade, unlocking the door to a crew that's clearly steamed.

"Sorry," I mumble as Wade and I slip into the hallway.

My phone rings with a call from Liam, and I know he's going to try and pull me off the case. "I'm fine," I say before Liam can begin.

"You're in the line of sight of a kidnapper," he barks. "That's hardly fine."

"Maybe it will help draw the kidnapper out?" I suggest.

"Give me a break, Kate," Liam spits and then tells me to hold. I hear arguing in the background, and then Liam's voice returns, ordering Wade and me to return to the car and to call in from there. He clicks off, and I convey the information to Wade.

We leave Arthur Ashe Stadium, wading through the crowd. "Remember that man from last night with the shoe-polish-colored hair?" I ask Wade as we walk toward the exit.

"Yes," he says.

"I think I spotted him earlier by the fountain."

"He was very careful to avoid the security cameras at the hotel. We got a partial hit on him, but it was kicked up to a different department. Classified." Wade rubs his chin. "Mae thinks we just stepped into someone else's case. She's convinced the man is not connected to the kidnapping. But if you saw him here—"

I think back to the person at the fountain and wonder if I got it wrong. Maybe I was just spooked. Wade and I exit the gates and walk past a father holding hands with a child, an oversize tennis ball tucked under his arm. The two are singing a Taylor Swift song, looking happy and carefree.

"I'll let Mae know," Wade says to me. "She can have an agent look through security cameras at the fountain around the time you and Alexis were speaking there."

The shuttle is full but not overcrowded, given that we are leaving a few hours before the day matches will end.

"Just think, you could have been parked so much closer if you weren't a producer," I say.

"And people say television is glamorous." He laughs as the shuttle jerks along the road.

Once in Wade's car, he blasts the air-conditioning and calls Mae.

"You both there?" Her voice thunders through the car speakers, and Wade adjusts the volume.

"Yes," I reply as a subway rumbles past.

"Kate." Liam's voice joins the conversation. "You know, I'd rather you don't do this."

"Shocker." I mouth the word to Wade.

"Liam's right to be concerned, Kate," Mae says, her voice even. "The kidnapper has singled you out. That's something we take very seriously. But I also believe you are in safe hands with Wade. And your cover remains intact—which helps us."

"There's no question I'm continuing," I reply. "Whatever you need. I trust you and Wade to keep me safe."

"We'd like you to drive to Glenport and pay a visit to Sophia James at the high school. Let's figure out why she didn't share the fact that Ian Reese hit her during that car accident. Also, probe her for more information, in general, about the Reese family. Let's regroup after that. We might have you swing by the pharmacy again. Kate, maybe you'll have better luck with Greggory than our agent did," Mae says.

"What if one of these people you're sending her to speak with is the kidnapper? He just sent a message for Kate to stay away." Liam explodes before the volume turns off, someone clearly muting their end.

Wade watches me, wondering, I'm sure, if I want to pull back. It's not like I'm running blindly into a burning building. An FBI undercover agent is with me, and field agents are all around. And if the kidnapper identified me, it won't be hard for that person to identify my kids. So, as far as I'm concerned, the sooner the maniac is caught, the better for everyone. And if I can help catch the jerk, then that's what I'll do.

Mae gets back online. "Kate, it's up to you."

"I'm still in," I reply as Wade starts the car and drives toward the exit.

"All right, but the minute you want to stop, you tell us," Mae replies. "Okay?"

"Okay," I agree and hang up.

"I admire you," Wade says, merging onto the Long Island Expressway, heading east. "You're very brave."

"Please." I feel myself blush, embarrassed by his compliment.

We pass exits for the fancier suburbs before getting off at Glenport and heading toward our destination. Wade stops at a school-crossing signal, graffiti sprayed over the flashing light.

At the driveway for Glenport High School, my stomach lurches as the digital message from two days ago flashes on screen: **Welcome Home, Lucy Bosco.**

An eerie feeling overtakes me as we wind our way to the school. My mind returns to my time here with Lucy. Wade parks, and we walk toward the door, the clouds threatening rain.

A security guard approaches us.

"We're here to see S.J.," I say, taking out my TRP Sports credentials.

"I remember you." He smiles. "You were interviewing S.J. a few days ago."

"That's right," I reply, happy I, we, won't have to explain our presence.

He offers to escort us around back to the tennis courts, telling us S.J.'s holding practice now. "You can't shoot any video," he says. "Those waivers were only for one day," he tells us, not registering that neither of us is carrying a camera.

"No problem." We follow him down a path that winds around the soccer field. "We just have a few quick questions."

"She's over there," he says, pointing to the three tennis courts past a large dumpster.

About a dozen high school girls are on the courts, some hitting, others sitting along the sides. "So, this is where the famous Lucy Bosco began." Wade examines the concrete surface.

"She played here freshman year but then went off to compete on the circuit. Junior ATP."

"And this coach was one of her BFFs back then?"

"They seemed really happy to see one another." I explain the hugs and smiles. "I got the feeling S.J. became a substitute mom for Lucy after her own mother died."

"Lucy's mother died in a car accident, right?" Wade asks.

I nod, remembering the story of how it was a hit-and-run. The police assumed the driver was part of a bank-robbery gang.

"A strange amount of car accidents associated with Lucy's circle; don't you think?" Wade says as I spot S.J. wearing a tight purple-and-yellow tracksuit, walking toward us.

"You think the accidents might be related?"

He shrugs as S.J. approaches, her arms flapping at her sides.

"I didn't expect you," she says, clapping her hands. "But, of course, I'm delighted to see you again, Ms. Green. And who is this handsome gentleman. Is this your beau?"

"This is my producer," I say as S.J. shakes Wade's hand.

"To what do I owe the pleasure of your visit?" S.J. says, her happy energy from days ago transformed into something jittery and exaggerated.

"We were in the area," I explain. "We just wanted to confirm some information from my interview."

Behind us a tennis ball flies into a tree as giggles erupt from the court. Someone yells, "Sorry."

"I assumed you would be canceling the story now that Lucy dropped out," she says.

I study her face for any guile. Does she know the truth or believe Lucy just left? She appears genuine. "We're still moving forward with the story. Although, it's obviously different," I say and explain again I have a couple of clarifying questions I hope she can answer.

"I'm a little uncomfortable talking to you without Lucy's permission," she says.

"Why don't you text Lucy and ask if she minds," Wade suggests.

At this recommendation, S.J. pulls at the edges of her tracksuit jacket. "I tried texting and calling her after she forfeited. She didn't respond." S.J. looks down at the ground.

"Does that surprise you?" I ask.

"Not really." S.J. shrugs. "Maybe a little," she says, eyes darting from Wade to me. "She disappeared once before. But that was decades ago."

Her comment gets my attention. We need to put S.J. at ease. "Could we sit down?" I point to the plastic picnic table on the grass. "My feet are killing me."

S.J. looks back at the courts and tells us to give her a minute. Is she stalling or just being responsible about her coaching duties? We watch her trudge to the courts and call the girls over to form a circle.

Wade and I move to the plastic picnic bench, which rests higher on one end. I drive my heel into the ground to keep from sliding into Wade, who sits next to me.

One girl on each court wheels a shopping cart of tennis balls to the far end and begins feeding lobs to the players lined up opposite them on the courts.

S.J. returns and slides onto the bench across from us. I need to be careful asking S.J. about Lucy disappearing, as it's not a question a sports reporter would necessarily focus on. But we want an answer.

"S.J." I lean forward, resting my head on my hands. "You've got me curious. Off the record, when else did Lucy disappear?"

"Oh, it's nothing really." S.J. puts her hands to her mouth. "I shouldn't have opened my big mouth."

Wade and I remain quiet, hoping the lack of conversation will encourage her to speak, especially since she's the chatty type who I'd guess hates awkward silence.

"It's just that when Lucy was in high school, she and Ian took off for a few days," S.J. says, explaining how terrified everyone was. "People thought they'd been kidnapped," she adds.

"That's awful," I respond, stuck on the word *kidnapped.*

"Ian was her boyfriend, right?" Wade asks, keeping his voice soft.

"Ian followed Lucy around like a puppy. But they were so cute together. Lucy smiled a lot more back then. They returned a few days later. Went off on an adventure, they said."

"What happened to them after high school? We know Lucy went on tour competing. Did Ian go to college?" I ask.

"He gave up an academic scholarship to Duke to stay close to Lucy." She sighs. "We all tried to convince him that was a bad idea. Young love." She shrugs. "He attended a local college here."

"How'd that go?"

"Fine for the first year. Great in fact because Lucy was training here in Glenport. Then Lucy landed a fancy coach whose tennis academy was four hours away. Too far to commute."

"That must not have gone over well," I say, imagining how Ian might feel giving up a scholarship to a top college to stay with Lucy, only to be left behind.

"Poor Ian," she says. "But I thought they were working it out."

"Do you remember the name of the fancy coach?" Wade asks S.J.

"It was the one who now coaches his own daughter—" S.J. says, confirming what we already know.

"Brynn Cole?" I say. "You're talking about Coach Zane Cole?"

"Yes," S.J. replies, slapping her hand against the table like she just won at bingo.

"It's a tough situation. Ian wanted Lucy around. But Lucy had so many people relying on her—a lot of family pressure. She supported everyone. It fell on Lucy to pay the college tuition for Conrad, their other brother, and her cousins. And her father gambled."

"That's a lot of pressure for a young kid," I say, remembering how stressed I felt just playing at a professional level at Lucy's age, let alone having family members relying on me.

"When I spoke to you a few days ago, you asked me not to discuss Ian's car accident with Lucy," I say, glancing over at the courts, where the girls have started cleaning up balls.

"It had nothing to do with Lucy," S.J. says.

"But it had everything to do with you," Wade replies. "Didn't it?"

"If you're asking, you probably already know." S.J. looks down at her hands.

"We'd like to hear from you," Wade says. "We're trying to decide if it's worth putting into the story. It's probably not—we just want to make sure."

"Oh, it's not," S.J. replies. "Ian and Lucy had a huge fight the morning of the accident. Ian was beside himself, according to everyone at the bar." She explains. "You know the rest; he drove drunk and injured me."

"Why didn't you mention that when we talked?" I ask her, trying to keep my tone calm.

"Because it had nothing to do with Lucy. It was sad, though. Ian ended up serving time in prison. Never was the same after that." She shakes her head, eyes on the ground. "I forgave him. But I haven't had a pain-free day since."

"One more thing," I say as S.J. starts to stir. "What happened between Lucy and her high school friend Heather Liu? They seemed so happy in the yearbook photos."

"It was a conflict over boys." She shakes her head. "Isn't it always about romance?"

"Conrad?" I ask, remembering Lucy's brother dated Heather.

"Hmmm, no, I don't think so," S.J. says. "I don't really recall the details." She stands up, and we follow suit.

"S.J.," Wade calls as she steps away. "Does it strike you as odd that Lucy's mom and then you, a mother figure, both were victims of car accidents?"

S.J. freezes, staring at us. "I never even thought of that," she says and then heads back to the tennis courts.

We turn to go in the other direction, walking past the security guard on our way back to the car. I wave goodbye as Wade's phone rings. He picks up, his eyes darting around as he listens.

"What?" I mouth, aware something major is going on, but he avoids looking at me while listening to the call.

"You won't believe this," he says, hanging up.

"What?"

"Mae just got a call that the Glenport police discovered a dead body at the Lucy Bosco Tennis Academy."

I take a second to digest this information, not wanting to know the obvious. *Is it Lucy?*

"Who is it?" I say slowly.

"They don't know," Wade replies, then tells me the body was discovered in the dumpster and only a hand was visible. "They aren't even sure whether it's a man or a woman," he says, expression grim. We walk to the car, dread pooling in the pit of my stomach as I start to fear the worst.

CHAPTER 36

As soon as we reach the car, Wade redials Mae.

"Before you ask, the answer is we don't know if it's Lucy." Mae fills the silence explaining the call came in from a worker at the academy. "He saw a hand in the dumpster and phoned the local police. Luckily, he was smart enough not to touch anything."

Wade starts the car, and I whisper for him to turn right as we leave the school.

"The Nassau County police are on the scene, but we won't have anyone from our team there for at least half an hour. Kate, I wouldn't put you in this position, but Wade's our closest agent."

"That's all right," I reply, "We're already on our way."

Liam's voice comes on the line. "You must stay in the car Kate. Promise us."

"I promise," I reply.

"Wade, the Evidence Response Team is on standby. If the body is connected to our case," Mae says, not mentioning Lucy by name. "Let us know right away."

"Got it," he replies and then hangs up. I point for him to turn, and we drive past abandoned storefronts and modest homes.

"Slow down here." I motion to the industrial park. He turns, passing the stone and granite yard and storage facility. The tennis academy is dead ahead—the simple concrete structure with a giant domed roof.

The action is to the right by a dumpster, where local police officers cordon off the area with tape as Nassau County Crime Scene Unit technicians pull on white coveralls and booties. One carries an evidence-collection kit as they make their way to the dumpster. Wade gets out and promises to update me as soon as he can. My eyes wander to the front of the building, and I notice a deflated blue balloon stuck amid the branches of a tree. A remnant of the grand balloon arch from the ribbon-cutting ceremony at the academy just two days ago. I look to where the dais was set up and remember Lucy's interaction with her former friend, Heather, the mayor of Glenport. We still haven't figured out what happened between them. My eyes return to Wade, who now stands with a few officers. He glances in my direction, and a text appears—No info. Face covered with debris.

I thank him for keeping me posted as a few raindrops splash against the windshield. Just what the police need. Officers rush to a vehicle and pull a tent from the trunk, carry it to the dumpster, and set it above the crime scene. The tent reminds me of the kind of canopy my mom and stepfather set up for tailgates at my college games.

There's a rumble of thunder. The rain picks up, pounding against the windshield and echoing through the car. I turn on the wipers to see better. Wade and the other officers step under the tent to protect themselves.

A technician places a ladder against the side of the dumpster and climbs up so she can peer inside. She carefully removes item by item, placing them in evidence bags, held open by an investigator below her.

From the car, I see someone with a camera trade places with the technician on the ladder. The person takes a bunch of shots and then steps down onto the ground and shows Wade the images. At this moment he knows if it's Lucy's body in the dumpster. Blood rushes through my veins, and I fight the urge to run out of the car. But a promise is a promise. I can wait another minute.

Wade takes out his phone, and I expect mine to ring. Nothing. I check the bars—five. He's talking into the device, body hunched. If it wasn't Lucy, wouldn't he send a quick text? Put me out of my misery? The rain picks up, battering against the car.

Wade pulls his jacket over his head and runs in my direction. As he opens the door, rain leaks into the car. Shutting the door, he turns to me, his expression giving nothing away.

"It's not Lucy," he says.

I feel my shoulders relax. Then notice Wade looks deeply troubled.

"What is it?" I say, watching him.

"It's Nico. Nico Pappas is dead."

CHAPTER 37

“The body in the dumpster is Nico?” I say, even though I know I correctly heard Wade.

“Yes.” Wade rubs his temples. “It looks like blunt force trauma. There’s a huge gash on the back of his head.”

On the one hand, as awful as it sounds, I’m relieved they didn’t find Lucy in the dumpster. But that doesn’t mean I wanted Nico dead. Or anyone, for that matter.

“I thought agents were watching Nico?” I look at Wade, the rain trailing down the glass window behind him.

“Agents found a fire ladder in the back of the Oyster Bay rental. Nico must have climbed out. We’re not sure how he got to Glenport—he might have hitched.”

“Nico Pappas hitching a ride.” I shake my head. “Why’d he come here at all? Do you still think he kidnapped Lucy? Maybe he was working with someone?”

“Discovering why Nico came back to Glenport is priority number one,” Wade replies.

Mae calls, and Wade hits the speaker button. “Brace yourselves,” she says, forgoing any greetings. “Thanks to Kate, we’ve been able to monitor the burner phone Nico used to communicate with Alexis. He used that same device three hours ago to phone someone else,” she says. “You’ll never believe who he called.” Mae raises her voice against the wail of sirens screaming toward us. "Nico called Conrad."

"Lucy's brother," I say, thinking about how much venom existed between these two men.

"Not only that," Mae says. "But Conrad's phone registered from a cell tower in Glenport."

"Conrad's in the area too?" I say, feeling a chill up my spine. I think back to Conrad attacking Nico, grabbing his brother-in-law by the shirt collar.

"It's six p.m.," Mae says. "We have three hours to find Lucy before the ransom deadline. I'd like you to swing by Conrad and Lucy's childhood home. Maybe Conrad's there. Wade, you can stay undercover, say you have some follow up questions for Conrad. But Kate—"

"I know, I know. Stay in the car."

"If Conrad's the kidnapper, and the murderer, he's very dangerous. We have agents heading in your direction, but they're a half hour away. If we weren't up against a deadline, I'd wait for Conrad to be apprehended by the local police and send an agent to interrogate him at the Nassau County police station. But—"

"The deadline," I finish her sentence. "I promise I won't go into their house," I say. Again.

We hang up, and Wade puts the windshield wipers on full blast as we drive out of the industrial park. My mind goes to Nico as I digest the fact that he's dead. Murdered. His death must connect to Lucy's kidnapping, but how? And why did he call Conrad just before he died? Did he suspect that Brynn had involved the authorities, so he reached out directly to Conrad? Did Conrad murder Nico?

Wade turns into the Boscos' neighborhood and drives by the tennis courts where I interviewed Lucy earlier this week. The interview comes back to me, and I remember how hard Lucy's early years were in the United States. How she told me the first words she learned in English were *Terrible. Lazy. Again.* The words her first coach constantly shouted at the seven-year-old Lucy, who'd traveled without her parents to a foreign country.

Wade turns onto the Boscos' block, and I recognize the ranch-style homes with large shingles on small plots of land.

"That's Conrad's car," I say, pointing to the Mercedes in front of the ranch with the peeling paint and weeds sprouting from the gutter. Water pools on the patchy grass in the front yard.

As Wade parks the car, Mae calls again. "CSI found Lucy's phone in the dumpster," she says, giving us a second to digest that information. Either Nico had Lucy's phone, tying him to the kidnapping. Or whoever murdered Nico had the phone, which meant Nico got too close to discovering the identity of the kidnapper.

"It's completely smashed." Her voice sounds agitated. "Like someone took a hammer to it."

Wade looks at me. We're both thinking the same thing—did the object that smashed the phone also kill Nico?

"The Nassau County police are five minutes away from you," Mae says. "Wade, you need to hurry."

Wade turns the engine off. "Going in now," he says, opening the car door as the rain stops.

"All right," Mae replies. "But if you feel you need back up, leave. I trust your judgment." She clicks off as Wade steps out and walks past the broken railing of the Bosco house to ring the bell. I watch Victor Bosco open the door and invite Wade inside.

I step out of the car to stretch my legs. My eyes pan from the Bosco home to the one next to it, where I spot the curtains in the front window move. The door swings open, and I see Estelle, the Boscos' elderly neighbor, peek her head out. She waves and marches down her front path toward me. She wears the same apron as last time, a little speck of flour on her cheek.

"Have you been baking again?" I ask, glancing at the Bosco house behind her. I don't want to alarm Estelle, but I also think she should go inside her house and lock her door.

"Yes," she says. "My grandson is coming over after baseball and requested chocolate chip cookies with sprinkles."

"I don't know if that sounds good. Or—"

"Gross?" She nods. "You here because of Conrad?" she asks, and my radar goes up.

"Why do you ask?" I turn to her, wondering if she's just a nosy neighbor or has some real intel.

"I live next door. It's hard not to know things. Conrad's a good kid. But that husband of Lucy's—the one with the long hair. He puts it in a bun."

"Nico Pappas," I answer.

Her phone buzzes, and she wipes her hands on her apron.

"Oh my," she says. "The cookies. I need to take them out of the oven. Come inside, dear, and I'll tell you something you won't believe about that good-for-nothing husband of Lucy's."

I know I promised Wade I'd remain by the car, but this woman can't be a threat, although the story of "Hansel and Gretel" does pop into my brain as I follow her. I shoot Wade a quick text telling him where I am.

The smell of fresh-baked cookies immediately hits my nose as I step into her hallway and walk to the kitchen. "Wow, it really smells good in here."

"Kate." A male voice calls my name, and I swing around, then freeze, as I stare into the haggard eyes of Conrad Bosco.

He must see fear on my face because he sits back down.

Estelle walks past me and places some cookies on the table. "Conrad's a good kid. When he saw you out the window, he asked me to get you. Give him a chance—hear him out."

"The police want to speak with you." I turn my eyes to Conrad, who keeps his distance, a towel hanging over his wet button-down shirt.

"I know. That's why I need to talk to you before they get here. They think I killed Nico."

Warning bells blow up in my brain. How does Conrad know that Nico is dead?

"My son is with the Nassau County Police," Estelle says, as if reading my mind. "He called and warned me to stay away from Conrad. But I trust Conrad. He wouldn't hurt a fly."

"Please." Conrad points to the chair across from him. "Hear me out."

I take the seat, reaching for my heart necklace to turn the device on.

"Nico called me a few hours ago," Conrad says. "He asked me to meet him at the academy. Nico told me he knew who kidnapped Lucy and he'd share the information with me if I wired $1 million to his account. I begged him to tell me over the phone, but he refused. He insisted we meet in person."

"Why didn't you call the authorities?" I ask, folding my arms across my chest.

"He told me not to." Conrad puts his hand over his head. "I just want my sister back," he chokes.

"What happened when you met with him?"

"When I got to the academy, his body was lying on the grass."

"He was dead?" I ask.

"He had to be. Nico's body was facing down, a gaping, bloody hole in the back of his head." If Conrad is lying, he's wily enough to suggest Nico's body was on the grass instead of in the dumpster, making us think someone else was also around to move the body.

"Why didn't you call the police when you found Nico's body?" I ask.

"I panicked," he says, glancing at Estelle. "I thought if I called the police, they'd think I killed Nico. Then they wouldn't keep looking for Lucy. I'm ready to pay the ransom." His voice rises in pitch. "I have the money together. But the police are going to arrest me for something I didn't do—"

As Conrad says these words, the front door bangs open, and footsteps charge toward us. Officers I don't recognize swarm Conrad, grab him, and jerk him to his feet.

"Please," Conrad whispers as they pull him past me. "Help Lucy."

I watch as Conrad is led away, wondering if any part of what he claimed could possibly be true. And if so, who is pulling the strings in this sinister web?

CHAPTER 38

Wade is waiting for me by the car, still playing the part of producer.

"An agent from our task force is heading to the station now to interrogate Conrad," he whispers to me.

"I'm not sure he did it," I say, then recount what Conrad shared with me.

"It seems like too big a coincidence that he went to meet Nico, and Nico just happened to be dead."

I nod; it is a crazy coincidence. "What if the kidnapper realized Nico knew his or her identity and figured out Nico planned to tell Conrad?"

"That certainly would be motive for murder."

My brain is spinning—Conrad could have just been trying to manipulate me, but if he wasn't, then someone else is holding Lucy. The patrol car with Conrad in the back seat pulls away, siren wailing through the air, the red and blue lights disappearing down the block.

"Since we're in Glenport anyway, let's swing by the Reese Pharmacy and see if we can get some information from Greggory," I suggest.

"I agree," Wade says, adding he wants to check in with Mae first, to make sure she's all right with the plan. He places a call and walks away from me. Leaning against the sedan, I wonder if they are discussing anything else. Anything about me? Why step away to run our idea by Mae? I look around the street as the sun, low in the evening sky, peeks out from the rain clouds. A teenager bounces a basketball in his driveway, taking shots at the hoop above his garage.

"We're on." Wade waves to me, getting in the car. I slide into the passenger seat, then pull on my seat belt.

"Why'd you step away to make the call?" I ask, staring at him.

"I didn't step away to speak to Mae," he says, sighing. "Today was my day with my kids—I had to call my ex and explain I probably wouldn't make it."

He turns the engine on and starts toward Main Street.

"That's hard," I say, understanding how he must feel. "How old are your kids?"

"I have two boys—one is seventeen and the other fifteen." Wade smiles as he tells me about them. His older son is a math whiz and into computer science, and his younger one is a talented baseball player. I watch how animated Wade gets as he talks about his children. "We're very close." He turns to me. "My ex just refuses to give me any slack with my schedule."

"What happened with your marriage?" I ask, immediately realizing I probably overstepped. "Sorry for prying—"

"No worries," he says. "What broke up my marriage is that she cheated."

"That's what broke up mine too," I reply, staring straight ahead. Wade turns onto Main Street, passing the nail salon and barber.

"This is the south part of the street," I say. "Didn't you say there were only traffic cameras on the north side?"

"I did," Wade says, both of us thinking that if Greggory happened to be involved, he might know that piece of information.

Wade parks in the lot where I parked only a couple of days ago. The lot where I overheard Greggory and Lucy arguing.

Ian's accident was your fault, Greggory said. *He gave up everything for you—*

We step out of the car and into the pharmacy; the jingle of the bell sounds discordant instead of quaint.

The familiar scent of talc powder now smells off, mixed with dust I didn't notice during my first visit. We pass the fudge and sweets, walking to the back of the store, where I recognize the young clerk from last time.

"Can I help you?" She gives a weary smile, her teeth crooked.

"We're looking for Greggory," I say, wondering if she's going to ask us why, but she seems indifferent and bored.

"He went to the Mac-n-Cheesy to grab dinner," she says, lifting her finger to point, the effort seeming to take a lot out of her.

We step onto the sidewalk and cross to the restaurant. The chandeliers cast a yellow glow inside. All the tables appear full, much busier today than when I was here with Lucy for lunch. I scan the place, looking for Greggory, and spot him at the bar. And, lucky us, there are two empty stools beside him.

CHAPTER 39

We sit down at the bar, with me taking the seat next to Greggory. He smells like his pharmacy, of talc and must. He's much bigger than I realized, tall and wide, with strong arms.

"Hello," I say to Greggory, who's wearing faded jeans and a black T-shirt.

He shifts to look at me. Up close, I see a once handsome face, now crisscrossed with deep lines and heavy rings around his eyes. I imagine his blue eyes formerly turned a few heads, but now they appear pained and tired.

"What do you want?" he says, and I wonder if he remembers me from visiting the pharmacy.

"I stopped by your store a few days ago—with Lucy Bosco."

His body stiffens at her name; anger clouds his face. The bartender places a hamburger and fries in front of Greggory.

"I imagine you're one of the few people opting for something other than mac and cheese?" I say, trying to get a little small talk going with the hope he'll open up.

"Any friend of Lucy is not a friend of mine," he replies, picking up his burger and then taking a bite.

"Greggory," the bartender says. "Civility." Greggory glares at the bartender, who shrugs at us in an *I tried* kind of way. "What would you folks like to drink?"

I would love a glass of wine but opt for club soda. Wade orders the same, picking up the menu and studying it. "What do you think about sharing two dishes?" he asks, trying to appear normal, but I can tell from his tight expression, he's worried too.

"I like that," I reply, suggesting the sausage mac and cheese for one.

"Good choice." He nods. "I feel like we should get a little bit of greens—" he replies, and I hope he's not about to suggest we split a salad.

"How about a broccoli-three-cheese mac and cheese?"

"Very practical." I smile, hoping the kitchen leans into the *three-cheese* part of the order, needing any comfort food I can get in anticipation of the stressful hours in front of us. Greggory chews loudly, the crunching of fries overtaking the clinking of glasses. He stands and walks toward the restrooms. Without a word, Wade follows him.

The bartender returns, and I give him our order. "What's up with that guy, anyway?" I ask, motioning to the empty seat next to me.

"Awww, Greggory's not a bad guy. Just has a lot of people relying on him. He used to wash dishes for me decades ago. This place was like a second home to him and his brother. Sweet guy, that Ian."

I'm about to ask the bartender about Ian when a customer sits down at the front of the bar and signals for his attention.

As I sip my drink, I reach my hand into the pocket of Greggory's jacket and feel around. All I can make out is a pack of cigarettes.

Greggory stalks back to his seat. I pull my hand back just as he grabs his jacket, throws money down on the table, and storms off.

Wade follows at a distance.

"What happened?" I ask, watching Greggory leave.

"I asked him about Lucy." Wade slides back onto the stool. "I introduced myself, explained you and I are working on a story about her. Then I asked him about his brother. Greggory pushed me against the wall and told me to stay away from Ian. That guy has a bad temper," Wade says, adding that he called headquarters to report the interaction.

"Could he just be overprotective?" I ask.

"Maybe. But he definitely strikes me as the kind of guy that could just snap."

"Here you go." The bartender places two steaming plates in front of us.

"Thanks," I say. "I'm excited to try something different. I was here a few days ago with Lucy Bosco—" I watch for his reaction.

"Lucy, what a great girl," he says and tells us how she used to work here too.

"Lucy mentioned she dated Greggory's brother—" I say.

"Ian." The bartender's eyes gloss over. "I thought they'd get married." He gives a sad smile. "I know they were young, but they seemed to really support each other. They were gaga over one another. But after Ian had that accident, well, it just, everything ended."

"What happened to Greggory?" Wade adds, "I heard he was very studious back in the day."

"Greggory wanted to be a doctor. You wouldn't believe it, but he was a real carefree guy back then. But once Ian had the accident, Greggory used his college money to hire an attorney, and you know, a couple of years pass, and everyone sort of just got stuck."

"Where's Ian these days?" I ask.

"It's so sad—he struggles with substance abuse. He came in here just a few hours ago drunk, trying to get another drink."

"Is he here?" I ask, looking around.

"Nah, I had one of our staff drive him home to his parents. He'll probably be back in rehab before the end of the week."

We thank the bartender and quickly finish up our meal, knowing our next destination. Wade calls Mae to get the address for the Reese parents as I step outside.

Across the street, I spot Greggory, smoking a cigarette and pacing outside the store. He spots me, holding my gaze a second too long. He drops the cigarette on the ground and grinds the object with his foot, eyes still on me. A chill runs up my spine as he glares, and I can't help but feel that he wishes it were me under his toe instead of the discarded cigarette butt.

CHAPTER 40

The dark clouds return as dusk falls over Glenport. We get back into the car. Wade turns on the engine and dials Mae. "You both there?" she asks, sounding exhausted.

"We are," I reply as Wade pulls onto Main Street, heading toward Ian's parents' home. "What have you learned from Conrad?"

"Conrad's sticking to the story he told Kate." Mae sighs. "He claims Nico called, told him he knew the identity of the kidnapper, and demanded $1 million for the information," she reports as we hear Liam's voice in the background, barking at someone; the tension everywhere rising as the deadline for the ransom looms closer.

Wade turns down a noisy street, where a net is in the road, kids with hockey sticks taking shots. He inches slowly past the action and turns onto another street.

"Liam and I are on our way to Glenport. We're over an hour away. Your job is only to gather information—don't do anything reckless."

"Got it," Wade says and clicks off.

Wade parks in front of a neat yellow house with flowers in the garden.

Across the street, I hear pop music and see a few kids playing jump rope.

We ring the bell, and a painfully thin man, with the eyes I recognize from the prom photo, opens the door. Ian Reese has aged, with sallow skin and busted blood vessels across his nose and cheeks.

"Ian," I say, extending my hand. "I'm Kate Green, and this is Wade Flanders, my producer—we're doing a story on Lucy Bosco and—"

"Lucy." His eyes flicker for a second before going dim.

"We were hoping to talk to you for a minute," Wade says as rain starts again. Behind us, the kids jumping rope run for shelter inside one of the homes. "Can we come inside for a minute?"

Ian opens the door to let us in, and we walk into a small living room with a worn love seat and a frayed chair. Ian sits in the chair, grabbing a bottle of vodka off the table and then putting it on the floor next to him in a poor attempt to hide it.

"Anyone else home?" I ask, sitting on the love seat.

"My mom went grocery shopping, and Dad's resting." He motions to the stairs.

I start by telling Ian that our station's been working on a feature about Lucy. "But she dropped out of the tournament, and we can't reach her." I leave that thought in the air, hoping he'll say something.

"Doesn't sound like her," he says. "She's not a quitter. Well, not about most things—" His eyes grow dark.

"What do you mean?" Wade asks, keeping his tone soft.

"She quit on me." His face twists, and I see flashes of a bitter man.

"When you were together? After high school?" I probe. "Is that what you mean?"

Ian scratches his nose as he looks from me to Wade. "Is this for your story?"

"Doesn't have to be," I reply. "Just trying to understand Lucy's path."

"*Her path*," he scoffs. "Took her from Glenport to a fancy tennis academy in New Jersey, where her coach gave her an ultimatum of him or me. She chose him, and that ended me."

We knew from S.J. that there was trouble between Ian and Lucy but not that she dumped him. I wonder if Lucy did end her relationship with Ian or if Ian just saw the inevitability.

"Lucy broke up with you after she started with Coach Zane Cole?" I ask.

"Not in so many words." He reaches for the bottle of vodka and pours some in a mug. "But she never had time for me—she might as well have ended it. Put me out of my misery. Then we had one humdinger of a fight—" He lifts the mug to his mouth and downs the whole drink.

"Was that the day of your car accident?" I ask.

He blanches, narrowing his eyes to study me.

"I don't like to talk about that," he replies, pouring some more alcohol into the cup.

"Do you blame Lucy for the accident?" Wade asks, keeping his voice even.

"Fucking reporters." He shifts in his chair. "I don't blame Lucy for that. Don't you dare say that in your story. I'm the one who got plastered. The accident was my fault." He shakes his head. "And Heather's."

Wade and I exchange a glance. Heather's name was the last thing we expected to hear at this moment.

"Do you mean Heather Liu? Lucy's high school friend?" I ask.

Ian nods and gulps down another round of vodka, seeming more comfortable with the idea of speaking about Heather versus Lucy.

"How was Heather involved in your accident?" Wade asks.

"The night of my accident, Heather was supposed to drive me home from the bar. I was—drunk." He starts picking at his fingers. "You already know that."

"Why didn't Heather drive you?"

"We had a misunderstanding." He looks down at his feet. "She thought something was gonna happen. I mean, I was drunk, but I wasn't about to cheat—"

Outside, I hear a car pull into the driveway and an engine turn off. That must be Ian's mother, and she may not be happy about Wade and me talking to her son.

The front door opens, and a woman's voice calls out, "What's going on in here?" She storms into the living room, glaring at Wade and me.

"They're reporters, Mom, want to talk about Lucy—"

"Are you out of your mind?" Ian's mom yells, her voice high pitched and angry. "Get the hell out of my house. Taking advantage of my son. Lucy Bosco betrayed our family," she hisses. "May she rot in hell."

The mom places her hands on her hips, staring at us. Wade and I scurry from the house. Before we're even a step off the stoop, the door slams. Wade and I exchange a look, and I can tell he's thinking the same thing—every member of the Reese family either hates or resents Lucy.

CHAPTER 41

Wade unlocks the car doors and calls Mae as I slip into the passenger seat.

"We heard everything through Kate's microphone," Mae says as Wade turns on the engine. "Liam and I are forty-five minutes away."

"More bad news." Liam's raspy voice comes through the speaker. "The kidnapper just texted and moved the deadline up."

"How much time does Lucy have?" I ask, checking the clock on the dashboard, which shows 7:00 p.m.

"Half an hour," Mae says. The exact message reads Be ready to deliver two million dollars at 7:30PM or I will blow Lucy's head off.

"That's an escalation in violence," I say, feeling my stomach twist. Are Wade and I the reason for the truncated deadline and perilous threat?

"We're pushing back," Liam adds over the sound of traffic coming through their phone. "*Brynn* texted that her family needs the extra time to secure the funds. But the kidnapper hasn't responded to that, and it's been"—he pauses—"eight minutes."

"Kidnappers tend to change direction or increase demands when they get nervous," Mae says. "The person must be nervous they'll be discovered. I think we're close."

There's silence as we process the new reality. We're all aware of the stakes. We might be closing in, but Lucy's chances of surviving just diminished exponentially.

"Even though Conrad remains in custody, he's ready to wire the ransom. But if it's paid—" Mae lets the words hang in the air. Paying is no guarantee the kidnapper will actually release Lucy alive. Especially if Lucy's seen his or her face.

"Our best bet is to find Lucy first. Conrad won't wire the money without proof of life. So, we know Lucy will be alive for the next half hour," Liam adds.

The next twenty-nine minutes, I think, watching the time change on the car's dashboard.

"We have a fresh lead," Mae says, and I hear honking through their phone. "The kidnapper got sloppy. The new ransom text pinged off a cell tower in Glenport. The kidnapper is there. And hopefully, so is Lucy."

Wade and I exchange a look.

"You won't make it to Glenport in time," I say to Mae and Liam, stating the obvious.

"We won't, but SWAT is ten minutes out. It's seeming more and more likely someone in the Reese family could be responsible. The task force is pulling up schematics of the homes and businesses owned by Greggory and his parents to compare with the photos the kidnapper sent of Lucy. Maybe we'll get lucky."

"Why don't you go to both houses and the pharmacy?" I say, thinking Lucy must be in one of the three Reese properties. My eyes move to the parents' house in front of us. Could Lucy be inside?

"The judge won't grant us a warrant for all three," Mae grumbles.

"And if we raid the wrong home, the kidnapper might panic and shoot Lucy," Liam adds.

"We need to do something." I look at Wade, who shakes his head and mouths that we can't.

"Hang tight," Liam says. "And don't approach anyone. SWAT is on its way. As soon as we narrow it down, they will be ready to move. We'll figure this out," he says, with forced optimism, before hanging up.

"We can't just sit here," I say, staring at the Reese home. My eyes move from the yellow clapboard down to the foundation. Concrete sticks out at the bottom, covered by squared hedges. Wade watches me. He knows what I'm wondering—is Lucy inside? Just twenty feet from us.

"If Lucy was here, I don't think Ian could keep it secret," Wade says. "He's too off-balance."

"I tend to agree with you there," I reply, although I can't take my eyes off the hints of the cellar. I roll my window down, point my camera at the hedges, zoom in, and snap a photo.

"Look." I hold the picture out for Wade. "There's a small window with bars behind the hedges," my mind going to the light source in the very first photo sent to Brynn. Light was shining from outside the image. Of course, it could have been a lamp or an overhead fixture.

"Greggory seems the most off-kilter to me," Wade says. "Although the mom is a close second. Why don't we head to Main Street and keep a distant eye on the pharmacy?"

I glance one more time at the house and then tell Wade I agree we should drive back into town. My mind returning to the angry image of Greggory standing outside his pharmacy, glaring in my direction.

Main Street is bustling, which surprises me. I imagined a cold, abandoned, haunted kind of feel for the place where Lucy might be held prisoner. The lights in the pharmacy shine through the small windows. An elderly woman walks inside, leaning on a cane.

I get out of the car and start across the street.

"What are you doing?" Wade quickly walks alongside me.

"We can't just wait." I look at my phone. "We have thirteen minutes."

A car passes in front of us. We let it go and then cross to the other side of the street. "Kate." Wade places his hand on my arm as we reach the sidewalk. "One second." His voice is strong. "I'm not saying no. What are you thinking?"

I peer inside the window of the pharmacy and see the young clerk handing the elderly woman a bag.

"Let's try speaking to the clerk again. We didn't ask her any questions. Maybe she saw something unusual without even realizing it." I raise a brow toward Wade.

He takes a deep breath but doesn't answer as the door to the pharmacy opens and the older woman steps out.

"Please?" I mouth and turn to the door, holding it for the woman and then stepping inside. Wade right behind me.

Wade motions to my necklace, and I turn it on.

"You still looking for Greggory?" the clerk says, snapping her gum. "He's in the cellar, getting some supplies."

Wade and I exchange a glance at the word *cellar*.

"You have so many different items in the store—is the cellar where you keep your inventory?" I ask, trying to sound as earnest as possible.

"Obviously." She rolls her eyes, as if I just asked her if the sky is blue.

"Bet you get stuck lugging all the boxes upstairs?" Wade laughs.

"Used to fall on me," she says. "But the last few days Greggory has been unusually helpful doing all the work. In fact, this morning I forgot he told me he'd take care of the inventory, and he nearly bit my head off when I tried to get some stuff."

We hear a door slam and turn. Greggory stands on the other side of the aisle. "You couldn't keep your mouth shut," he shouts at the clerk. Wade takes a step forward to wind his way around. But Greggory's too quick, shoving his body against the shelving.

The sound of metal falling pierces the air, and I see Wade dart in my direction as the shelves wobble, then fall. Wade grabs me, placing his body over mine as we're pelted with shelving, boxes, and cans. The smell of detergent and alcohol overtakes my senses, mixed with screams from the clerk.

"Get up," Greggory orders the clerk as more metal falls around us. I try to move toward the clerk, but Wade holds me back.

"Wait," he whispers. "Greggory has a knife. Slowly—" Wade releases his hold, and I push myself to all fours, wiping a sticky minty-smelling substance from my face.

"Stay down," Greggory demands, and I feel a foot kick my gut. My muscles spasm as I double over, a fiery pain running through my insides as my face hits the cold floor. More screams reach me through the fog, and I try to get my brain to focus.

"You don't have to do this." Wade's words float into my ears. I turn my head and blink my eyes open, seeing Greggory pushing the knife against the clerk's neck.

She starts to scream, but he presses the weapon closer, blood dripping at her throat. "You," Greggory says to me. "Couldn't leave it alone. Fucking reporters."

"You don't need to hurt anyone," Wade says again, voice calm. "Let her go."

"Shut the fuck up," Greggory howls. "Shut up. Let me think." He pulls the clerk with him, deeper into the store. "Reporter," he yells at me. "Grab those zip ties." He motions to the back of the store, where the shelves remain intact.

I force myself to my feet, wiping a slimy substance off my hands as I plow through the debris on the ground.

I take the long zip ties down from the shelf, my eyes on the clerk, who's trembling with fear.

"On the ground, man," Greggory says to Wade, who slides onto the floor. "First, constrain him," Greggory orders me, and I place the zip ties around Wade's wrists and legs.

Greggory walks behind me, pushing his knee into my back. "Tighter," he shrieks. "You think I'm an idiot?"

Wade nods to me, indicating I do as I'm told. We both know that SWAT is outside and ready to enter. But if we don't calm Greggory down, the clerk won't survive. The knife sits too tight on her throat.

"Now her," he says, moving the knife from the clerk's neck to mine, the blade pushing against my skin. He puts his arm around my shoulders, bending with me so I can secure the ties around the clerk. His breath is thick and heavy. "See what you made me do?" He hisses into my ear. "You had to get in the fucking way."

The blade feels cold against my skin, and I'm aware of the pressure increasing as I take shallow breaths.

A loud crash pierces the air. It sounds like it comes from downstairs. Lucy? Greggory loosens his grip for a split second—enough time for me to elbow him and slip away.

"Get down," a voice thuds from the front entrance as fog fills the pharmacy and feet thunder inside. I drop down, arms reaching around the clerk, pulling our heads together. Through the vapor I can't tell how close Greggory stands. Feet crash by. Hands reach for my arms. "You're okay, let's go. Let's go."

Coughing, I let myself be led away from the noise and onto the sidewalk. Two SWAT members usher Wade, the clerk, and me to the ambulance.

"I'm fine." I motion them away. "She needs help." I point to the clerk, who's pressing her hand to the spot on her neck where the knife cut her.

Wade retrieves a handheld police radio and turns up the volume as we sit in the back of the ambulance.

He's gone downstairs, comes through in static.

The door's locked.

Break it down.

Loud movements echo through the radio, footsteps on stairs. Crashing of objects.

"Don't get any closer," Greggory's voice calls. "Or I'll kill her."

"You don't want to hurt anyone," a woman says.

"You're wrong," Greggory shoots back. "I want to hurt her. She ruined my family—"

Through a different channel we hear an agent confirm he has eyes on the target. And then someone gives the order to take the shot.

An object falls; feet scurry.

We've got her. She's alive, a voice crackles through the speaker.

I turn to Wade, tears pouring from my eyes. "I was so worried." I choke on the words.

He puts his hand over mine. "I know. She's okay."

But is she? Over the radio, we hear the EMTs talking. "We're losing her," someone says as Wade turns the radio off.

"Maybe we didn't find her in time." I gasp, all the tension from the last few days bubbling back up.

Wade puts his hand on my back. "Don't jump to conclusions."

More ambulances arrive, and medics rush in with multiple stretchers.

"Here she is." Wade nudges me as EMTs wheel her out of the pharmacy, followed by a second stretcher with Greggory.

I twist to see Lucy, who is covered in a blue blanket, her face purple with bruises, one eye swollen shut. I try to reach her, but the police keep me away. An EMT makes eye contact with Wade and shrugs as Lucy's lifted into an ambulance and quickly hooked up to equipment. She's clearly not out of the woods. My heart sinks at the realization she might not pull through after all.

CHAPTER 42

It seems like everyone in Glenport is in the street, pushing against the police tape around the pharmacy. Even the rain does nothing to discourage people from remaining on the street. Whispers and speculation reach us where we remain sitting in the back of the ambulance.

"I always knew something was off with Greggory."

"And his older brother, too—spent time in prison."

The young clerk slides off the edge of the truck, her hand covering a bandage around her neck.

"Are you all right?" I ask her as the EMT moves from bandaging her to checking me.

She nods. "Thank you for protecting me," she says. "Was someone locked in the cellar?" she asks, eyes filling with worry.

"Don't blame yourself," Wade says. "You couldn't have known."

Sirens sound in the night sky, louder and louder, whining as more vehicles pull onto the street.

"I should have picked up on it. I told you Greggory offered to get all the boxes from the basement these last few days. He was acting so strange. He had a fight with a customer this afternoon," she says.

"Do you remember anything about that person?" I ask.

"It was a man," she replies, her hand still pressing against the bandage on her neck. "As soon as he showed up, Greggory told me to grab him a cup of coffee from across the street."

"Do you remember what the man looked like?" Wade asks, keeping his voice even. We both stare into her face, waiting as she squints into the night.

"Umm, it was a guy," she says, even though she already told us that.

"Did you notice anything about his height or clothes or hair?" I ask.

"His hair!" she yells. "It was long and pulled back in a ponytail."

That must have been Nico.

"Did Greggory go anywhere after the guy with the ponytail left?" Wade asks.

"Yes! Greggory left for about an hour to do an errand shortly after." She looks at us, eyes wide.

Wade says the police will want to talk to her.

"They already told me," she says. "Thanks again." She takes my hand in hers and squeezes it, then walks away.

I spot Liam rushing down the street toward me. Mae behind him. "Are you okay?" Liam asks, giving me a full hug.

I nod.

"Are you injured?" He pulls me away and stares into my eyes, a mix of anger and fear in his gaze.

"Just a bit sore." I point to my stomach. "And dirty." I motion to the detergent and moisturizers that have soaked through my clothing and now transferred to Liam's shirt. "How's Lucy?"

"I want you and Wade to go to the hospital and get checked out," Liam says, ignoring my question. "That's nonnegotiable."

We agree, even though both of us have been looked over by the EMTs. "But how is Lucy?"

"She's alive," Mae says, voice solemn. "That's all we know."

CHAPTER 43

In the car, all my worries resurface. The recent report from the hospital was that Lucy suffered a skull fracture and was heading into surgery in an effort to avoid brain damage. Her shoulder was also dislocated. And the bones in her right hand shattered—her dominant hand. And to imagine Greggory once wanted to be a doctor? I feel sick thinking about it.

I have so many questions about Greggory and Nico, but all my mind can focus on is Lucy and hoping she'll survive. Wade parks in the visitor lot of the hospital, and we rush inside and find the agents in the waiting room.

"What's the latest?" Wade asks them.

"She's still in surgery," the older one tells us. "Greggory didn't make it. Dead on arrival."

"You two need to get checked out," the other agent says, handing us clean sweatshirts and sweatpants and leading us over to the hospital staff.

It doesn't take long for the doctor to diagnose me with a bruised rib and for a nurse to clean up a large cut on my hand. Wade needs a few stitches on his arm.

Once we're cleared, Wade heads to the cafeteria to get us coffee as I stare at the nursing station, where the staff are joking around. For them, it's just another day at the office, while here, just yards away, we wait for life-or-death news.

My phone beeps with a text from the TRP producer—Leah Fulton.

Lucy Bosco was kidnapped. Get to hospital!!

That's ironic, I think, putting my phone down without answering. Wade returns with the coffee, and I take a sip, even though it looks like sludge. Across from us, a woman is sniffling, a younger man trying to console her.

My phone rings. Charlie. I know better than to ignore him; he'll keep calling until I answer. "Hello," I say, bracing myself against an expected order.

"Are you okay?" he says, his tone surprisingly calm.

"I thought you'd be yelling at me about the Lucy story," I respond as the doors to the hallway open and a doctor walks over to the woman and young man.

"One of the photos on the internet showed you by an ambulance," Charlie says, and I hear televisions blasting in the background. "Are you heading to the hospital?"

"I'm already here." I hear my voice tremble. "She might not make it."

Someone interrupts Charlie with an *urgent* question, and he asks me to hold. I hope he knows I'm here out of concern and not to do a report.

"Kate"—he returns to the line—"don't worry about the story. Make sure Lucy's all right. We'll report what's on the wire service for now. And if Lucy decides to go public with the details at some point in the future, it's yours. Obviously."

I feel an overwhelming surge of gratitude for Charlie. "I don't know what to say—"

"Say you always knew I was a good guy, even though I kept it hidden," he replies, then hangs up before I can get another word in.

I feel someone gently shake my arm. I blink myself awake, my head resting on Wade's shoulder.

"Lucy's out of surgery," Wade says, his voice soft.

"Is she okay?" I look up at him.

"She survived the operation." He gives a tired smile. "That's something."

I nod, still full of worry.

Wade then tells me Lucy won't be able to have visitors for a while and suggests we get some rest. But I don't want to leave. He doesn't seem surprised when I tell him I prefer to stay. He stands up, stretches, and offers to get us breakfast.

Wade returns with large coffees, two muffins in plastic wrap, and Conrad, who looks like he hasn't showered in days—shirt wrinkled, hair disheveled, stubble uneven around his chin.

"I came straight from the police station," he says by way of explanation, sitting across from me as Wade hands me the coffee and muffin.

Before I can focus on Conrad, I need a caffeine boost and down the whole cup despite the taste. The muffin is a step up from the coffee and a welcome injection of sugar. Next to me, Wade finishes his coffee, too, but leaves the muffin untouched.

One of the morning shows plays on the screen mounted to the wall—bright, happy people cooking tacos in a studio kitchen. The waiting room is more full than last night; anxious faces mimic what I imagine mine looks like.

"When did you get here?" I ask Conrad, who taps his foot against the floor in quick, nervous beats.

"A few minutes ago." He looks at me. "I still haven't spoken to the doctor. I tried calling a bunch of times, but no one was available." How different he seems from the bossy publicist of just a few days ago. Or even from that afternoon in Estelle's kitchen before the police rushed in and arrested him. A broken man now, full of anguish and worry.

"It doesn't seem real, does it?" he says, and I nod. "I feel like it's my fault—" he continues, choking on his words. "I was the one who suggested going to the Reese Pharmacy. If only—" Conrad's voice trails off as he wipes a tear from his eye. "It had to have been us. Our sudden appearance must have triggered Greggory." He covers his head with his hands, body heaving. I think back again to Lucy's fight in the parking lot with Greggory. And Nico listening behind me. I wonder how Nico figured out that Greggory was the one who kidnapped Lucy.

Heavy footsteps take my attention away from Conrad, and I see a doctor rushing with a team of residents through the hallway and disappearing. Another doctor walks toward us, looking around and spotting Wade, who she must have spoken to while I was asleep. We stand as she approaches our group and introduces herself.

"This is Lucy's brother, Conrad," Wade tells her.

"Your sister has woken up," the doctor says, giving him an encouraging nod. "She has a long road ahead of her, but she's doing about as well as we could hope."

Tears of relief sprout from my eyes, and without thinking, I hug Wade, who hugs me back. Behind us, the doctor continues to talk to Conrad about Lucy's prognosis, but all I needed was to know she's awake and doing well.

The doctor takes Conrad back to see his sister, and I call Liam, who's finishing up paperwork, to relay the good news.

Conrad returns, his features softened with relief. "She's really banged up—but she's Lucy. She's going to be fine." He gives a soft smile. "She asked to see you," he says to me.

I walk down the corridor toward another reception desk, for the neuro ICU, where the lights are dim and the chatter almost nonexistent.

"I'm here to see Lucy Bosco," I say quietly to the nurse.

"She needs rest, but you can go in for a few minutes," he says, pointing to a room behind the glass wall.

I step into the private room, hearing the beeping of monitors and the whoosh of the blood pressure cuff. Lucy's eyes are closed, and I pull up a seat next to the bed. Her head is wrapped in bandages, stopping halfway down her forehead, where purple bruises are starting to yellow.

"Kate?" Her voice is hoarse and barely audible. I stand up and move closer to her so she can see me.

"You're going to be all right," I say.

"Nico," she whimpers, and I wonder if she knows he's gone.

As if reading my mind, she whispers the word *dead*.

"Nico," she says again, opening her eyes wider, and I realize she wants to tell me something about him. I lean down close to her mouth so I can hear her. I listen in shock as she whispers the troubling information.

The nurse comes in. "Excuse me." His voice causes me to jerk up. I'm not sure if I'm more surprised by his sudden appearance or the words Lucy whispered in my ear.

"Sorry to startle you. But Mrs. Bosco needs her rest," he says.

"I understand." I turn to Lucy for one more second. "Don't worry about anything. I'll let the police know."

She gives a hint of a smile and closes her eyes as I leave the room, still stunned by what she told me.

CHAPTER 44

Back in the waiting room, exhaustion rushes through my bones—I'm so tired my body aches. Wade offers to drive me home.

"I don't want to take you out of your way," I say, unable to stifle a yawn.

"You won't," he says. "I live in Stamford, Connecticut. You're on my way home."

Wade doesn't need to offer twice. My car remains in the US Open parking lot; Liam made sure security knew not to tow it.

I walk with Wade to the car, surprised to learn he is one town past mine. The sun shines along the horizon as the world around us starts waking up.

"What did Lucy say to you?" Wade asks.

"It's so awful," I reply, staring out the window. "From the cellar, Lucy heard Nico confront Greggory at the pharmacy," I say, recounting Lucy's words. "Nico told Greggory he figured out that Greggory kidnapped Lucy. He found Greggory's name badge on the driveway."

A motorcycle roars past as Wade changes lanes on the expressway. "Is that why Nico got murdered?" Wade says. "Because he tried to save Lucy?"

"That's the horrible part," I say, shaking my head. "Nico didn't try to save Lucy."

Wade glances at me before returning his eyes to the road. I take a deep breath, remembering the next part of Lucy's story. "Nico told Greggory he'd keep quiet as long as Greggory split the ransom."

I see Wade's hands clench the steering wheel; he's working hard to stay focused on driving. "What a disgusting human," he mumbles.

"Lucy heard Greggory refuse," I continue. "Then Nico threatened to expose Greggory. That's when Nico must have called Conrad; meanwhile, Greggory made sure Nico would never be able to talk again."

"You need to tell Mae and Liam," Wade says.

I dial Liam and recount the story as Wade drives over the bridge, the Manhattan skyline peeking through the morning haze.

Wade whispers to me to ask Liam about Oliver. I shiver, remembering the stalker who stared through my living room window in the middle of the night, pressing his face against the glass. "Is Oliver still locked up?" I ask Liam.

"Yes," he says, telling me agents discovered hundreds of photos Oliver took of women without their knowledge. "The judge ordered Oliver held without bail. Go home, get some rest. And—"

"Put on my alarm," I reply, laughing.

"Yup," he says.

I direct Wade through the town of Greenwich and to my block, which looks welcoming and safe. "Well, partner," I say, unbuckling my seat belt. "Thanks for the lift."

"You're welcome." He smiles back, turning off the engine and then stepping out of the car. "Mind if I walk you to the door and just check around?"

"Are you trying to make a good impression on my father?" I joke as he accompanies me along my brick pathway.

"Maybe." He shrugs as we enter my home, and I wonder what it looks like through his eyes. He goes upstairs first and then returns to the hallway.

"I love your place. It has so much character," he says as we head to the kitchen, where I find myself embarrassed by the mess on the counter.

"I'm glad you're not a neat freak," he says. "I'm a little messy myself."

"That's what made us such good partners on the case." I laugh, finding myself a little sad to be saying goodbye, having enjoyed spending time with him, despite the circumstances.

Even though he's done checking the house, he lingers in the kitchen, staring into my yard.

"Would you like a coffee or something?" I ask.

He glances down at the floor, appearing nervous. "Actually, I wanted to ask if you'd like to grab dinner one night?" He looks up at me, giving a little smile.

I feel my cheeks flush, nervous too.

"I'd like that very much," I reply.

"Great." He seems relieved. "It's a date," he says, and I walk him to the front, aware that a silly smile is plastered across my face.

CHAPTER 45

I wake up disoriented, no idea how long I was out. Checking my phone, I see it's 7:00 p.m. I pad downstairs in my sweats, switch on the television, and settle into my worn leather couch.

I click to the US Open, raising the volume as I watch Brynn stride onto the court. Clad in a blue-and-green tie-dyed tennis dress, she waves while pointing her phone at the crowd. The announcers discuss how she's roared onto the scene—a prodigy, much in the vein of Lucy Bosco.

"This is the biggest stage Brynn's ever played on," the female announcer says, referring to the Louis Armstrong Stadium, which holds just under fifteen thousand fans. "If she wins here, Brynn's next match will be at Arthur Ashe," she continues. "One of the most famous arenas in tennis."

The announcers change topics to discuss the shocking news of Lucy's kidnapping—I mute the volume, wanting to focus on Brynn's match against the aging Barbie-doll Jill Wallace. The mere fact that Brynn is even playing fills me with admiration for her.

Jill takes the first set in a tiebreaker. Brynn appears nervous, making unforced errors. The camera pans to Alexis, who sits rigid, her sunglasses covering her face. The shot widens to show Coach Zane, who remains uncharacteristically quiet. While Alexis and Zane are seated next to one another, their bodies tilt apart, as if the wind were blowing them in different directions.

Nikki calls, and I pick up to her enthusiastic voice, a balm to the last few days. "Mom," she gushes, "I can't wait for you to visit—I found the best pizza place ever," she says and tells me about a spot that's all pink called Pizza Girl. "It's the best! My new favorite."

"Better than Connecticut pizza?" I ask, laughing.

"Yes!" she says, moving on to tell me about her last few days and a new trip to go skiing at Lake Tahoe.

"I'm so happy you're happy," I tell her.

"Not just me—" she says. "Jackson's doing great. He's already in the new dorm with his friend. I told you he'd be fine."

"Yes, you did," I reply. "I'm lucky to have two wonderful kids."

She makes a gagging noise, but I can tell she appreciates my comment. We hang up, and I return my attention to the match, where Brynn leads the second set. I watch as she finds her rhythm and easily evens the score. Barbie-doll Jill appears frazzled as the two women get ready for the final set.

The camera pans again to the Cole family. Zane is animated, pumping his fist and yelling out words I can't hear. But Alexis remains still, her lips tight, her eyes hidden behind the sunglasses despite the fact the sun set a while ago.

My phone pings with a text. It's Liam—Got the note you left in the book.

And? I type back, staring at the phone as I wait for his response. The grandfather clock in the hallway, marking the passing time. Three dots appear and then the words. Meet me at my apartment tomorrow at 10AM.

I send a thumbs-up, ready to get to the bottom of this. I'm glad I left the note in Liam's book. And I meant every word too. But I'm also nervous how he will respond when I see him.

I refocus on the match as Brynn takes the third set, looks at her father, and then does a victory cartwheel before running to the net to shake Jill's hand. Brynn Cole is moving on, despite everything. "Good for her," I say out loud to no one. But I still can't help feeling a pang of sadness for Lucy and all she lost, the least of which was her final chance to win at the US Open.

CHAPTER 46

Liam meets me at the door with a half hug, which feels like a formality given the circumstances. Only five days have passed since Lucy's kidnapping, but it feels like a lifetime. He holds the door open, and I step inside, immediately noticing a cardboard box on the table. Is that Nancy's box?

"Coffee?" he asks, and I nod. He's ready with two mugs, offering one to me and keeping the other as he leads me to the chairs.

I cradle the hot cup in both hands, waiting for him to speak, my brain thinking of how much rides on this moment.

"Message received," he says, holding up Mayor Compton's book, waving it back and forth. "Loud and clear." He removes the piece of scrap paper hanging out and tosses it on the table. I read the words I left for him—Tell the truth or lose me forever.

I swallow but don't respond. The words are harsh, but it's time to stop playing games. I need the truth. Did Liam leave my brother and me because he didn't care about us, or because he wanted to protect us from something dangerous?

Liam leans back in the chair, crossing his arms over his T-shirt. "As much as it would have pained me, I was going to choose the second part of your message—lose me forever," he says.

I feel my breath exhale.

"Not because I want that, but to protect you. The problem is, you've stirred up quite the hornet's nest," he says. "You know that man you spotted with the shoe-polish-colored hair?"

I nod. "He was following you. You wouldn't stop poking around." Liam shakes his head.

"Did you catch him?" I ask, breathless.

"He's been detained," Liam replies. "For the last time, I wish you'd drop the subject. For all our sakes—really. Can you do that?"

"I can't," I reply, my voice soft.

"Please," Liam says; his voice cracks. "I really need you to drop it."

I stare at the wall above him, unable to meet his gaze. "I can't," I say again, my voice a whisper.

"I was afraid that would be your response," he replies.

I look up and stare into the same blue eyes I see in the mirror.

"If I tell you," he says, lips tightening. "You won't be able to share this information with a soul. Think about that for a minute. It's a terrible burden. If you remarry, you can't tell your husband. You won't be able to tell Nikki and Jackson." He pauses and looks toward the photos on his shelf. "You won't be able to tell your brother—and you will want to."

"I understand," I reply.

"Do you really?" He shakes his head. "Because I thought I understood that price once, but I regret the arrangement I made."

I lean forward, staring into his eyes. "I'm sure, please tell me."

He nods, stands, and opens the cardboard box, then pulls out a cassette tape. "I figured you'd say that." He gets up and retrieves an old cassette player, then places the tape inside.

There's static and beeping and then a voice.

911, what is your emergency?

My boyfriend, he's beating me with a coffeepot. Please hurry. I locked myself in the bathroom. He's trying to break the door—

What is your address?

There's shouting and yelling in the background; then the woman mumbles the address of the apartment in Washington Heights.

Are there weapons?

No! No weapons. Hurry.

Is anyone else there?

Just my boyfriend, please hurry.

Liam hits stop and looks at me. So many thoughts go through my mind, the main one that I was right—he and his partner Harley were set up.

"Did they know you and Harley would respond to that scene?" I ask as he sits back down.

"Yes," Liam says. "Harley was working undercover with Internal Affairs. He was close to busting a network of dirty cops on the take."

"Did you know Harley was undercover?"

"No." He shakes his head. "He made one mistake. Said the wrong thing to the wrong cop." Liam pauses and lowers his gaze. "Then they knew." Outside a bus screeches to a halt. "They set him up that day."

"After you recovered from your injuries, you worked for Internal Affairs?" I ask, trying to piece the rest of the information together.

"I did," he says. "It involved very dangerous people," he adds.

"Like Mayor Compton's father?" I ask. "Were you part of the task force targeting all the departments she helped bring down?"

"Yes," he replies.

"But why did you hide it from Anthony, Mom, and me?" I ask, thinking about how my brother, Anthony, still refuses to even speak to Liam.

He sighs as regret settles on his face. "Because these people are very dangerous. And they never go away. Sharing the information with you puts you in danger."

"But you solved the crime. You put them in prison," I say, tears welling up.

"Kate." He sighs. "This will never be over. The city, this country is sick. Their organization is like a cancer spreading through the entire body. I just removed a small tumor."

"And if I tell someone, it will put them in danger?" I ask.

He nods, giving me a sad smile. "Let me tell you something. The moment that sealed it for me. The moment I knew I had to let you go."

I stare, my eyes glued to him.

"Your mother was away visiting a friend. I had the two of you for the weekend. I took you and Anthony to Macy's to buy shoes. Anthony was in his stroller. I was leaning down helping lace his shoes. It was just a flash, and you wandered off. I scanned the area and found you immediately. You were holding hands with a woman dressed in a checkered black-and-white dress. You weren't looking for me. You were smiling. I could see you pointing and admiring her large diamond necklace with matching earrings. The woman walked right up to me holding your hand. She knew what she was doing. She let go of your hand and placed it in mine. "You should really do a better job watching out for your family, *Officer*," she said. I will never forget the tone and the emphasis she placed on the word *officer*. She knew who I was. It was a message."

I'm stunned. We both sit there quietly for a moment, eyes locked, both our cheeks flushed and wet with tears. I get up and give him a hug, whispering that I'm glad he told me.

He wipes a tear from my face. "You say that now, but you may come to regret your decision."

I look at him and register the worry in his eyes. Suddenly, I understand the stress sharing the information will put on him—the additional burden he will feel worrying for my safety. And while somewhere deep down I know I should feel guilty about the cost to him, I'm relieved to finally know the truth.

CHAPTER 47

I sit next to Bill in the third row of Arthur Ashe Stadium, my foot bouncing with anticipation. After everything Brynn went through, she's about to play in the women's finals at the US Open. Only the sixth woman in history ranked outside the top fifty to make it this far.

"Why are you so nervous?" Bill nudges me. "It's like your daughter is out there."

"I feel a bond with her," I reply, smiling. What I don't tell Bill is Brynn's connection to the kidnapping of Lucy. Or how involved I was in solving that case. The entire Cole family agreed to keep their association with Lucy's kidnapping under wraps. It's about all they've agreed on since Lucy was found.

Brynn struts onto the court, wearing a yellow-and-purple tie-dyed outfit and matching sneakers. The choice of yellow a tribute to Lucy Bosco, whose outfits always featured a yellow stripe. While Brynn's ordeal remains a secret, the tennis world knows of Lucy's. Every international media outlet is after her for the story.

Lucy's already told me she'll tell her saga to me when she's ready. For now, that's good enough for Charlie, who knows not to push, or we might lose the opportunity. Meanwhile, tomorrow night TRP will air my feature on Brynn's rise to tennis stardom. The piece is almost done, but for what happens tonight. Brynn also agreed to appear live on set with me tomorrow at the TRP studio.

"I know I shouldn't have a favorite." I raise my brow, aware that as a sports reporter, I should remain neutral, but I can't help cheering for Brynn over her opponent, a top ranked French player.

"No one needs to know." Bill winks at me. It's not like me hoping Brynn beats her opponent will impact the results.

Brynn, Brynn, Brynn, the crowd chants, excited to have a US player in the finals. The energy is electrifying, and I feel my feet pound along with the spectators'.

"How was your week with David?" I lean over to Bill as two women in front of us take their seats in anticipation of the match starting.

"He's a tool." Bill smirks. "And all he kept doing was asking about you."

I wrinkle my nose but don't say anything.

"I told him you're dating someone new," Bill adds when I don't respond.

"One date is someone new?" I reply, feeling my face flush at the memory of my dinner with Wade.

"It's a start," he says.

Brynn takes the first set in a tense tiebreaker, the crowd erupting as she wins the final point on an ace. I glance over at the player box, where Alexis sits next to Zane. She sees me and nods, hands pressed against her lips. Alexis and I had coffee yesterday, and she told me Zane plans to file for divorce.

It's a relief, she explained, adding that Zane agreed to let Brynn live with her. *He decided it's better for Brynn's tennis to have time away from him,* she reported.

I put up my fist in a little celebration, and she smiles at me as Brynn and her opponent return to the court.

The second set goes to Brynn's opponent; the whole crowd seems to deflate, like a balloon losing air. "Want a snack?" Bill asks. "I have carrots and celery sticks." He pulls a Tupperware container out of his backpack.

"Look at you," I say, taking two carrot sticks.

Brynn bounces up and down on her feet before striding back on the court for her third set. She breaks her opponent and then wins her game, quickly up 2–0.

"Your girl's looking good." Bill smiles.

"She certainly is," I reply with a big grin.

CHAPTER 48

I don't know what draws me to Nico Pappas's funeral, but I find myself traveling to the cemetery on Long Island. The sun is bright; a cool breeze whispers through the branches, hinting of fall.

I drive down Main Street, past the pharmacy, which is shuttered. Someone graffitied the door, spelling out the word **KILLER** in bright-red spray paint. A chill runs down my spine. I shake it off and continue to the cemetery.

Only a handful of people are here. A head turns, and I see Lucy, bandages over her forehead. Her right hand in a cast. The purple bruises around her eye have given way to yellow.

It's a small affair, a graveside funeral. The clergyman finishes, and mourners start back to their cars. Lucy remains in the front row, and I walk over to sit in the chair next to her.

"You're wondering why I bothered with this?" she says, turning a man's gold wedding ring over and over in the fingers of her uninjured hand.

"Yes," I say, noticing how her face is void of emotion.

"He needs to rest somewhere," she replies. "He may as well rot in hell here."

She continues to play with the ring, and I notice blisters on her skin.

She sees me staring at the angry welts. "I'm allergic to gold," she says, tossing the ring into the grave.

My eyes lock on Lucy's face. I can almost hear the gears in my head click into place. Brynn also has an allergy to gold. Despite Lucy's bruised eye and swollen lip, I see the resemblance. "You're Brynn's mother."

She nods.

"Is Zane the father?" I whisper.

"No!" She flinches and jerks from the pain of the movement. I need to remember how fragile she remains. "Ian's the father. But I never got the chance to tell him. By the time I realized I was pregnant, Ian was already in prison."

"Is that what you and Greggory were arguing about in the pharmacy parking lot?" I ask.

She doesn't answer, but stares at the dirt piled next to Nico's grave. A breeze rustles the trees as Lucy raises her eyes to look at me. "I forgot you heard that," she says.

I nod, remembering Lucy's words—*I gave up everything for him.*

She tells me that Greggory didn't put the pieces together then. "The next morning, he came over to the house to confront me." She trembles at the memory.

"It just slipped out." She stops speaking, and shifts in her chair. "He taunted me—*Lucy Bosco thinks she's too good for the rest of us. Left Ian high and dry.*

"*Ian left me,* I yelled back at him. *He left me pregnant and alone.*

"At that moment, it was like time slowed down. Greggory's eyes darkened; his lips twisted into a snarl. I never witnessed anyone that enraged. He punched me across the face, then in the gut. I fell to my knees. I couldn't breathe." Lucy pauses, closing her eyes.

"*You had our family's child and didn't tell us?* Greggory's words slowed as he reached down and smacked me with the back of his hand. My breath returned, and I stood, spun, and tried to run away. He followed, tripped me from behind, and my head hit the pavement. It dawned on me in that moment that my baby represented the last chance Greggory or Ian had to continue the Reese family name.

"I was on my hands and knees, trying to crawl away, when he stepped on my fingers. I could hear the bones break."

She glances down at her cast, shivering at the memory. "I remember he stood there, silent, looming over me for what felt like an hour. Every time I moved, he kicked me. Finally, he lifted me up and dumped me in his car. *Hell if I'm going to leave you here to rat me out—you're not getting the opportunity to put another Reese in prison.*"

"He never meant to kidnap you?" I ask.

"I don't think he did at first. But he couldn't leave me either. I guess he thought he'd get some money by ransoming me before getting rid of me." A tear forms in her eye. Clouds descend over the cemetery, casting the tombstones in gray shadows.

"Why did he involve the Cole family?" I ask. "Was it because of Brynn?"

She coughs. "That's the sick irony. Greggory had no idea Brynn was his niece. Once he kidnapped me, he was out for revenge. He blamed Zane, too, for breaking me and Ian up."

"What made you give Brynn to Zane?"

"It seemed to make so much sense at the time. He and Alexis desperately wanted a child. I was a teenager, and my baby's dad was in prison. Zane was really nice about it, paid for all my health care, created the cover story that I was recovering from an injury—" She bites her lip. "I really thought Brynn would be better off. I think she was."

"Does Alexis know that Brynn is your daughter?" I ask.

"I don't think so," Lucy says. "One of the conditions Zane and I agreed on was that no one else would know Brynn's identity. Zane told Alexis that an adoption attorney reached out—Alexis was so desperate to have a child, I don't think she asked too many questions."

Lucy stands up, and I see a limo waiting for her on the road. I put my hand gently under her uninjured arm to help guide her across the grass. "Are you going to tell Brynn?"

"I don't know. Not yet," she says. "I worry that she's already been through too much. Maybe someday. And thank you for agreeing not to tell anyone."

"It's not my secret to share," I reply. "Either way you must be proud," I say, helping Lucy into the limo. "Seeing her win a US Open Championship at her age. Certainly, a chip off the old block."

"Yes." Lucy gives a sad smile. "For now, I'm going to cheer for her from a distance. She's done well."

I close the door and watch the limo pull away, wondering if I'd make the same choice as Lucy.

I appreciate that Lucy believes she's doing the right thing for Brynn by keeping her true identity secret. But I'm also well aware of how parents' efforts to protect their children, despite best intentions, can hurt them in the end.

EPILOGUE

Two months later

Nikki walks downstairs wearing a witch's hat and black cape.

"It's Thanksgiving." I laugh. "What are you doing in your Halloween costume?"

"Jackson and I decided to start a new tradition," she says as Jackson appears from the kitchen with a Harry Potter wand and glasses. "It's called Thanks-Halloween."

"Since your favorite holiday is Halloween and we're at school for it, we decided to improvise," she adds.

"Which means," Jackson says, leading me into the kitchen, "candy corn pancakes for breakfast." Sitting me down at the table, Jackson places the concoction in front of me, along with a coffee and orange juice.

"If I'm eating these—then both of you need to also." I laugh, not sure if these look great or awful.

"Absolutely," Jackson says, bringing two more plates to the counter.

Nikki passes me the maple syrup, and I pour a generous portion over the pancakes as I watch Jackson wrinkle his nose.

I break off a big bite, stuff it into my mouth, and chew. "Not bad," I reply, getting a second forkful. "I was skeptical," I admit.

"Jackson's been working on the perfect recipe for days," Nikki says, taking a forkful too.

"It's not just about dumping candy corn into pancake mix," he says. "It's also balancing the sugar and vanilla."

"Look at you," I say. "Mr. Chef."

After breakfast, the kids force me upstairs to put together a costume for dinner. Apparently, all our guests are under orders to come dressed up for the occasion.

I decide to go old school and dress in all black, with painted whiskers on my face.

"That's the best you could come up with?" Nikki laughs as I walk into the living room.

I shrug, just happy to be with my family, celebrating with the people I love.

The doorbell rings, and I go to answer it. Wade and my father arrive together, both in costume.

"Happy Thanks-Halloween," Liam says, dressed as Zeus, handing me a bottle of wine wrapped in tinsel paper. I give him a full hug, marveling at the change in our relationship since he finally told me the truth. He may feel apprehensive about the potential danger, but I needed to know him, fully, to truly have a relationship with him. He releases me from the hug and smiles, and I return the expression.

"Hey, Gramps." Nikki walks up to my dad and gives him a hug. "We made chocolate mashed potatoes. Want to try them?"

"Definitely," Liam says, following Nikki into the other room.

I look up at Wade, who's wearing a cowboy hat and cowboy boots. A bandana tied around his neck. "It's the best I could do on short notice." He leans down and gives me a kiss.

"It's not bad," I say, taking his hand, grateful he's here. So much could have gone wrong. I think back to the moment in the pharmacy when Greggory pushed over the shelving, burying Wade and me under the metal racks. But Greggory is gone, and there's no need to worry about him.

"I wish your kids could have joined today," I say, knowing it's his ex-wife's turn with them for the holiday.

"They can come next year," Wade says, squeezing my hand.

"So . . . you see us together next year?" I give him a smile.

"And many years beyond that." He grins.

"You may want to try the chocolate mashed potatoes before you make that kind of commitment." I laugh, leading him into the other room, grateful for new traditions and our expanding family.

ACKNOWLEDGMENTS

The title *Close Call* is apropos to the book, as I found myself working round the clock to make my deadline. And this wouldn't have happened without the incredible support of so many people. First, my brilliant literary manager, Liza Fleissig of Liza Royce Associates. Your sharp editorial instincts, tireless brainstorming, and unwavering support are truly unmatched. Period. The end. No one has her clients' backs like you. And to her partner, Ginger Harris, I adore you and deeply appreciate your support.

To my absolutely incredible editor, Liz Pearsons, thank you for your invaluable guidance, sharp editorial eye, and steadfast support throughout this process. Your thoughtful feedback and encouragement made this book stronger at every stage. Not to mention your good cheer and warm friendship. I am so grateful for you!

Thank you to my developmental editor, Andrea Hurst, who has been with me for all the Kate Green books. Your keen eye has made each book better. A big thank-you to Grace Doyle and the wonderful team at Thomas & Mercer and Brilliance Audio, including Andrea Nauta, Alicia Lea, Will Fairless, Angela Vimuttinan, Jarrod Taylor, Laura Stahl, cover designer Caroline Johnson, and narrator Chanté McCormick, whose tireless work and kind guidance made *Close Call* better.

I have the absolute best team supporting me from marketing to publicity to social media. A huge thank-you to Erin Mitchell, Sean Grabin, and Jordan Upchurch. Thank you to the indomitable

Debbie Deuble Hill, Alec Frankel, and the whole IAG team for their commitment and support of my work for film and television.

The US Open was always one of my favorite events to cover as a reporter, and it was such a joy to revisit it through *Close Call.* To supplement my firsthand experience, I also turned to the wealth of incredible content focused on professional tennis—particularly the Netflix series *Break Point* and Andre Agassi's autobiography, *Open*, both of which I recommend for all fans of the sport.

While this book is fiction, I made every effort to make the law enforcement sections as realistic as possible. To that end, I want to thank retired FBI agent and author Jerri Williams for generously sharing her time and knowledge. Also, a huge thank-you to Unit Chief Adam Hoogland of the Violent Crime Unit in the FBI's Criminal Investigative Division and FBI Public Affairs Specialist Tina Jagerson for taking the time to answer all my questions.

To my mighty beta readers and brainstorming buddies, who, without hesitation, accommodated my tight deadline with open arms and sharpened pencils (okay, keyboards). I love and appreciate each of you: Tracy Kellaher, Naana Obeng-Marnu, Linda Coppola, Erin Mitchell, and author extraordinaire Tessa Wegert.

I'm extremely grateful to the amazing and welcoming crime fiction author community—the most supportive and friendly group out there! I'd be lost without all my author pals. I'm honored to be the cofounding president of Sisters in Crime Connecticut, a member of the board of the Friends of Key West Library, and a writing instructor at the Westport Writers' Workshop.

Thank you to my Hartstein family for shouting out my novels everywhere, from book events, to dinners, to launch parties (hosted by Bonnie and Gal Shweiki and Julie and Brian Hartstein), and even at funerals (if you know, you know). A huge shout-out to the Tulletts and Grays for their steadfast support and love. I'm so lucky to have you in my life. I'm also very appreciative of the support I receive from the Kipnesses, Kalverts, Hargraves, and Richmans. I am very grateful for all of you. To my mother-in-law, Dorothy Kipness, and Larry Broder—I cherish your support.

A special thanks to the best friends a girl could have, including Michelle and Greg Marrinan, Tracy and Michael Kellaher, Rachel Sherman and Ben Kessler, Cindy and Gregg Schwartz, Gigi Georges, Pam Gerla, Stacy and Jason Novoshelski, Anne and Chris Strahm, Caroline Holl, Gayle and Geoff Alswanger, Scott and Jessica Samet, Alison and Rob Weikel, Emily and Surf Mendell, and Rosa and Michael Kucza.

To my "sister" Michelle Zelin for always having my back, for listening to my endless ramblings about this book and everything, and for being one of my biggest cheerleaders. You're the best! To my parents, Joyce Hartstein (also a cherished beta reader) and Marvin Hartstein, who have supported me in every way imaginable. Your love, encouragement, and belief in me have been the foundation of everything I do. To my husband, Rob, who is not only the best partner in life but an integral part of my work. Thank you for listening to every plot idea, reading *every* draft, and providing insightful feedback and encouragement. I love you to the moon and back. To our sons, Justin and Ryan, thank you for cheering your mom on. This journey would mean nothing without both of you.

To the incredible support of the booksellers, libraries, Bookstagrammers, podcasters, and content producers, thank you for helping my dreams come true. And, most importantly, to the readers; none of this matters without you!

ABOUT THE AUTHOR

Photo © 2018 Adam Regan

Elise Hart Kipness is a national television news and sports reporter turned crime fiction writer. *Close Call* is based on Elise's experience in the high-pressure, adrenaline-pumping world of live TV. Like her protagonist, Elise chased marquee athletes through the USTA Billie Jean King National Tennis Center and stood before glaring lights reporting to national audiences.

In addition to reporting for Fox Sports Network, Elise was a reporter at New York's WNBC-TV, News 12 Long Island, and the Associated Press. She is the cofounding president of Sisters in Crime Connecticut and a member of the board of the Friends of Key West Library. Elise also is an instructor at Westport Writers' Workshop. When not writing,

Elise loves reading and binge-watching thrillers, and she will fight you for the last scoop of coffee ice cream.

A graduate of Brown University, Elise has two college-age sons. Elise, her husband, and their three labradoodles split time between Key West, Florida, and Stamford, Connecticut.